Captives: Kingdoms Rule Hearts

EMILY MURDOCH

Copyright © 2014 Emily Murdoch

All rights reserved.

ISBN: 1505627346
ISBN-13: 978-1505627343

DEDICATION

To my husband, Joshua Perkins.

No one could ever ask for a better man in their life.

CONTENTS

Acknowledgements	i
Prologue	1
Chapter One	4
Chapter Two	8
Chapter Three	13
Chapter Four	18
Chapter Five	27
Chapter Six	37
Chapter Seven	44
Chapter Eight	53
Chapter Nine	61
Chapter Ten	71
Chapter Eleven	77
Chapter Twelve	86
Chapter Thirteen	94
Chapter Fourteen	100
Chapter Fifteen	108
Chapter Sixteen	116

Chapter Seventeen	124
Chapter Eighteen	131
Chapter Nineteen	141
Chapter Twenty	148
Chapter Twenty One	157
Chapter Twenty Two	163
Chapter Twenty Three	168
Chapter Twenty Four	175
Chapter Twenty Five	181
Chapter Twenty Six	192
Chapter Twenty Seven	199
Chapter Twenty Eight	204
Chapter Twenty Nine	212
Chapter Thirty	221
Chapter Thirty One	224
Chapter Thirty Two	230
Chapter Thirty Three	239
Chapter Thirty Four	243
Chapter Thirty Five	249
Chapter Thirty Six	252

Chapter Thirty Seven	257
Chapter Thirty Eight	266
Chapter Thirty Nine	272
Epilogue	274
Historical Note	278
About the Author	281

ACKNOWLEDGMENTS

Thank you to Endeavour Press, who have continued to show their faith in me. My husband Joshua Perkins is the reason that I started writing, and I could not continue without him. My wonderful editor – also known as my mother – has once again proved that I cannot do without her. Thanks as always are due to my entire family, although it has certainly expanded since my last book. My parents Gordon and Mary Murdoch, my brother Haydon Murdoch, my parents-in-law Stephen and Jane Perkins, and my new siblings-in-law Sophie Perkins and James Perkins should all receive a mention for supporting me through yet another book. I owe much to Bella Harcourt, who encouraged me through the latter stages of writing – I shall always remember our walks with a smile. And lastly, to my team of bridesmaids, who kept me sane through a wedding, moving to the other side of the world (and back), and the writing of this book: Becky Callaghan, Georgia Bird, Sophie Perkins, and Stephanie Booth. Thank you.

PROLOGUE

The prisoner had not spoken for weeks.

None had expected it to last this long. The journey over the wide sea, back to Normandy, had been a troubled crossing. Of the five ships that had left England's shore, only three had arrived safely, and even those had lost men to fear and sickness. Those that had not died or fled muttered underneath their breath.

The prisoner had not complained.

Dressed in clothes that had seen better days, the prisoner had been forced upon a horse, despite their protestations that they were not strong enough to ride. The cloak had become torn and stained over the fortnight-long ride to the castle of Geffrei, and the hood was pulled across the prisoner's face, obscuring the night. Despite the cold, the prisoner was not offered a warmer cloak, or a kind word.

The prisoner had barely noticed.

As the sound of the horses' hooves slowed, the prisoner looked up. Through bleary eyes, only a vague impression of the place at which the company had arrived could be seen, but it was imposing even in its vagueness. A stone building with several floors, and no light emitting from the few windows to pierce the darkness of the evening. No flags hung from the walls, and the door outside which they stood was bare, save for one small handle.

The prisoner closed both eyes.

"You awake?"

The prisoner was dragged down from the horse, and made to stand, although every bone cried out for rest. The brim of the hood fell down over their eyes. The murmur that the prisoner attempted made no sense.

"Walk! If you know what's good for you."

There were almost a dozen knights that had ridden with the prisoner, but one was more splendidly dressed than the others. His cloak was lined, offering warmth against the bitter autumnal breeze, and it was he only that had been fed thoroughly during the journey.

"My lord Geffrei!"

The man with the lined cloak turned to face one of his men. The others were lowering themselves from their horses, and pulling up their belts over their empty stomachs.

"Yes?" he replied bluntly.

"Food is required," said the man, pointing at the prisoner. *"If you do not want it to die."*

The prisoner fell.

"Up!" shouted Geffrei, pacing towards the prisoner lying on the ground. *"You'll walk, not crawl, into my home, you dirty animal!"*

A hand reached up, cracked and sore, from the prisoner lying on the ground, but no hand went down to meet it. Eventually, the prisoner raised themselves up from the ground, and hung their head.

"Now," breathed Geffrei with malice in every tone, *"on you go. You're the guest of honour."*

Cruel laughs rang out as the prisoner stumbled forwards against the door, clutching at the handle. It turned. The prisoner leaned, exhausted, against the door.

The room that the prisoner fell into was the Great Hall. A small brazier glinted at the far side of the room, and a medley of dogs unravelled themselves to meet their guests. Feet sounded around the prisoner as the men strode in, desperate for warmth.

Geffrei threw himself by the fire in the only chair in the room. He turned his eyes to the prisoner, who had pulled themselves up to stare into his face.

"Well," he said with a smirk. *"Here we are. We have finally arrived. What do you think of your new home?"*

The prisoner stood up, and with a great effort, spat onto the rushes on the floor.

Geffrei shook his head with a smile on his face. "Now, that's no way to treat your new home," he chastised. "What do you have to say for yourself?"

The prisoner pulled back the hood from their face, and shook her long hair and veil out from the mud-splattered cloak.

"Where's my daughter Annis?"

CHAPTER ONE

The room had fallen silent. None had seen such beauty, and yet such pain across one face. The woman had long hair, but it had long since lost its youthful shine. It was now covered in mud, and a ribbon that could once have been blue was entangled in it.

The woman ignored their stares, and the muttering that began at the edges of the room. She had only eyes for one man, and he grinned at her.

"Your pups are none of my concern," Geffrei said lazily, "but if this Annis did survive, you can be sure that it would not take many moments for her to wish that she had not."

The woman said nothing, but sank to her knees. A serving girl entered, bringing hot bread and ale to the men. They fell upon it quickly, desperate for sustenance. None was offered to the woman.

"You lie," she said, with a tremor in her voice. "If my girl lives, then she is well. I would know…would I not know?"

Her belief in her maternal instinct had clearly been shattered. After so many weeks of travelling, it was a surprise to many that she was alive at all.

"Enough," Geffrei waved a hand. "I am tired of you. Someone take her to a room far from mine, and leave her there."

None of the men moved. Geffrei's whims altered so frequently that it was often a grave mistake to act upon his first order. Not until he threw something at them did they know that he was serious. This time it was a goblet.

"If that woman is not taken out of my sight," he thundered, "you shall all spend the night with the pigs! The pigs I say!"

The droplets of wine slowly fell out of the goblet like drops of blood. The woman almost reached her hand out for it. The goblet was but inches away from her, and it would provide her with the only liquid she would have received for days – but too late. Rough hands once more pulled her to her feet.

Two men pulled her out of the Great Hall into a corridor, lit with flaming torches. The woman could not take in much more of her surroundings. Before she could be aware of how long they had been walking, she was thrown into a room, which was locked behind her.

The floor smelt terribly. As the woman opened her eyes, they met with a pest, slowly crawling through the rushes. It looked like a maggot. She pushed herself away hurriedly, bringing her knees under herself and clutching at her ankles.

She was completely alone.

"Why is she even here?" one of Geffrei's men called out, as they feasted on their first good meal for days. "Who is she?"

Geffrei snorted as he reached for another piece of bread. "You did not recognise her?"

The men shook their heads, except one that was more concerned with fitting more onto his plate than finding out the identity of the woman that they had dragged across Normandy for the last weeks.

Geffrei smiled. "She is Catheryn, daughter of Theoryn, wife of Selwyn."

There were some understanding nods from men who had seen too much of the world, but the man that had previously been so consumed by his meal looked up.

"Catheryn? Wife of Selwyn? And who is Selwyn to us?"

Geffrei's smile disappeared as quickly as it had come. "Do you know nothing?" he spat. "Did you not even think about the land that we went to take for King William, and for God? Idiot!"

The man's face faltered, but he continued. "My apologies, my lord. I merely wish to become better informed."

Geffrei's frown softened, but there was still a harshness across his features. "Peace, Henri," he said, begrudgingly. "Catheryn's father was a rich man in England, and Selwyn hailed from a noble line. Their marriage was intended to create a dynasty – a dynasty that could prove very useful to befriend."

"Or befoul," said Henri, slyly.

Geffrei guffawed. "Well spoken!"

A small gesture brought the same serving girl to pour more wine into Henri's goblet. The other men relaxed, and began to murmur amongst themselves. The petty concerns of this woman did not worry them.

"It is true, I cannot deny it," Geffrei continued. "Being in control of Catheryn certainly offers her captors a certain amount of power in the new creation of England. Now that her husband is dead, she will control a large area in the South. Her daughter, too, would have been useful – but I have heard Richard of Bleu-Castille has taken her into his keeping."

He spat on the floor.

"And so," Henri spoke up once more, "you intend…to marry this Catheryn?"

The men fell silent, and they turned to their lord. A marriage would certainly change things.

Geffrei looked at his loyal followers.

"Do you wish for a mistress?" he asked quizzically.

None of them knew the answer that Geffrei was looking for, and knew that it would be dangerous to offer a remark that could so easily offend.

"Hmmm," Geffrei pondered. "I think not."

More than one man breathed a silent sigh of relief.

"I do not consider her connections important enough. Perhaps if the Conquering of England had not been so absolute, so brutal…if there had been a chance that the Anglo-Saxons could have risen up, it would have been convenient to create a line with Catheryn."

Geffrei picked up a chicken bone from his plate, and considered it.

"But England is no more," he said softly. "It has been killed, and its finest feathers have been plucked. Now it will be consumed by William, and his family, and the rest of us can expect no better than the bones that slip from his table."

He flung the bone over his shoulder, which was immediately snapped at by one of his hunting dogs.

"So why is she here?" returned Henri.

Geffrei shrugged. "She is certainly a great prize. A prize to show the battles that we fought. And we should keep an eye on her; we may see no use in her, but that does not mean that no one else does."

CHAPTER TWO

When Catheryn awoke, it was not because of a gentle breeze, or a caring nudge, but instead because she realised that a grub was trying to burrow its way under one of her fingernails.

She opened one eye, and carefully pulled it out of the cut that it had already made there. Flinging it across the room, she raised herself up into a sitting position, and thought.

Annis. Her daughter, still left in their homeland, now defenceless. Catheryn had thought she had undergone the greatest sadness of all: seeing her beloved husband ride out to battle once more, and not seeing him return. When the news of his suspected death had come, she had cried out with a scream that had told the whole household the news. Words had not been needed. She had cursed the wind as it had fallen on her face, because it may not be falling on his. Every piece of food was ashes in her mouth, because it could not guarantee his return to her.

But before there was time to grieve, to even consider organising a burial for the body that they had not yet found, or recount his glorious deeds, the men had come. They had taken her away, and she had not seen Annis since.

Catheryn put her hand to her hair, and absent mindedly pulled out a few strands. Surely, she thought, she would know. I would know if my own daughter had died. But she had not known when Selwyn had gone, until that messenger brought such dark tidings.

A scraping coming from the doorway told her that someone was outside. Struggling to her feet, Catheryn rose to meet the intruder.

But it was only a girl – barely out of childhood. Her long blonde hair fell down to her waist, and she smiled hesitantly at the woman she had been told was their prisoner.

Catheryn blinked tired eyes. "A…Annis?"

The girl wavered in and out of focus, and the sunlight glinted on her golden hair.

Catheryn fainted.

When she awoke, Catheryn was exactly where she had fallen. The only difference to the room was the softness beneath her aching head. Moving slightly to the side, she saw that a small rag had been placed underneath her face where she had fallen.

Catheryn pushed herself up from the floor, and shuddered when her fingers brushed over things that she would rather not think about. Sitting upright, she tried to remember why she had fallen – forgetting that she had not eaten a full meal in days.

The girl. She had thought that the girl was Annis. Catheryn shook her head, and instantly regretted it as throbbing pain swept across it. Her daughter was much older than the timid servant girl that she had clearly terrified.

Catheryn leaned against the cold stone wall, and sighed deeply, trying to rebalance herself. There was no point in standing, and it was surely better to save her strength. After all, she had no idea how long she was to be in this place.

Within moments, Catheryn had fallen asleep, exhausted.

The small window in the room that Catheryn was forced to live in was high in the wall, but it did give Catheryn the opportunity to gaze at the stars when the clouds were good enough to reveal them to her. It was through the same small window that she watched the moon wax and wane, wax and wane.

The longer Catheryn spent in the room, the more every crevice became as known to her as the walls of her home in England. It was a square room, about three paces each side, and the rushes on the floor were never changed. The only furniture in the room was a small table, only large enough to fit a small plate on, and a chair that was made of wood, and had no softness lent to it by fabric or fur. It was not a room built for comfort.

Catheryn's health struggled on, but she did not lose any of her strength. She was determined to return to England, and to find her husband Selwyn and bury him with all honour, and find her daughter Annis. Sometimes she would dream that she was there, and the dream would be so strong that when she awoke and found herself still trapped in the disgusting chamber, hot tears would fall.

The servant girl, who Catheryn learned was called Lina, would bring an inconsequential meal to her each day, which largely consisted of a stringy broth with some sort of vegetables in it. On good days, there was bread. Most days, there was not.

One day, after the moon had changed completely three times, Catheryn managed to coax Lina into conversation.

"Thank you," Catheryn said softly. "For the food."

Catheryn's Norman was not as good as it had once been, but she had always tried to keep the languages that she had learned, and she was pleased to see that Lina had understood her.

"It is nothing," Lina whispered, her face turning red.

"It is good of you to bring it."

"No," Lina shook her head, her feet unconsciously moving her back towards the door. "I am ashamed to bring it. I would not feed it to the pigs."

Catheryn smiled bitterly. "And yet I thank you."

Lina paused, obviously wrong-footed by the kindness from the woman she had been told was a wild beast, and should be ignored.

"How long do you think I will be here, Lina?"

Lina began backing to the door again, keeping her eyes fixed on Catheryn's feet, seemingly unable to look at the prisoner properly.

Catheryn realised that she had made a mistake. "I only ask, Lina, so that I can understand why my lord Geffrei keeps me here. I want to go and see my daughter." Lina stopped. Her hand was on the door, but she could not move any further.

"Tell me…tell me about your daughter."

If Catheryn had not heard Lina's timid tones, she would not have realised she had spoken; her lips had barely moved.

Catheryn moved from the wall where she was standing, and went to sit in the chair.

"Her name is Annis," she said quietly, her voice full of love. "She would be a couple of years older than you, I think."

She paused, waiting until Lina said something.

"I am but twelve summers."

Catheryn smiled. "Annis is nearing sixteen. She has beautiful blonde hair, and she loves to cook."

Lina's mouth fell open. "But – but she must be a lady!"

"She is indeed," Catheryn laughed, "but that does not mean that she cannot enjoy herself."

Lina's mouth was still open. It was clear that she didn't consider working in a kitchen to be anything close to enjoyment.

"What colour does she like to wear?"

Lina's question came out in a rush, as though she was shocked at the impudence of asking such a personal question of a great lady, even if she was wild.

Catheryn shrugged. "I do not think she has a favourite dress, but she loves deep colours. Red, blues, greens. Not purple."

Lina didn't reply, but a smile instantly dazzled her face. The idea of having more than one dress was incomprehensible to her – the thought of having to pick a favourite had almost stunned her.

Catheryn was enjoying talking about her family, and Lina was a particularly good audience. "What do you want to know about my husband?"

The smile on Lina's face disappeared as quickly as it had appeared.

Catheryn's heart slowed. "Lina?"

"I have to go," Lina gabbled, trying to locate the handle of the door behind her without turning her back on Catheryn. "I cannot stay – "

"Lina?" Catheryn said uncertainly. "What do you know about my husband?"

"I don't know anything about Selwyn!"

Ice flowed into Catheryn's veins. "How do you know his name?"

Lina gave up the fight, and turned around. She pulled open the door, and then turned back around to face Catheryn, who was astonished to see tears in those young eyes.

"I am sorry," Lina's voice was so quiet, Catheryn could barely hear her. "I am sorry to speak his name to you, my lady. I know it must give you pain as…as he did not survive the Conquest. I know that he was killed, with honour, on the battlefield. I am sorry."

CHAPTER THREE

Catheryn no longer watched the moon. She no longer realised what she was eating. She could not even have sworn that it was still Lina that came every day. Nothing mattered. Not now all of her family had been taken from her.

The tears that eventually came threatened to drown her. Catheryn sobbed one day, and the next sat in silence, unable to understand that the man that she had loved, that she had built a life with, that she had raised their children with, was no longer on this earth. It did not make sense that there was not a place that she could go to find him.

The dreams that had comforted her for weeks now took a terrifying and violent turn. Instead of sitting with Selwyn, of riding with him and watching Annis with him, Catheryn watched in horror, every night, as Selwyn was cut down from his horse by faceless men, all wearing Norman armour. She wanted to rush to him – to protect him in the only way she knew, by putting herself between him and the swords that glinted in the sunlight. But Catheryn could never move, and she could do nothing but watch the swords bury themselves in her husband's flesh.

Every night, she awoke screaming.

There seemed no end to the pain. Every evening, Catheryn tried to tell herself that tomorrow, a new day, could bring a fresh start for her. Not to love Selwyn any less, but to learn to live without him.

Every morning, the pain had not left her.

It seemed to possess her like a spirit. Every muscle seemed to ache of love for him, and every breath seemed a betrayal of him, the man that she loved that no longer took a breath.

At times, Catheryn would fall asleep, exhausted from whispering his name under her breath.

There was no way for her to tell how long it was, but there was a day when she woke up and realised that she had almost forgotten Annis. Her daughter. She was now alone in England, with no parent or sibling to protect her. What on earth had become of her?

Catheryn was dwelling on the thought of her daughter alone in their home one night when she fell asleep.

She dreamt of the night that she was taken. The Normans had stormed the village, and set each and every home alight. The children were shepherded away from their parents, and the sword taken to them. Mothers, fathers that attempted to prevent the slaughter were killed themselves.

She had seen the flames from their home, and had known that Annis was down there in the village. Her daughter, her only daughter. Her son had been playing at her feet, but she left him playing there, in the home that she had assumed would be safe. She had run out into the darkness, without even putting on a cloak. As she neared the village, she could hear screams. Screams for the dead, screams of the dying, screams of the living that knew their lives were over.

As Catheryn had entered the village, girls and boys that she couldn't recognise in the dark raced past her.

"Get away," she yelled in the dream, just as she had done on that fateful night. "Run!"

No child paused, but continued. Then she saw Annis, helping some of the smaller children that could not run clamber up into a tree. Annis could not stay here. She knew what the Norman men would do to any girls of Annis' age.

Annis' eyes had shone in the darkness as they were illuminated by the flames. She climbed up the tree, and gestured for her mother to join her.

In the dream, as in her memory, Catheryn had shaken her head desperately, and turned away from the fiery village. She needed to get back to her son, to the other sons and daughters of the village that had hopefully taken sanctuary in her home.

But she had arrived there just to watch the last child be slaughtered by a Norman that had grinned as he saw her. She was dragged back to the village, and forced upon a horse. With the last look that she cast upon her home, she looked upwards.

In reality, her daughter had been in the tree. Staring down at her in horror.

But in the dream, the branches were empty.

"Annis?"

Catheryn could not help but cry out in the dream, but she was ignored. No Annis appeared.

"Annis!"

Catheryn awoke, and the name of her daughter was still on her lips. But it was not the dream that had woken her: before her stood a tall man, with a bitter smile on his face.

It was Geffrei.

"My lord Geffrei," Catheryn said stiffly. "Forgive me if I do not rise from my bed."

Geffrei looked down at the woman lying on the dirty rushes. His smile widened, and lost some of the bitterness.

"Why, let me help you."

Geffrei reached down and grabbed Catheryn's shoulder, pulling her up sharply. Catheryn gasped in pain as her shoulder jolted painfully. Forced upon her feet, Catheryn glared at the man that had kept her a virtual prisoner for months.

"What do you want?" she spat, all pretence at civility abandoned. "You know that no one will pay my ransom, now that my husband and son were brutally murdered!"

Geffrei shrugged, and lowered himself gracelessly onto the wooden chair.

"You are not worth much anyway," he said carelessly.

Catheryn hated him, but she knew that her life was hanging in a balance that she didn't understand. "Then why are you keeping me here?"

Geffrei studied her silently.

"You don't…you don't want to marry me, do you?" Catheryn asked quietly.

Geffrei laughed. "You are not a particularly exciting proposition, you know. No good name, no wealth, now that the Normans have taken your lands. Besides, I am looking for someone somewhat younger than yourself."

Catheryn could not help but be relieved. "Good, because you disgust me, and I would not have married you."

"Quiet, woman!" Geffrei spat, goaded too far. "You are worth nothing, you hear? You have no sons to carry on your line, and I cannot even sell you back to your worthless husband so that he can make use of you."

"Then why am I even here?" Catheryn snapped back.

Geffrei smiled. "You have a daughter, I believe?"

Catheryn did not immediately understand what he meant. "Yes," she said uncertainly. "Annis. Why?"

Geffrei's smile widened.

"You are revolting," Catheryn said. "You would never have my daughter even if I did know where she was."

"And you would like to know, I presume?"

Catheryn's heart leapt. "You know where my daughter is?"

Geffrei shook his head slowly. "As much as I would dearly love to taunt you with that knowledge, it is not something I possess."

Catheryn sighed sadly. "Then what are you going to do with me?"

Geffrei rose, and shrugged once more. "I am not sure, to tell you the truth. I have certainly gained an interesting amount of grandeur by holding a woman such as yourself prisoner. The wild woman of England. Strikes just the right amount of fear into my tenants, don't you think? I am also waiting for members of her family to claim her ransom, but I under-estimated the extent of King William's wrath. Few remain."

Geffrei swept towards the door, but Catheryn desperately lurched forward.

"I demand better accommodation!" she said, trying to speak calmly. "Chambers better suited to the ranking you have just admitted I possess."

Geffrei paused. "You," he said quietly, "are an Anglo-Saxon. You do not ask, you do not get, you cannot barter, you receive nothing, you deserve nothing." His eyes scanned around the dirty and bare room. "Besides, compared to what you are surely used to, this is comparative luxury."

He left the room, and left Catheryn shaking with anger and fear.

CHAPTER FOUR

It was not until Catheryn felt the heat pouring through the window that linked her to the outside world that she realised that it must be summer. Summer of the year 1067 – a year in which she had never seen more than the tiny square of sky visible from her room.

She spent most of her days pacing up and down the room, trying desperately to keep her mind occupied. Lina's daily visits had gradually returned back to normal, but Catheryn could never entreat her to discuss much more than the weather outside, and the time of year.

Catheryn awoke one morning, not from the light that usually fell on her face, but instead due to shouting.

"Careful!" A rough voice shot through the semi-darkness. Catheryn opened her eyes slowly, and saw that the sun had not yet risen. "If you break that, it'll be our heads!"

Grumbles were the only reply that Catheryn could make out. Suddenly, a loud crash startled her. She stood up, and once again craned her neck, attempting to see whether she could gain a view through the window in the wall. Once again, she was unsuccessful.

"You oaf!"

There was the dull sound of a fist hitting a man's chest, and a groan.

"They won't like it!" The same voice was obviously angry, but there was a hint of fear and trepidation in his tone. "And it'll be me they blame!"

The voices began to argue, but they must have been moving away from the wall because Catheryn could no longer catch what they were saying. She stopped trying to clamber up the wall, and sat sleepily in the uncomfortable chair.

Something was obviously about to happen here at Geffrei's home – something important enough to unnerve the servants. But Catheryn could not think what on earth it could possibly be.

She started at a noise, but it was only Lina, bringing her the daily ration of pottage that she was now being allocated.

"Good morning, my lady," she mumbled, as she set down the plate on the table, pulling a spoon out of her apron pocket and laying it down beside it.

"Lina," Catheryn said quietly, hoping this time to entice some information out of the girl without terrifying her. "Is your lord Geffrei...has he got celebrations planned?"

At once Catheryn regretted her words. Lina stumbled away from her, shaking her head.

Catheryn spoke quickly. "But something is happening, isn't it Lina? I heard voices, they were moving something...carrying something I think. What is – "

And then an idea struck her that was so fantastic, so marvellous that Catheryn felt that if she even breathed it, the idea would disappear in an instant. And yet she had to ask.

"Has Geffrei found my daughter?"

Lina shook her head once more, but Catheryn pushed aside the negation.

"Now, Lina, you can't just shake your head to everything that I say! What is happening?"

But Catheryn's forceful voice had gone too far. Within a moment Lina had left the room, and Catheryn was alone again.

It had barely been three hours since Catheryn had once again disconcerted Lina into leaving quickly when she heard the key turn in the lock of her door. Catheryn was sitting against the wall opposite the door, and felt no need to rise. It would only be Lina, or perhaps Geffrei determined to taunt her once more.

But it was not Geffrei that appeared as the door swung open. It was, instead, a man who was very tall with dark hair. He was richly dressed, with a large sword hanging from his belt. There was a short, dark haired woman by his side, and a crown on his head.

Catheryn scrambled to her feet.

"And this is she?" The woman was speaking over her shoulder, and as she entered the room Catheryn saw that Geffrei was not far behind them. His voice contained an oily tone that she had not heard before.

"Yes, my lady Queen, this is the woman I have spoken of."

The three of them walked into the room, and the door was shut behind them. The woman was not as short as Catheryn had initially thought, and much of her was covered with a large blue travelling cloak. The dress that flowed underneath it was of the Norman style, but Catheryn could not help but begrudgingly admit to herself that it had some merits. Catheryn did not know what to do, where to look, or whether she should say anything. Thankfully, that conundrum was quickly solved for her.

"What is your name, my lady?" King William the Conqueror's voice was deeper than Catheryn had heard the gossips say, and the strength in each word was undeniable. It was the voice that men would follow, would fight for, would die for.

"I am the lady Catheryn, wife of Selwyn *eadlorman*, Ælfgard's daughter."

Catheryn did not know how she managed to command her tongue, but it formed the words that she was thinking well enough. She could not believe that the lord of Normandy – the man that had taken England for his own, and demanded that it be his, was standing before her in her cell.

"Well met, my lady Catheryn," William clearly did not know or appreciate the formal Anglo-Saxon greetings, which grated on Catheryn's senses like sand upon silk. "You know who I am."

His last was a statement, not a question, but Catheryn was polite enough to incline her head. There were probably few people now in England that did not know the visage of this man. The woman beside him, however, was unknown to her.

"This is my wife, the lady Matilda, soon to be Queen," William continued. "She had heard of your presence here, and wanted to see you."

Catheryn's eyes widened. "You had heard of me?"

Matilda smiled. "It is common knowledge at court that various women of high-born status from England are now in Normandy."

"There are more of us?" Catheryn couldn't believe it. "More women, other than myself, that have been torn away from their families to rot in Norman castles?"

There was an edge to her voice now, but she tried to control it. It would not do to lose her temper with the King's wife, and she was sure Geffrei would have her punished once the royal couple had left.

Matilda's smile weakened slightly. "Indeed," she said, more quietly. "Many of our kind have taken the journey across the sea."

"You mean women?" Catheryn shot back, unable to hold back her outrage any longer. "When you say 'of our kind', you mean women, don't you? You mean mothers, wives, daughters — females that could not defend themselves, and looked to men and their honour to protect us? And what has become of these defenceless people?"

Matilda did not look away, but kept her eyes on Catheryn. Almost imperceptibly, she bit her lip. "Many were widows, and now many are wives and mothers once more."

"You sicken me," Catheryn said shortly. "You force us to marry the men that killed our sons, our lovers. There is no honour in it."

Matilda said nothing, and her husband cast her a look, waiting for her reply. Eventually, she spoke again.

"I cannot deny what you say," Matilda said simply. "I love my husband, and it would be death to me to wed his enemy. But," and here her voice took on a new strength, "that is the way of this war. Or any war. It is a man's game, and although we women may pay the price, some of us will gain the rewards. That is the gamble that we all take."

"It is not a gamble if we do not choose to play."

Catheryn's voice caught, and she fell silent.

"What of your husband?"

It was King William now who spoke, but there was no shake in his voice.

Catheryn opened her mouth to speak. No sounds came out.

"You do not need to ask," Matilda said softly. She moved forward as if to comfort Catheryn, but she shrank away from her touch.

"I do not need your pity," Catheryn said stiffly. "I just want my daughter."

Matilda looked confused. "My lord Geffrei, I was not aware that you were maintaining two Anglo-Saxon women."

Geffrei, momentarily forgotten, leaped forward to speak once more to his Queen.

"Please ignore the prisoner, my lady Matilda – Catheryn's daughter is somewhere in England, and yet she continues to complain about it."

"Do you have daughters, my lady?"

Catheryn's question seemed to have caught Matilda off-guard.

"Daughters?"

"Yes. I have heard of your sons, of course, but often daughters are forgotten until they are wed."

Catheryn saw immediately – she did not need Matilda to speak. She had daughters.

Matilda nodded. "I have three. Perhaps another on the way."

Her hands consciously moved to her stomach, and her husband snorted.

"God's teeth woman, it's a boy!"

Matilda ignored her husband. "Or a girl."

Catheryn smiled. "God grant you health, whatever He blesses you with. My lady, if you had a daughter in England, alone, with no father, mother, or brother to protect her, what would your thoughts be?"

Matilda could not help but smile at the audacity that the woman was showing. Her hair was dirty and unkempt, and there was a disgusting smell emanating from the rushes on the ground – and yet she stood, defiant.

"I would not be thinking," she confessed. "I would already be on the first ship to England."

Catheryn returned the smile. "Then you can understand why I am anxious to finally leave this room after months and months of wondering if my child is safe."

The smile dropped from Matilda's face, and she turned on Geffrei.

"My lord, this lady, of high Anglo-Saxon birth, has been a prisoner in this small room, since she arrived here last year?"

Geffrei's face was full of terror as he looked over the shoulder of the bristling woman to her husband standing behind her, a scowl on his face.

"She is but an Anglo-Saxon, my lady Matilda," he said smoothly, "and as such, does not deserve such quality treatment." He shot a disdainful glance at Catheryn, who glowered back. "She is but an animal, and I treat her that way."

Geffrei little knew King William, and he had never met his wife Matilda before. Had he done so, he probably would not have been so rash.

One glance at her face was enough.

"My...my lady..." was all that he was able to manage.

"Oh!" Matilda exclaimed, swivelling around to face her husband. "This is awful. This disgusts me. That a woman of such nobility has been caged here like a beast for so long – it is not to be borne. I demand that she be removed immediately."

"I shall have a chamber prepared – "

"Removed to another lord's keeping," Matilda interrupted Geffrei without even giving him a look. "You agree, do you not, husband?"

Catheryn looked at the tall man that had begun a ruinous campaign on her home. He was looking down at his wife with such love, such devotion that Catheryn felt almost embarrassed to be in the room.

"Your commands are, as ever, to be followed," he said gruffly. "Although I cannot pretend to understand where you will send her."

Matilda sniffed. "I may not be a man, but that just means that I have some sense still in me." She cast a smile at Catheryn, who could still not quite believe what was happening.

Geffrei, on the other hand, seemed to be stuck in a mad panic.

"My lady, I must protest, I did not mean…" His voice trailed off as both King William and Matilda stared at him coldly. "I only thought that…perhaps…" After waiting a few moments, and after a deep breath, he said quietly, "I did not want the expense of caring for her."

"Then you should have let her go home."

Catheryn started. She couldn't believe that those words had been uttered by the King himself.

"My lord King," she said uncomfortably, "it is my dearest wish that I can return to my homeland. Will you not grant me safe passage?"

"And what would you do there if you did return?" questioned the King. "Your home and lands are no longer yours. I gave them to my lord Richard myself."

Catheryn's voice caught in her throat. To think of another man walking down the corridors of her ancestors, taking her husband's place…but she must be clear of thought, she must concentrate on the most important bargaining she would likely ever do.

"I must find my daughter, my King," she said hoarsely, finally giving way to the hunger in her bones and half sitting, half falling to the floor. "I must find my Annis."

Although Catheryn could not see it, Matilda's face had softened again. Any mother would die in the attempt to rescue her child, and she was no different.

"My lord," she said formally to her husband, "would you not expect half of me, if I had become separated from our children?"

King William nodded his head, slowly. "And yet she is too powerful, too important to have in England at this time. Just one of the pretenders would need to marry her, and already they would have an alliance that may try to challenge our rule."

Matilda cast a quick and thoughtful eye over the woman that had collapsed, albeit gracefully, onto the floor.

"She is past child-bearing," she said softly. "No heirs will be blessed to her now. There would be no profit in it for any man."

"And yet she could offer prestige," her husband counters. "No. I cannot allow her return."

Matilda sighed. "You are right, of course." She moved forward, and then in an elegant movement, knelt by the woman that had attempted to follow most of the conversation, but was having difficulty keeping conscious.

"My lady Catheryn, I sympathise," Matilda reached out an arm to comfort the woman that looked up at her with wide eyes. "But you are too precious to lose. Do not fear – we will not leave you here with this repugnant man." She cast a look over her shoulder at Geffrei.

"I know a lady that has children like you, and will be a much better carer of you. Her name is Adeliza. Adeliza de Tosny, wife of William FitzOsbern."

CHAPTER FIVE

The rain was falling steadily, as it had been for the last three days. Anything that had started out dry was now drenched, and many of the men felt that they would never be dry again. They cursed against this English weather, and longed for home.

The tents sagged under the weight of all the water, and small boys, wet to their skins, were going around the encampment attempting to remove the water from the tents into buckets. The task had at first seemed a fun one, but as each day dawned to further rain, they now bitterly regretted volunteering.

A man sat at a tent opening, looking out at the clouds that showed no sign of moving. His hair was dark, but smatterings of grey threatened to start to overtake his temples. His plain and simple clothes belied their price, and the sword by his side showed he was a knight.

William FitzOsbern sighed. He shut his eyes against the water splattering down onto his shoulder, and thought of home.

"Fitz?"

Forced to open his eyes, he saw a small man, dressed in the regalia of a bishop. Odo of Bayeux.

"My lord Odo," Fitz rose to greet the man that had been left in charge of England whilst the King was visiting his family back in Normandy. "How goes your day?"

Odo spat on the ground, his hair plastered to his face. "The same as it always does in this God-forsaken country. Can I come in?"

Fitz bowed his assent, and moved so that Odo could pass him and enter the shelter of the tent, small as it was.

"It does not feel that there is much to do, in truth," Odo continued, lowering himself gingerly onto a stool in Fitz's tent. "I hope I don't get this too wet," he added, looking up at Fitz.

The owner of the stool shrugged. "Nothing will stay dry forever. Not in this weather."

Odo barked a laugh. "You wish to be in Normandy?"

"I wish to be anywhere," Fitz emphasised, "but here."

He sat back down on the chair that had been his resting place when Odo first arrived, turning it first so that he could face his guest.

"I appreciate that you have stayed," Odo's voice was more serious now. "I need good men here while our King is away. Strong men. Men that can be respected as well as liked."

Fitz looked at the King's half-brother, and smiled to himself. Odo was determined to prove himself, everyone knew that. He should never have joined the Church, but it had to be. His father had been determined to have at least one son gain power within a cathedral, and so Odo had had no real choice. But his bishop's robes had not prevented him from riding out in the battles that had won England for their own.

Fitz's eyes darkened as he remembered the day that they had landed. The foreign beaches, and the villages of people that had no idea that they were coming…

"…don't you think?"

Odo's voice brought Fitz back to where he was. Ashamed of his lack of attention, Fitz shook his head slightly, trying to regain his concentration.

"Back in Normandy?" Odo smiled again. "We shall have to send you back, at this rate, if you cannot keep your mind attentive to the job at hand."

"No, my lord Odo," Fitz said hastily. "I am perfectly content here. I am honoured to protect England with you for our King."

Odo's glance took in the tired eyes and sore leg that Fitz had been attempting to hide from his men for some time.

"It is an honour." Fitz repeated himself, and caught the eye of Odo once more. The two men smiled at each other.

"It is indeed," Odo conceded.

There was a moment of silence between them, broken only by the continuing pattering of rain.

"I have a favour to ask of you." Odo spoke abruptly, looking over at his companion. "I have to be honest with you, and tell you that it is not a pleasant one, and it is one that I would rather not do myself."

Fitz smiled, in spite of himself. "You are not making the task seem any more enjoyable, my lord."

Odo's barking laugh sounded again. "You are right of course – but I think it right that I do not give you fair warning. You may decide to delegate it to another man."

Fitz shrugged. "I may, I may not. What do you require of me?"

It was Odo's hesitation that caused Fitz's first real concern. Odo was a man that had ridden screaming into battle with only a mace to protect him. He had managed to persuade forty Norman lords to follow William to England in the first place. If there was something to be done that he did not like, it was almost certainly dangerous, foolish, or both.

"I need a message taken," Odo said reluctantly. "It is quite a simple one, but could be disastrous if it fell into the hands of our enemies."

Odo did not say who the enemies were, but they both knew it. The English: every man, woman and child within this country was against them, despite the invasion happening almost a year ago. There were still very few people that openly welcomed the Normans, and not even they could all be trusted.

It was a perilous time to be a Norman in England.

"And where does this message need to be taken?" Fitz asked.

Odo would not look at Fitz when he spoke. "London."

"London?" Fitz could not believe it. "You want me to take a message that would be victory in our enemies' hands to London?"

"I know what I ask seems foolishness." Odo spoke in haste. "But – "

"Foolishness? Nay, call it what it is – madness! I am a FitzOsbern, not a servant to carry around messages. Is there not another with time to take on such a task?"

"There is none that I would trust more to complete this favour but you."

Fitz stopped. He looked at the man that was attempting to prevent a country from falling apart. The weight of it was showing in his eyes, and in the way that his hands curled about in his lap.

"There is none," he repeated, "but you. Will you take this burden from me?"

Fitz breathed out heavily. "We are in Canterbury now. How many days travel is it from here to London?"

"Three days. Two, depending on the horse. One if you decide to ride like the devil is chasing you."

"Which he may be." Fitz smiled. "My lord Odo, why have you asked me to do this?"

Odo swept an arm across him as he spoke. "Fitz, you know why."

"My lord," Fitz looked confused. "There are many men here that would be honoured to do this for you."

"And yet," Odo said thoughtfully, "there are few men here that have mastered the heathen tongue."

"I suppose," Fitz said slowly, "that I have. And yet Anglo-Saxon is not a difficult language to comprehend."

"You joke, surely!" Odo looked amazed. "The very sound of it confuses me, and I know very few that have even managed to remember a few phrases. Your skill with languages must be prodigious."

Fitz shrugged. "My aptitude is no surprise. It is always useful to speak one's enemies' language."

"And it is why you are so highly valued by the King, and by myself. There are few that can converse so well with the savages of this isle."

Fitz coloured slightly. "I am not accustomed to being so highly praised, my lord."

"You will need to – I think you have a long and prosperous career ahead of you."

Fitz looked at the man opposite him.

"I will take this burden from you."

Odo visibly relaxed. "I knew that you would. Your reward will be waiting for you here when you return."

"Make it sunshine!" Fitz rose, and his guest followed his lead. The two men stood, side by side at the entrance of the tent. The rain that had been falling slowly was now pelting into the ground, churning up the mud that had barely had time to dry.

Odo turned to his companion. "Be safe."

"I always am."

"When do you intend to leave?"

Fitz peered out of the tent. "If I waited for the rain to stop, I may never leave. First light tomorrow, I shall be away."

Odo clapped Fitz on the back. "God speed, my friend."

Fitz knew that the journey to London the next day was not going to be pleasant. Even if he ignored the fact that he would almost certainly have to undertake the journey whilst soaking wet, the roads – if you could call them roads – were now filled with bandits, men that had barely survived the invasion and were now determined to wreak vengeance on any man that even partially resembled a Norman. They were not very discerning.

Pulling his cloak tightly around his shoulders, Fitz left his tent. A young man, tall and with a head covered in black hair, quickly ran up to him.

"My lord?"

"Ah, Marmion," Fitz nodded. The young man was of a good family, but his father had died in the invasion. He was the younger son, and had needed a man to take charge of him – and as Fitz had no squire, he had taken him on. Marmion was vicious only when he needed to be, and a gentle spirit off the battle field. Just what a Norman should be. Moreover, he was one of the best horse riders that Fitz had ever seen, and he hoped that before too long, Marmion would be able to teach him.

"You are going, my lord?" Marmion's deep voice was full of concern. "The roads are dangerous."

"This is a favour for…a very great friend."

Marmion understood immediately what Fitz meant. "Well then," he said with a lazy smile, "I hope your friend has a lot of gold to reward you with when you return home!"

Fitz chuckled. "I think we can safely say that there is more than enough that my friend can do for me."

The two men smiled at each other, but Marmion's smile was the one that disappeared first.

"You will be careful."

It was a statement, not a question.

"I will," said Fitz reassuringly. "You'll be making hot baths for me again in no time."

Fitz turned to walk away, but Marmion put a hand on his arm.

"You cannot think of going now!"

Fitz shook his head. "I need to visit the city for a few items that I will need on my journey."

"Let me go," Marmion said. "I can easily gather for you whatever you need."

"I know," said Fitz. "But I have not seen Canterbury, and I have heard it is quite beautiful. I will not be long. Ready a horse for me – I shall be leaving early tomorrow morning."

Marmion bowed his head, and walked away.

Fitz walked along the corridor created by the mass of men, standing on both sides in the doorways of their tents. Almost one hundred men were camping here on the grounds of St Augustine's Abbey – one of the largest areas in Canterbury where the locals would refuse to bring their weapons. Their reverence for the holy ground was not felt by the Normans; every man that Fitz passed carried a sword, and their hands never ventured too far from its handle. The Normans had become accustomed to living in fear of their lives.

As Fitz entered the city, the sounds of traders and hawkers began to reach his ears. Even in this terrible weather, money must be spent.

"The best lace, the best lace that money can buy!"

"Get them hot, get them here, get them now…"

"…and I dare you to find better!"

Fitz smiled as he heard the babble of voices. It was almost second nature for him now, streaming out the Norman from the Anglo-Saxon, but he still struggled for some words within the Anglo-Saxon tongue. It was so different from anything he had ever encountered, just like this wild island where the rain almost always fell.

As he walked, some traders carefully approached him in broken Norman.

"Lord, lord see these, see these lord…"

Fitz waved them aside with a quick sweep of his hand, and was amazed to see them melt back into the general bustle of the street. He turned, and saw that the men were hurriedly talking amongst themselves, trying desperately not to be noticed by him. He caught something of what they were saying.

"…go back to his own country…"

Fitz sighed, and continued back along the main street within Canterbury. If only he could return home to Normandy.

The rain had subsided to a drizzle, but Fitz was still struggling to ignore it. His feet slipped on the wet stones of the street, and he muttered an obscenity under his breath. The last thing he needed now was an injury that would prevent him from fulfilling his promise to Odo.

Several of the shop fronts that he passed were boarded up, and a couple seemed empty, abandoned. Fitz poked his head into one. The door was unlocked, and the ribbons and silks that were laid across the shelves were covered with a thick layer of dust.

"My lord?"

A small child was peering in at the doorway, staring with wild, frightened eyes at the man in Norman armour standing in an Anglo-Saxon shop.

Fitz smiled at the child, although he wasn't quite sure whether it was a girl or a boy.

"Hello," he said softly in Anglo-Saxon. "My name is Fitz. What's yours?"

The child hesitated, clearly unsure how this strange man could be looking so odd and foreign with familiar and safe words pouring from his mouth.

Fitz smile broadened. "Is this your shop?"

The child shook their head slowly. "It is the shop of Cyneric."

His or her voice was soft, and didn't give away any secrets.

"And where is Cyneric now?"

"Gone."

"Gone?"

The child took an uncertain step backwards, but did not run away as Fitz suspected they wanted to.

"He went away to fight the bad men."

Fitz froze.

"The bad men?"

The child nodded slowly. "Bad men like you."

Shame coursed through Fitz, and he almost opened his mouth to argue – but then, where could he start?

"I am not a bad man," Fitz lowered himself onto his haunches, trying to make himself look smaller to this slip of humanity. "I'm really quite nice."

The child shook its head slowly, and said nothing.

"Did Cyneric not come back?" Fitz knew the answer, knew it as plainly as he could see the dust coating the man's livelihood, and knew that it would almost break a small part of him to see this child say it out loud. And yet he had to ask.

The child shook its head again. "Cyneric did not come back. No one did."

Fitz didn't know what to do with himself, but he arranged his face into what he hoped was a sensitive and thoughtful pose. The child ran. It obviously did not work.

Fitz turned on the spot, taking in everything that was left of a man's life. This man probably thought that he would be back home within days, ready to pick up the threads of his life again.

He shivered. A cold breeze swept in, bringing with it a scattering of rain. It reminded him that he should continue, that he needed to purchase a few items before evening fell.

Leaving the shop, however, Fitz saw that the child he had been speaking to had returned. With him – or her, he reminded himself – were four other children, all of various ages, and only two of them were definitely boys. The other two, like the first, was garbed in a mixture of shirt and off-cuts that hid exactly who they were.

"Hello," Fitz said uncertainly. "Who are these people?"

It was now Fitz's turn to take an uncertain step backwards. He had heard of bandits, but if these children really hoped to overpower him, surely they could not possibly think about doing it during daylight – in the centre of a busy street?

"I wanted you to see," the child stared up at the man that looked so frightening, but swallowing, maintained its composure. "I wanted you to see some of the children that have been left behind."

Fitz smiled sadly. "Your fathers did not return after the invasion? So your mothers and you are all alone?"

The children looked up at him, confused. One spoke up, a boy.

"Mother was taken away."

Fitz felt physically sick. He had heard – of course he had heard – of the unspeakable things that some Norman soldiers had done to the local women. He had assumed that it was a mix of bravado and lies. He had been sure that no man could ever…would ever…

The children looked up at him, confused. There was no self-pity in their faces.

Fitz thought about his family. About the wife that he had left behind.

He shuddered.

CHAPTER SIX

It had taken four days of hard riding, but at last the journey was over. Catheryn patted her horse gently on the shoulder. It was, like her, unaccustomed to such long days, but Catheryn had the added problem of blinking in the sunlight. It had been too long since she had been outside.

Her destination, she had been told by a man that wore the colours of Queen Matilda, was but a short journey around the hill that they had stabled their horses at. The sun shone high in the sky, and Catheryn adjusted herself on the horse, trying to find a place that wasn't uncomfortable.

She was weary, and saddle sore.

Turning a corner in the path that curled around the hill, Catheryn's eyes caught sight of the place that was to be her home for…a long time, if these Normans had anything to do with it. The castle rose high over the village that nestled in front of it.

"Not long now, mistress," the man that was accompanying her, with a name that Catheryn could not pronounce, said. He cast a smile at her. "Soon you will be cared for in a manner better suited to your station, my lady."

Catheryn returned the smile wearily. "I'm not entirely sure what my station is, at present," she admitted. "In England, I am a lady, in Normandy, I am a prisoner."

"No reason that you cannot be both," said the man stiffly. "The FitzOsberns are a noble family. They will treat you well."

Catheryn opened her mouth, but closed it again. There was no point in her trying to explain – trying to convince a man that there was a great deal of difference between commanding an entire household to being alone in a room for half the year.

By this point, they had reached the edge of the village. Many of the locals lifted their heads, but saw just another two travellers, and thought no more of it. A gaggle of young girls looked up at her shyly, before a woman shouted at them and they scattered, giggling and shrieking with laughter.

Catheryn looked around, and bitterness crept into her heart. These people were very like the villagers that she had left behind – but these people knew nothing of real pain and loss. They had lived in relative safety all of their lives. Not for them the coming drums, the fires, and the screams of their children…

"…my lady?"

The man had obviously been talking to her, and Catheryn blushed at her rudeness.

"My apologies," she said awkwardly, "I am tired."

"It is nothing," he replied. "I just wanted to welcome you to your new home."

Catheryn realised that they had arrived at the castle gate. The place where she would be a prisoner once more. Now the journey was over, she already missed it. The change from room to wilderness had been a welcome one, and for a few days she had managed to convince herself that she was truly free.

The man knocked solemnly on the great door, and within moments it was opened by a man in dark navy blue.

"Who knocks?"

"The lady Catheryn, sent by the Queen."

The answer was formal, and Catheryn was glad that she was not required to contribute anything. Despite the fact that it was only midday, she thought longingly of bed. Of a real bed, with a coverlet, and no rats to crawl in with her.

The man that had answered the door nodded, and pulled the door wide open so that the two horses could pass through.

As her horse walked on, Catheryn's eyes widened. What she had taken to be the outside of the castle was in fact a wall that surrounded it. Between the two was a grassy area with several tents, and people bustling between them, shouting out for more arrows, or a mug of mead.

Geffrei's home had seemed monstrously huge to Catheryn, and yet this castle was larger still. Catheryn's heart sank: this place, surely, would have a dungeon of some sort, not just a room in which to abandon her. She had been a fool to trust the words of Matilda.

Sinking lower on her horse, she meekly followed the man that had brought her so far. He walked his horse slowly to what Catheryn now saw was the actual entrance to the castle.

"And the name here is FitzOsbern?" she said quietly.

The man nodded. "A noble house, much beloved by the royal family. The lord here is in fact the cousin of our King."

Catheryn caught the reverence in his voice, and tried desperately not to roll her eyes. Another man easily impressed by birth. Her husband had been of low birth, but had earned his way to his position. This FitzOsbern was undoubtedly some sort of idiot, but his family had given him this place.

"The FitzOsberns," she repeated. She had never heard of them in England, and had no idea whether it was just the lord or whether or not he was married.

But that question was readily answered by the entrance of a woman, near Catheryn's own age, draped in rich silks and wearing a necklace of stones that glinted in the sunlight. This was obviously the lady of the house.

The man dismounted from his horse, and bowed low to the lady.

"My lady," he said deferentially.

The woman inclined her head, but said nothing.

"I bring greetings from our Queen, Matilda, and good tidings to you and yours," the man continued formally. "She bids you welcome this lady, a lady of the Anglo-Saxons, into your home. She asks that you care for her as a distinguished...guest."

The pause emphasised that her position was not that of a guest, but that of a prisoner. The fact that it stuck in their throats did nothing to help her.

Without waiting for assistance, Catheryn gracefully dismounted from her horse.

"I bid you thanks," she said slowly, her tongue stumbling slightly over the formal Norman greeting that she had memorised. "I honour the family that offers me shelter."

Her curtsey was in no way as low as the servant's, but it was a curtsey – something that Catheryn had debated on doing on the road, and eventually decided that there was no way of avoiding it.

The woman looked at her, coldly. There was no welcome in her face, and no hand to clasp. Turning away from Catheryn, she said to the man briskly, "I cannot follow her heathen tongue. Tell her to come inside."

She swept away into the castle.

Catheryn laughed in shock. The rudeness that the woman had shown her was beyond belief! She would never have admitted a guest into her home in that sort of manner, even if they had been unwelcome.

The man looked at her uncomfortably, shuffling his feet slightly and examining them hard rather than look at her. "My lady bids you – "

"I know exactly what your lady said," Catheryn cut across him.

He flushed. "My lady is nervous. I serve the Queen, but I trust my lady Adeliza just as much. Her husband is away, and she is not accustomed to greeting strangers."

Catheryn did roll her eyes this time. "Then she should learn. If I can learn to be a prisoner hundreds of miles from my home, she can learn to keep me in hers."

Ignoring his hissed reply, Catheryn walked past him and into the castle.

The woman that was so insistently rude to her was standing by the fire, which was slowly smouldering in the centre of the room. It was a hall, and many different rooms led from it. Catheryn could hear the entire household working away, despite the thick stone walls that were covered with gorgeous tapestries. The fire sparkled in the gold threads, and on the necklace hanging around the neck of the woman that was to be her jailor.

"My name," the woman spoke stiffly, "is Adeliza. Adeliza de Tosny FitzOsbern. My husband William FitzOsbern is across the water, caring for England for our King."

"I think England was doing rather well without your help."

Catheryn gasped and put her hands to her mouth.

"My lady, I must apologise – I am weary, and road-sore, and – "

"Enough."

The cold tones immediately stopped Catheryn from continuing. The woman had barely moved, but there was a power in her that caused Catheryn to look at her with fear.

"You are not a guest here, my lady," Adeliza looked at her with cold eyes. "You are not welcome, and you are not wanted. You are a prisoner of our lady Queen Matilda, and it is only due to her request that you are here."

Her eyes scanned the newcomer. Ragged clothes and dirty hair barely covered by a strange veil. She was thin, and could hardly stand. Adeliza shook her head.

"You will keep to your chambers, and you will know your place. Meals will be our only meeting, and I do not expect you to talk to me."

Catheryn tried to speak, but Adeliza spoke over her.

"You are a prisoner, and you will be treated as such. Do not think of attempting escape: our lands stretch far and wide from our home, and every man, woman, and child are loyal to us. They will see you, and they will bring you back."

Catheryn stared at the woman who was to be her jailor.

"You are not wanted, lady Catheryn of England."

Turning her back, she quickly left the room.

Catheryn almost laughed in shock. If she and that woman had met in England a year ago, it would be Adeliza scraping the knee. Catheryn greatly outranked this woman who did not think her good enough to give a proper welcome.

Catheryn realised that the man that had brought her to this place had gone. She was standing alone in the hall of a castle, miles and miles from everyone that she knew and cared for. She was truly alone. Tears welled in her tired eyes.

"My lady?"

Catheryn turned quickly, and the servant girl took a hasty step backwards.

"My lady Adeliza bid me take you to your chambers," she said quietly.

Catheryn frowned. "And does your lady Adeliza bid you be polite to me?"

A look of confusion blossomed over the servant girl's face. "My lady?"

Catheryn sighed. "Forget my hurried words," she said quietly. "I am too tired to argue. Take me to a place where I can sleep."

CHAPTER SEVEN

The moon had changed from old to new twice, and Catheryn had barely settled in the castle of the FitzOsberns. It felt like every day was a new exercise for the household to remind her that she was not wanted, an outsider. Their prisoner.

Each morning, when the household broke their fast together, Catheryn would sit between Adeliza and a young woman who never spoke to her. During the first few days after Catheryn had arrived at the castle, she had tried to speak to Adeliza. Catheryn knew that there was no reason that she, an Anglo-Saxon, could not have a rational conversation with a Norman. She was too old, and had seen too much of the world to believe that there was really that much difference between them. And yet still, Adeliza forced silence onto the table.

Catheryn was beginning to crave the small conversations that she had had with Lina, when she had been a prisoner of Geffrei. At times it made her laugh – she could never have imagined wishing herself back to those days of silence and solitude. And yet she had at least had someone that acknowledged her presence once each day.

The summer was hot, and heavy. Much of the castle's household would try and spend their days outside in the shade, where the heat was not trapped and fires were not still burning. Within the first week of her staying with the FitzOsbern family, Catheryn had discovered the way to their kitchen. Her love for creating something delicious with only her hands and a fire was a skill her husband had always mocked her for, and yet done it with a smile, and a kiss.

"You're not a servant!" Selwyn would say. "Let someone else do that…"

But Catheryn could not deny the passion that she had for feeding the stomachs of those that she loved, and she had passed that fire onto her daughter. Annis. Would she be in a kitchen now, Catheryn wondered. Would she be eating?

Catheryn had hoped to find solace in the kitchen of the FitzOsbern castle, and yet she was denied it. The servants there could not seem to understand why she wanted to be there; they suspected her. Catheryn knew that they had probably been fed lies about Anglo-Saxons poisoning all the food that they prepared…and yet it would give her great peace to lose herself in the kneading of some dough.

"Please," she said to a stony face. "I will not be any trouble."

"You are trouble," was the reply. "Do not return here."

The chambers that had been given to her by Adeliza were not large, but they were comfortable. The first room that led off the corridor had a small fire in it, two chairs that had beautiful silks draped over them, and a chest that she had put her meagre belongings in. A cloak. A second dress that had been given to her by a servant girl, who had muttered that her mistress Adeliza no longer wanted it. A flower she had picked.

A doorway beside this chest led to her bed chamber. This room was just as sparsely furnished; the bed was the only item within the entire room, but it had a straw mattress and several rugs. For Catheryn, it was palatial, and it was all hers.

But as the sun rose each morning, the stifling heat would become oppressive, and she would have to leave the castle. Adeliza had not warned her about trying to escape, but each time she meandered past the stables, the men would stiffen, and rise from their jobs. They would watch her walk past, and only return to their duties once they were sure that she had gone.

It was clear that she was not permitted to ride.

And so Catheryn went to the only place where she knew she would feel comfortable. She found a field that had been left fallow this year, full of grasses and butterflies, and lay down in the centre. She had always done this when a child, had always felt safest surrounded by the tall grasses that whispered to her in the wind.

That childhood was long gone, and yet the feeling of being swept away by the wind brought Catheryn more peace than she had known since leaving her home.

Catheryn closed her eyes. She was alone, as if on the ocean, where none could touch her.

She could almost have fallen asleep, were it not for the dry sobs that broke into her daydream. For a moment, Catheryn could not fathom what the howling noise was, or where it was coming from. Eyes still shut, she brushed her hands through the long grass, feeling the snag of flower heads against her fingertips. If she just ignored it, it would go away.

But of course, it would not. After several minutes, Catheryn sat up, eyes open, scanning the horizon for the source of the commotion.

It was not difficult to find. A girl, perhaps fifteen years, perhaps slightly older, was hunched in a tangled heap in one edge of the field. The racking sobs were coming from her, and although Catheryn could not see her face, it was clear that she was deeply distressed.

Annis would be about the same age, Catheryn thought. Her heart wrenched at the thought that her own child could be just as distraught, but hundreds of miles away, with no one to comfort her.

But then, this girl does not seem to have anyone to comfort her, either, Catheryn thought. She looked around. There was no one but her within earshot.

A swell of maternal nurturing swept through Catheryn, and she knew that she would not be easy until she had spoken to the crying girl.

Pulling herself upright, and dusting the soil off her clothes, Catheryn began to hesitantly move towards the girl. She was so distracted by her own tears that it was not until Catheryn was without reach of touching her shoulder that the girl suddenly lifted her head, her face full of shock.

"What?" The girl said, her voice shaking slightly. "Wh-what – who are you?"

Catheryn smiled gently. "My name is Catheryn. What is yours?"

The girl pulled a hand up to sniff at her nose, and Catheryn saw that the clothes that she wore were no peasant's garb. This girl was of a good family.

"Emma," the girl said slowly, eyeing Catheryn up and down warily. "Who are you? You're that woman that eats with us, aren't you?"

Catheryn dropped to the ground next to her, and pulled her legs underneath her body. "I am no one in particular," she said. "I hope you do not find my question impertinent, my lady, but what has caused you to lose so many tears?"

The girl called Emma sat up a little bit straighter, and Catheryn stifled a laugh. She had known the title 'my lady' would soon brighten up the girl's spirits.

"I have a sister," Emma began, turning her body slightly so that she was facing Catheryn more. "She and I are twins. She is slightly older than me, by but an hour or so, and yet she uses it to taunt me, to claim power over me."

"Do you not love her?" Catheryn asked quietly.

Emma sighed, and looked around at the field they were sitting in. "It is impossible for me not to," she admitted, "for she is my second soul in this world, and we do adore each other. It is just…difficult." Her gaze suddenly focused back on Catheryn. "Do you have a sister?"

Catheryn shook her head, and plucked some grass from the ground. She twirled it between her fingers as she spoke. "I was the only child of my parents."

Emma's eyes widened. "Just you, alone?"

"Yes, but we had a large household, so I was never lonely. In fact, one of the boys that I grew up with eventually became my husband."

"I could not imagine being a child alone in a family," Emma confessed, and added in a whisper, "although sometimes I wish I was."

She looked up at the older woman nervously, but Catheryn laughed.

"I think we all of us ladies wish that, at one point or another. Tell me about your family."

Happiness spread across Emma's face as she considered her beloved family.

"Well…"

"Emma?"

A voice rang out over the field, and both Emma and Catheryn turned to see from whence it came. The figure of a woman, draped in a blood red dress, was hurtling towards them from the castle.

"Emma!"

As the figure drew nearer, it became clear to Catheryn that the woman running towards them in such disarray was none other than Adeliza. Catheryn turned to the girl that she had been comforting.

"Is that…?"

Emma sighed deeply, and nodded.

By this time, Adeliza had reached them.

"Emma, my darling, Isabella has told me – "

But Adeliza stopped short. Her eyes flew between her daughter and the woman that had arrived to be their prisoner. It was clear that they had been talking, and the tears on her daughter's face that she had rushed to dry were already gone.

"My lady Adeliza," Catheryn quickly rose, and smiled at her hostess – or jailor. "We had just been discussing your family. Emma tells me that she has some wonderful siblings. You must, of course, take the credit for that family bond."

Adeliza's mouth opened, but nothing came out. Emma, in her turn, rose also.

"I must apologise, my lady mother, for not coming to you about this. I needed somewhere to be alone, and then this woman – "

"I see," Adeliza cut her daughter's apologetic speech off, but Catheryn was relieved to see that she was smiling. "Run back home, my love, and speak to your sister. She is almost as repentant as you are."

The mother and daughter smiled at each other, and then moved together quickly for an embrace.

Emma ran back to the castle, skirts flying in the breeze – leaving Catheryn and Adeliza to a slightly awkward silence.

Catheryn waited and waited, but Adeliza said not a word. Both of them had turned to watch Emma go, but Adeliza had not moved around to face Catheryn after Emma was out of sight. Catheryn was not sure whether it was worth raising her voice; but then she did not know the Norman customs. Was it permissible for her to just simply walk away?

"My youngest," Adeliza said suddenly, still facing away. "You think that you have learned everything that you can, and yet each one continues to surprise you."

"You are blessed," Catheryn said. "I had but two children, one daughter, one son, and both as different from each other as summer and winter."

Adeliza swivelled on the spot, and Catheryn saw that she was smiling.

"It is so often the way," she said. Then her smile faltered. "You say that you *had* two children?"

A fist of iron clenched around Catheryn's heart, and she felt her legs shake. She sat down – out of desire or out of necessity, she knew not which.

Something passed across Adeliza's face that Catheryn had never seen before. It was not until the woman she had barely spoken to knelt to sit down with her that she realised what it was: tenderness.

"You lost a child?"

The voice that Catheryn expected to be full of disdain and indifference was instead a strange combination of interest and respect. Adeliza looked sad, and yet embarrassingly intrigued.

Catheryn forced herself to respond. She nodded. "My son."

There was silence between the two mothers, two women that suddenly had more in common than any two men could possibly imagine.

Adeliza's voice was almost a whisper. "I lost my first born son."

Catheryn's hand reached out to the woman that was strangely both her captor and her sister.

"Tell me about your boy," she said gently.

Adeliza smiled wanly. "He was never really mine to begin with," she confessed. "We had him for such a short time. The Lord only blessed us with him for five days, and then he simply did not awaken."

She clasped Catheryn's outstretched hand tightly.

"It does not matter how long we have them for," Catheryn said softly. "They are still precious to us."

Adeliza nodded. "And your son?"

"He was much older," Catheryn confessed. "And yet still very much my baby. He was but six years when...when he was taken."

"Taken?"

Catheryn swallowed. She had never thought that she would discuss this with another woman, let alone a Norman woman. And what about her husband? As a Norman lord, it was almost certain that he had been one of the invaders, one of the fighters. It could easily be he that had taken the two most important men from her.

"In the invasion," she managed to say. "They...they came to our home, and they killed him."

The hands that were entwined were quickly dropped. The two women sat in silence, knowing exactly who 'they' were.

"But then," Adeliza said quietly, "is this not our lot? Is this not what it is to be a woman: to create life, and then to have it snatched away from us before our eyes?"

"You speak truth," said Catheryn, "and yet I wish it were not so."

"I thought, once," Adeliza smiled ruefully at her companion, "that my daughters would live in a better world, and have a different life. But the longer I spend in it, the more I realise that it is exactly the same."

"Your two daughters — what are their ages?"

"A month before your arrival they celebrated their fifteenth year." Adeliza smiled at the thought of those happy memories. "And your daughter?"

Catheryn sighed. "Annis is perhaps just a year older. She does not look much older, but she is."

"Where is she?" Adeliza said curiously.

"She remained in England. I was taken during the Conquest, taken here to Normandy against my wishes.

Annis stayed behind...and I do not know what fate I have left her to," Catheryn said bitterly.

Shock covered Adeliza's face. "She is still there?"

Catheryn nodded.

"But – you are all that she has of family left in this world! Should you not go to her?"

Catheryn tried not to let the bitterness of her soul seep into her words, but she could not help it. "You are the one keeping me here, Adeliza. If I could will myself to her through sheer power of spirit, I tell you, I would be there. But I am not permitted to return to her."

"But...but..." Adeliza stammered, "but anything could happen to her!"

"You think I do not know that?"

A soft breeze floated through the field, and the grasses murmured their secrets. The sound of two girls laughing was carried by that same breeze, and the two women turned to see Emma, and a girl that Catheryn assumed was her twin sister, running and laughing around the castle walls.

"Blossoming into womanhood," remarked Catheryn.

Adeliza laughed. "And yet the child remains!"

Catheryn thought of Emma and her wailing tears, and joined in the laughter.

After their giggles had subsided, Adeliza voice turned serious once more.

"I must thank you," she said formally, "for calming my daughter."

Catheryn smiled. "I would that some woman is doing the same for mine."

CHAPTER EIGHT

Evening had drawn in faster than anyone had thought possible, and once more, a feast was being held in the castle of the family FitzOsbern. For the first time since she had arrived, Catheryn finally felt like her presence was not an insult.

Sitting beside her was Adeliza, and the two women talked together quite happily. In fact, they had barely stopped speaking since they had joined together at the table.

"So you have three children?" Catheryn asked. She looked around the room, with the four tables set out as a square, and saw Emma laughing with a girl that looked remarkably like her. The younger woman caught her eye, and they shared a smile of understanding across the room. It appeared that Emma and her twin were back on speaking terms.

On the other side of Adeliza was a tall, pale young man with a rich cloak and a highly decorated belt. Catheryn had assumed since the first day of her arrival that he was a son of the household, but he had said nothing to her and, from what she had seen, very little to anyone else.

"Four," Adeliza replied with a smile. "The three youngest you can see here. Emma, you have met, and her sister Isabella."

Catheryn looked over once again at the twin sisters.

"It is strange to think that Isabella is but a short time older," she said. "Does that affect – "

Catheryn stopped suddenly, and reddened.

Adeliza looked puzzled. "What is it?"

"I must beg your forgiveness," Catheryn said awkwardly. "In my country, it is normal to ask such questions of a host, but I think perhaps it is not so acceptable here."

Instead of a frown, however, her words were met with a laugh.

"Oh, Catheryn," Adeliza smiled. "It is almost expected between us Normans to enquire about marriages amongst our children. Do not be embarrassed; it is natural to wonder."

Catheryn's smile returned. "Is it really so accepted?"

Adeliza shrugged. "Some ask because they are curious, and some ask because they have someone in mind – a friend, a cousin, a mistress – and some just ask because they need to show an interest. Not to ask would in fact have drawn more attention!"

"And so," asked Catheryn eagerly, "your girls' prospects. What are they?"

Adeliza's smile flickered. "Not so certain as they once were," she admitted, lowering her voice so that the babble of the room could mask her words. "Ever since the invasion…"

Her voice trailed off as she looked at Catheryn.

"I do not wish to offend."

Now Adeliza looked anxious and embarrassed, but for Catheryn, it was with just as little cause.

"Come now," she said, "was it you that invaded my home? Was it you that decided to go across the water? Did you decide who should and who should not die? No. And so continue, my lady Adeliza," Catheryn's smile encouraged her to speak, "please go on."

Adeliza swallowed, and continued.

"You must remember, my lady Catheryn," formality slipping back into her phrases again, "that many things that once were are no longer are because of the invasion. Some families that were once great lost all of their sons, and now have only daughters. Others that had no land are now rich men."

"The game has changed."

"Exactly," Adeliza nodded at Catheryn's words. "It is becoming more and more complicated, especially as the girls are now much older."

Their faces turned to the subject of their conversation.

"They will soon be married," Catheryn said slowly. "Who do you have in mind?"

Adeliza pursed her lips thoughtfully. "Isabella is the eldest, which means that she is most likely to marry Ralph de Gael."

Thoughts stirred in Catheryn's memory.

"Do I not know him?"

Adeliza nodded. "I would not be surprised. He was born in England, but fought on the side of our King William during the invasion. He is a little…older than my Isabella, but he is a good match."

"What is his age?"

"He is nearing thirty years," Adeliza confessed, and then continued quickly, "but really, it takes that time for a man to be worth marrying!"

Catheryn laughed. "In too many cases, you speak the truth!"

"Well," Adeliza said after they stopped chuckling, "he would be a good match for Isabella – but now I think it more likely that he shall marry Emma."

Catheryn screwed up her nose in confusion, and ripped some bread off the loaf before her.

"Why?"

Adeliza looked around her, as if to check that no one was listening to their conversation.

"I have not spoken of this with anyone," she said conspiratorially, "not even my husband, for I have not seen him since he left to go with our King to England. But there is now no limits on the type of man that my daughters can marry – no limits of country, especially."

Catheryn's eyes widened as she began to understand what Adeliza was hinting at.

"You mean...?"

Adeliza nodded. "Having a husband that is English is no longer a problem, and there is one man that is the prize."

Catheryn spluttered out her words, "you can't mean...Edgar Ætheling?"

"You don't think that my daughter is worthy of him?" Adeliza's voice was frosty once more, and Catheryn was brutally reminded of their first meeting.

"Wait, wait," she said hurriedly, "you misunderstand me. I just did not realise that Edgar was still an eligible match for any young woman. I would have thought that King William would not want him to marry a woman of such a high status family. Surely Isabella and Edgar's children would be a great threat to the royal family?"

Adeliza waved away that concern with her hand. "Edgar cannot seriously consider himself an alternative to William. His marriage to Isabella will only secure her and her children's lands both here and in England. Ralph de Gael will then marry Emma."

"God forbid."

Adeliza and Catheryn turned in shock to look at the man that had spoken. He blushed: it was the young man sitting beside Adeliza. He turned away from them, and started talking to his neighbour.

The two women couldn't help themselves. They collapsed into giggles. They only paused in their laughter to help themselves to more succulent pork that was being offered to them by a servant. The man sitting on the other side of Adeliza leaned forward to help himself too, but before either woman could speak to him, he returned to his seat and began eating silently.

"That," Adeliza said in an undertone, "is my son, Roger."

Catheryn stole a glance at the boy – or rather, young man. His hair mirrored his mother's, but she had to assume that his face was closer to his father's, as there were no similarities there.

"Tell me about him," Catheryn said, turning back to Adeliza. "He seems very…different from his sisters."

Adeliza smiled happily. "He is a little shy, perhaps, and a little too concerned with the way that people think about him, but Roger is a good man. He is seventeen years, and very good with our villagers. The people love him."

Catheryn nodded. "Those are good traits for a son – but then, did you not say that you had four children? Where is the fourth?"

"William is my oldest, named for his father," Adeliza drained her goblet, and gestured for a servant to bring her more wine. "In fact, he is lately married."

"Congratulations! Who is the lucky woman?"

"There is no reason why you would know her – Maud is her name, but she comes from no family of particular repute."

Catheryn hesitated, but then continued to say what she thought. "I would have expected the eldest son of such a house as yours to marry a woman of great power and wealth."

Adeliza smiled. "You forget that everything has changed. Before this time last year, this house was ancient, and yet had accrued little honour. But my husband is the cousin of our King William, and our power rises with his. William married almost three years ago now. Maud may not have a title or a name worth keeping, but she is beautiful, well-learned, and came with a large dowry. What's more, they are fond of each other. We saw no reason to prevent a love match as it brought so much."

Catheryn looked approving. "That is indeed a good match; for both you, and her family. It is rare indeed to marry for love. When do you hope for children?"

Adeliza shrugged. "I do not expect it, although I certainly do hope. I think she is a little young to be a mother. She was but fourteen when they wed."

"I do not know," mused Catheryn. "I was near her age now when I was blessed with Annis."

"Tell me about her," said Adeliza. "I feel that I have spoken far too much about my brood."

"I do not blame you." Catheryn watched as Emma and Isabella pushed their plates aside, and they leaned together to whisper. "But really, there is not much to tell."

"Nonsense – I know that every mother has almost too much to say about her children!"

Catheryn smiled unwillingly. "I suppose you are right. Annis is…I suppose she is a wilful child. She has long blonde hair and bright blue eyes, and loves being in the kitchen, at the centre of any home."

Adeliza looked shocked. "You – you let her serve you?"

"It is not as it seems," Catheryn said hastily. "It is not that Annis is a servant, but more that she loves it…and who am I to deny her."

"I agree with you there," Adeliza said heavily. "It has never been in my power to refuse my children anything."

Silence fell between them, but it was a comfortable one. Catheryn knew that she had to break it.

"Adeliza?"

"Yes?"

Catheryn swallowed. She knew that what she was about to say would probably end the friendly accord between herself and the mistress of the house, but there was no way that she could forgive herself if she did not speak now.

"I was hoping – "

"You know," Adeliza interrupted, "I must apologise for my behaviour when you first arrived here. I am ashamed to admit that I saw you as more of a burden on my household than a blessing. Having you here brings greater scrutiny from the royal household and…" Her voice trailed off, but it regained its strength again. "And that is not always welcome."

Catheryn opened her mouth to speak, but Adeliza put up a hand to stop her. A dark ruby ring encircled her middle finger.

"I know that you have done nothing to deserve the treatment that you and your people have suffered. But in these last few hours, you have become a wonderful mixture of friend and stranger to me. I hope," Adeliza smiled nervously, "I hope we can continue to be friends."

Catheryn was overwhelmed. "I don't know what…I don't know how to respond to that. That I have gained your faith and friendship – it is too much."

The two women smiled at each other, but one of them knew that she had to speak up now, before it was too late. And so she did.

"Adeliza. I cannot hear you speak of our friendship without asking one great favour from you."

The smile that covered her friend's face fell slightly.

"Catheryn – "

"I know that what I ask is much," Catheryn said in a rushed voice, "but I must ask. Can you help me…can you help me find my daughter?"

Adeliza looked at the woman sitting next to her. Still in the vigour of life, Catheryn unmistakably showed signs of difficult living. Grief was etched into the lines around her eyes, and there was a sadness in her mouth that never really left.

"Catheryn," Adeliza said gently, placing a hand over

her companion's, "I know something of the pain that you feel, and if it is even half of that which I imagine, I know that it is agony. But I cannot help you. You forget. As much as our friendship may blossom and grow, you are still a prisoner here."

CHAPTER NINE

Fitz dropped his head into his hands. The haze of voices around him washed over his sore head, with a few phrases managing to reach his tired mind despite himself.

"It simply cannot be – "

"It must be him, or I shall forbid it!"

Raising himself to attention once more, Fitz tried to smile.

He was sitting in a room with some of the most important and noble people in both England and Normandy in London, and his head hurt. The more the discussion continued, the more fractious everyone became – and the more wine was drunk. The letter that he had carried to London for Odo had concerned this meeting, and once again Fitz cursed the moment that he agreed to carry it.

A tall man stood up, and without saying a word, the din settled down to silence.

"Now," said King William, "this has bored me. My wife's coronation is not a matter of discussion. It is a stupendous event, which all of you are *honoured* to be a part of, let alone consulted on."

His fierce eyes scanned the room, and men that had charged into battle roaring dropped their gaze, ashamed.

"You." The King pointed at Fitz. "And you two. You may stay. Everyone else must leave."

"But your majesty," protested a bishop that Fitz could see was swaying slightly from the sheer amount that he had drunk.

It did not take a single word from the King. He simply looked at his subject, and the argument was won. Without a moment's hesitation, the room had emptied.

Fitz looked around him, barely aware of who else King William had wanted to stay. He saw that Matilda was exactly where she had been throughout the entire evening; sitting by the fire, a piece of embroidery work in her lap, her delicate hands working her needle whilst her vibrant eyes followed the intense discussion that had surrounded her since she had first sat down. Beside her was the chair of her husband, who was still standing.

A man stirred to Fitz's left, and he saw that his brother Osbern was there.

"Osbern?"

The man looked up, and smiled nervously.

"My lord?"

"God's tears, you cannot fail to know me?"

But then, it had been several years since the brothers had last met. Their father Osbern had always wanted both of his sons to succeed, and for all of his lowly beginnings, had powerful relatives. His aunt had been not only the grandmother of the previous King of England, Edward, but was also the grandmother of its current King, William the Conqueror. This in some way made the FitzOsbern brothers cousins to royalty, and their father had taken advantage of that fact in a way that had been brilliant and daring. Placing his eldest son in the care of William's father, Robert, he had made sure that his younger son, Osbern, became King Edward of England's chaplain. And so the seeds were sown: whatever happened, the FitzOsbern boys would have a friend.

"Fitz!" Recognition covered his brother's face as he searched out those familiar features that made them almost look like twins – and yet it had been almost ten years since he had seen it. "Goodness, what are you doing here in my country?"

Fitz laughed, almost with relief to see a familiar face that he did not have to speak to with care lest he offend.

"Your country?"

The heavy tones of the King swept over their smiles. Osbern's face dropped in horror, but Fitz touched him reassuringly on the shoulder.

"It is an expression, my lord King," Fitz said to the man that commanded two of the largest kingdoms in Europe. "Our father made sure we were loyal to one country each: Osbern went to England, and I remained in Normandy."

The King nodded briefly. "Then all is well. Come, draw close with us and Ealdred; there is much to discuss."

Fitz saw that an elderly man in the robes of an archbishop now sat next to Matilda. The two brothers picked up a bench that was nearby, and moved it to the fire so that the five could continue to talk to make preparations for the coronation.

"It has taken too long," King William said ruefully, shaking his head. "I had meant for you to be crowned with me, my love."

The two shared a look that radiated understanding and joy. Fitz was almost embarrassed to witness it.

"It is of no matter," Matilda said softly, finally putting down her needle. "It was more important then for you to take the crown properly. I could never have travelled across the sea in time."

William snorted. "It should still not have taken two years to get to this point. Now it is May, and you are still Queen in my eyes only!"

"I must protest, my King," Osbern spoke up properly for the first time, and Fitz was astonished to see just how confident his little brother had become. He was still only a chaplain, and yet he spoke to King William as if they were trusted friends. But then, Fitz reminded himself, Osbern was accustomed to speaking to Kings, advising them, being trusted by them. It was he, Fitz, that was new to this. "Your lady is hailed as Queen throughout this land."

"And my lord," the man called Ealdred finally began to talk, "you could have done nothing these last few months. The rebellions by the Welsh, and the troubles in Exeter – it was more important to deal with them first."

William sighed. "You both speak the truth. But this is not the time to dwell on my mistakes and misfortunes – the day grows late, and I am sure that more than one of us would not say no to a comfortable bed."

His eyes moved to his wife. Matilda was once again with child, although it was not widely known. She had recently moved into her sixth month, and in certain lights and fabrics, was beginning to show.

Matilda smiled. "It matters not to me when I return to my chamber. Our kingdom is more important than that."

The royal couple shared a smile, and then William turned to Ealdred.

"Which date do you think would be best to organise the coronation of my lady?"

Ealdred considered for a moment, and then spoke. "It is usually preferable to link the day of the coronation with a holy day. You remember, my lord, that Edward was crowned on Easter Sunday, and you yourself were crowned by me on the day of our Lord's birth."

Fitz realised now who this man was – the Archbishop of York. Despite being of English birth, he had survived the Conquest, and had even crowned William on Christmas Day of 1066. But he could not remember why it had been he, and not the Archbishop of Canterbury. It was usually his role and right. But he was falling behind the conversation.

"So it is decided," William stated in a voice full of relief. "The coronation will occur on Whit Monday. Which day is that, exactly?"

"Easter this year was the twenty third day in March," chimed in Osbern quickly, "making Whit Monday the eleventh day of May."

Ealdred raised a white eyebrow, and Fitz could not tell whether he was impressed or shocked at the quick way in which his brother had spoken to the King.

"Excellent," said Matilda, "some of the best flowers will be blossoming. It will be beautiful."

"It is your presence that shall make the event a success, my dear," William smiled softly, but then turned a serious eye to the Archbishop.

"I shall begin the preparations," Ealdred said with a smile on his face. "And I thank you, my King, and you, my lady, for this honour."

"The honour remains with me, my lord," Matilda smiled wickedly, "for do not you think I am blessed to be crowned by a man that has made three Kings?"

The smile that had cut across Ealdred's face disappeared, and Fitz saw a similar change in William. He could not believe that Matilda could be so bold – by saying such things, she claimed that both Harold and Edgar Ætheling were rightful Kings, something that was treason under William's reign.

But Matilda was clearly more comfortable than any other man in the room.

"Now," she said, glancing at each man in turn, "what other arrangements must be made?"

Ealdred coughed, and all present turned to him. He was, Fitz reminded himself while trying not to smile, their leading authority on king-making.

"The Anglo-Saxons," and Fitz noticed that the old man's hands trembled as he referred to his people, "have a typical way of doing this, but never before has a Queen been crowned in this way. It is totally new."

"New?" William looked confused. "But there have been other Queens before – Emma was Edward's lady and companion."

"But that," Ealdred smiled, "is precisely my point. They were always called companions, and never were Queens such as our great Matilda."

"I do not understand the difference," Matilda spoke up. "Why change what has gone before? Surely if the English are to love me, we should keep to their old ways."
Fitz's mouth opened, but before he could say anything, his brother chimed in.

"But you are a different Queen, my lady. You are to rule Normandy when our King is here, and rule England when he returns across the sea. You are the mother of a new dynasty of rulers. There must be a distinction between you and those that have gone before you."

Matilda still did not seem convinced.

"What say you, Fitz?"

Fitz swallowed. He knew that Matilda was more intelligent than almost any other woman that he had ever met, and that if you had suggested to most men but three years ago that a mere woman could have so much power over a nation, they would have laughed. None were laughing now.

"My lady Queen," Fitz said slowly, "a coronation is a sacred moment. It is a vow that you take to honour and protect the people. But if you are going to be a different Queen than the Queens that this land has seen, it makes sense that the moments that make you a Queen are different in their turn. I see no harm in adding to the ceremony."

"Exactly," William said. "Exactly how I would have said it. Thank you Fitz. We do not have to alter the old, but simply extend it. Ealdred, can I leave this to you?"

Ealdred nodded. "I will also create the *laudes regiae*."

The unfamiliar words grated on Fitz's ears, and he could not help but ask.

"The what, my lord archbishop?"

Ealdred looked at Fitz properly for the first time, and smiled. "The *laudes regiae*. It is a song that is sung at every coronation – a prayer in song. Every monarch has their own created for them, although it follows a similar pattern each time. I would be honoured," he directed this last part at his King, "to create one for our marvellous Queen."

William did not reply, but turned to look at Matilda.

Fitz's eyes were beginning to sting with tiredness, and he fought the urge to rub them. He must stay awake – it was an incredible mark of respect that he had even been included in these discussions. He would see them out to the end.

"The only things that I think need to be addressed," Osbern was saying, "are the regalia that our lady will be presented with."

"Regalia?" Ealdred said sharply.

Osbern nodded. "If we are to distinguish our lady Queen from all others that have gone before her, if she is to lead in our lord King William's stead when he is gone from us, if she is to make decisions that are just and true…it is vital that she be seen to be just as endowed with gifts as our King."

"Just as endowed?" William said gruffly. "Would you that I handed over the kingdom to her?"

But Matilda laughed. "I think Osbern speaks truth, my love. Without an orb and a sceptre, I am just another companion. With them, I am a Queen."

William sat in silence for a while as he considered. Fitz had to hold his breath from yawning aloud.

"So be it," he said finally with a wry smile. "I see that you are to claim everything that I am, Matilda."

"Just as you promised me on the day of our wedding," she reminded him with a matching smile.

Osbern opened his mouth nervously. "My lord King?"

William raised an eyebrow in answer.

Swallowing, Osbern continued. "May I make another suggestion?" Without waiting for a reply, he spoke more. "Every King of this island has been presented with a coronation ring. It is a visible reminder of their power and responsibility, both of the monarch and their people. Should not our Queen Matilda receive such a gift?"

There was an intake of breath in the room, and Fitz was unsure whether he was alone in it or whether he was joined by others in a medley of shock. A coronation ring?

Fitz looked at William, waiting for his King to speak, but to his surprise it was a female voice that broke the silence.

"I thank you, Osbern, for your kind thoughts and words," Matilda's voice was soft, but there was a power within it that made Fitz relax. "I think that you are right to suggest a coronation ring. But let it not be one as great as our King's – instead, a more simple one would be appropriate. Is that possible, my King?"

The more formal phrase was clearly intended to appeal to her husband, and judging by the smile on his face, Fitz guessed that she had succeeded.

"One day," the King said, "I will be able to refuse you something. But today, I offer you whatever you want with my blessing."

Ealdred stood slowly, his bones creaking in a way that made more than one person flinch. "I apologise, my King, my Queen, but I must retire. An old man such as myself cannot help but feel his age when the stars are bright."

Matilda rose. "Sleep well, my lord archbishop," she said, "and I apologise for keeping you awake for so long."

"It is high time we each returned to our chambers," William rose, and placed a protective arm around his wife. "Let the preparations commence tomorrow, at first light."

Ealdred, Osbern, and Fitz all bowed as their monarchs exited the room.

"I shall speak to you once the sun has returned," Ealdred said to the two brothers. "Until then, my lords."

Fitz watched the elderly man leave the room, but before he could say anything to his brother, a figure walked through the doorway.

"My lord?"

"Marmion," Fitz relaxed. It was unnerving, being in a place with too many corridors, full of places for men to hide and hear information never meant for their ears. "We are not finished, I shall return shortly."

Marmion reddened as he looked at the two men.

"I am sorry, my lord," he said gruffly. "I did not mean to disturb you. It is only – I saw our King leave, and I wanted to speak to you about the coronation."

Fitz looked at Osbern, who shrugged. Fitz turned back to Marmion.

"Speak, Marmion – and do it quickly, my brother and I are quite exhausted."

Relief emanated from Marmion's shoulders as he breathed out a large sigh.

"My lord," he said, addressing Osbern, "I did not realise that you were also of the house of FitzOsbern. It is an honour to meet you, and – "

"Yes, yes," Osbern waved a hand. "To your point, my man. We have been talking these few hours."

Marmion blushed again, and Fitz wondered once more how a man that large and powerful could ever be embarrassed.

"I had a thought, my lords, on the coronation. A way to increase the spectacle, to make it memorable – to make sure that no one doubts our King William and Queen Matilda."

Fitz smiled.

"And you think that you can organise this idea? Will it cost much?"

"Nothing at all," Marmion said eagerly. "And if you do not wish to be named as a part of it, I shall take responsibility for the outcome myself."

"Then we are agreed; make your plans," Fitz said quietly. "Now go: I have one final piece of royal business to discuss with my brother."

Marmion bowed, and left the room. Fitz waited until he was completely sure he was out of earshot before speaking.

"Is it really necessary..." Fitz started, looking around him to ensure that they would not be overheard. "Is it really necessary to go to all of this trouble for Matilda?"

Osbern shook his head. "Without this coronation, Matilda is no Queen. Without Matilda, William is no King."

CHAPTER TEN

Matilda was dressed in the most elegant dress that Fitz had ever seen. Her shoulders were covered in a rich fur cloak, and gold was embroidered around the edges. Unlike her neck, which was encircled with several necklaces glittering with jewels, her hands were bare.

Fitz craned his neck from where he was standing in the Old Minster. There had been some debate whether the Old or New Minster in Winchester would be the best place to crown Matilda as Queen, but once again, tradition had won. This was where King Edward had been crowned, all of those years ago, and that's exactly where Matilda would be crowned.

Hundreds of people were standing in the large nave, but a careful path from the door to the altar had been marked out with petals of flowers. Matilda was standing in the doorway, framed by two women. Fitz recognised one of them – Madeline was a Norman woman of great beauty that he had seen many times at the royal court across the water. The other woman was a mystery to him.

"That's her!"

Fitz titled his head to watch a pair of Anglo-Saxon men whisper eagerly.

"No, truly?"

"On my honour," said the first man, a wide smile across his face. "That is her – Queen Edith!"

Fitz's eyes widened as he turned back to the trio of females by the door. So that was her: the wife, now widow of King Edward.

Matilda and her two companions began to slowly walk through the crowd. As they passed, men and women bowed their heads at the woman that was to become mother and sister to them.

Ealdred cleared his throat noisily.

"We, the blessed people that live here and across the water, are gathered to witness this glorious day in which our Queen is crowned. Just as our God gave the people of Israel Saul as a king to guide them, so too has William been sent to us…"

"Sent? Sent!"

Fitz did not turn around, but could still hear the muttering of an Anglo-Saxon woman behind him.

"If he was sent by God to protect us I'll eat her crown," the voice continued.

Around her, several people murmured in agreement. Fitz reddened. There was nothing that he could do now, there was no way that he could interrupt the royal proceedings for some gossipers. But he had not realised that public opinion against King William was so strong. The invasion felt so long ago.

"…and just as Esther did, our Queen will entreat our King for justice and mercy throughout the lands."

Ealdred stepped forward. "Who brings this woman to be our Queen?"

"I do."

William's strong voice carried throughout the entire cathedral. There was nothing but strength and power in the two short syllables, and Fitz smiled.

Adeline and Edith took a step back, and William walked over to stand beside his wife. He placed a hand on her shoulder.

"I, William, lord of Normandy by birth and King of England by right, bring this woman to be our Queen. She is my wife, the mother of my children, the lady of my heir, and the keeper of my house. By my hand I bless her. I bring to you Matilda, Queen of England."

Ealdred stood before them, and smiled – a rarity.

"Hail, Matilda, Queen of England," he said.

"Hail!" The cry was echoed by everyone present. At least, Fitz assumed that it was everyone.

"And who," Ealdred continued, "supports this woman to be our Queen?"

"I do." Both Adeline and Edith spoke, the Norman language pouring out of both their mouths. Fitz's eyebrows raised – did Edith actually speak his tongue? The women stepped forward, vowing to protect and serve Matilda. The words were soft, but they could still be heard.

Ealdred began to murmur some prayers over the royal couple, which Fitz could not catch from where he was. The mutterings of the people around him could now be heard once more.

"She may be a Queen," one person said just in front of Fitz – a tall man, bearded and full of bitterness, "her grandfather was a King. But who is he? Who is William to rule over us?"

Fitz grimaced, without being able to stop himself. This was a complaint that he had heard time and time again. The fact that William had been born...well, the wrong side of the blanket, was a fact that he had clearly never managed to escape.

"Amen."

The murmuring stopped as Ealdred came to the end of his prayers. His sharp eyes looked out to the congregation, and Fitz was suddenly struck with the idea that Ealdred, despite concentrating on his prayers, knew exactly what was being said by the Anglo-Saxons that were watching.

"My people," the archbishop said grandly, lifting up his arms as if he were about to embrace them, "there is nothing greater than seeing a partner in royal power such as this. Our Queen Matilda is not only the wife of our lord King William, or the mother of our future King, but she is a glorious beacon of life and love. It is she that will beg for mercy, and seek justice. It is she that will have the ear of our King, and use it wisely. It is she who knows the things that every mother seeks, and will seek it for us. Let us welcome her as a gift to our people that we have not deserved."

His words were not met by a cheer, although Fitz was almost glad that it did not. A cheer would have broken the silence, and it was delicate. No one cried out in anger, but no one cried out in support. It was a balance of wills between the Normans in the crowd and the Anglo-Saxons, and thankfully there was balance to be found.

Ealdred moved around the thrones to the altar, upon which many objects were sitting. Fitz craned his neck, but he couldn't quite make them out from where he was.

A crown. Two crowns, in fact. Ealdred placed one on the head of King William, and then slowly placed the other on Queen Matilda.

"In the name of the Holy Trinity," Matilda said softly, "I promise three things to the Christian people who are subject to me: first, that God's church and all Christian people in my dominions preserve true peace; the second is that I forbid robbery and all unrighteous things to all orders; the third, that I promise and command justice and mercy in all judgements, so that the kind and merciful God because of that may grant us all his eternal mercy, who liveth and reigneth."

Fitz breathed a sigh of relief. Trying to memorise such a speech would have been difficult for many people, but Matilda had grappled with it like any great leader, and had beaten it.

"The Christian Queen who observes these things will earn for herself worldly honour," Ealdred said seriously, "and if she fails to fulfil that which was promised, then within a very short time things will grow worse among her people, and in the end it will all turn out for evil. Heed the warning, my lady Matilda."

"I heed your warning," Matilda smiled at the numerous people watching her, clearly unworried about the attention on her.

A small boy ran up to Ealdred, almost tripping over his long ceremonial robes. On any other occasion, a great cry of laughter would have risen up from the crowd. But not today. Not here.

Ealdred took the small glass vial from the boy's trembling outstretched hands, and bid him leave softly under his breath. He turned back to Matilda, unstopping the vial as he spoke.

"Just as Kings and Queens have for ages past, I anoint you with this holy oil."

Allowing three or four drops to fall slowly onto his fingers, Ealdred then made the sign of the cross on Matilda's forehead. Her eyes were closed, and her mouth seemed to murmur words of prayer.

"Hail Queen Matilda!" A shout began somewhere to Fitz's left, and he immediately took it up.

"Hail Queen Matilda!" he called, and soon everyone was cheering. Sneaking a look over, Fitz saw his brother Osbern grinning.

Ealdred waited for the commotion to calm down, and then continued.

"To remind you of this sacred moment, I present to you a ring, made of gold to show the value that you are to your people, and an emerald, the stone for this glorious month of May, to remind you when you became our Queen."

Matilda held out her hand, and Ealdred carefully put the ring on her finger. As she had abstained from wearing any others, the gold ring shone out from the light that poured through every window. It was beautiful.

Ealdred smiled briefly. The ceremony was almost over; his job was almost done. He turned to the congregation.

"I present to you your King and your Queen: King William and Queen Matilda!"

William and Matilda rose.

"King William and Queen Matilda!"

This time it was Fitz, and not his younger brother that began the cheers, but it did not take long for the men and women around him to carry it on.

"King William and Queen Matilda!"

"Long life to William and Matilda!"

"Hail to the Queen!"

Fitz sighed heavily. There had been so much worry about what they would do if the Anglo-Saxons had risen against them, no one had really considered what they would do if nothing went wrong!

"Really," Fitz heard the same woman behind him speak again, "she is very beautiful. You cannot deny that, and after having so many children too."

Fitz smiled. Osbern had been right: the people here did really love Matilda. And why not – she was a woman who had taken a clear interest in her people, of both races.

Now all they had to do was survive the coronation feast.

CHAPTER ELEVEN

Fitz put a hand on his stomach, and groaned. He could not remember eating so much before in his life, and his tunic was stretched uncomfortably. Every time he thought that the feast was over, another set of servants brought out more food.

Osbern was sitting beside him, and laughed at the sight of his brother.

"Truly, you cannot eat another bite?"

Fitz groaned in response.

He looked around him at the grand banquet that had been organised for Queen Matilda's coronation. Anyone who was anyone was there, and thanks to the wine that had been flowing for the last few hours, the noise in the room was almost unbearable. The musicians in the corner were almost drowned out by the shouting, the laughing, and the talking that flowed out of everyone's mouths. In one corner of the room, a group of men were gambling, surrounded by a gaggle of women avidly watching the game unfold.

The tables were set as a square in the room, with men and women sitting on both the inside and the outside. A large fire was at the centre, over which some meat was still cooking. Fitz watched some of the juices splash down into the fire, causing a sweet aroma to drift his way. It smelt delicious – perhaps one more portion of food…

King William and Queen Matilda were sitting at the top of the table. On William's right hand side was Ealdred, looking more inebriated than was proper for an archbishop. On Matilda's left hand side, Fitz saw with astonishment, was Edith. She looked uncomfortable, and yet sat there silently, picking at the bread that was being torn apart by her fingers.

"She lives in Winchester now," Osbern said, seeing where Fitz's gaze had fallen. "Since her husband's death, she has remained here, in the city of Winchester."

Fitz stared at the woman who had been Queen of England. She looked older than he had thought her, but then she had seen much pain and much suffering throughout her time as the mother of England. After seeing that she would not be able to provide the King with children, it was then her fate to watch him waste away, and see the peaceful country that they had built together fall around her.

And now, here she was: not the host, but the guest of the Queen's coronation feast. Fitz wondered how it did not taste bitter in her mouth.

"She is a fine lady," Osbern said softly.

"Of course," said Fitz, "you were her husband's chaplain, and counsellor. You must have spent much of your time with her – what is she like?"

Osbern considered for a moment. "She is a quiet lady," he said finally. "Not a woman that looks for a debate or a fight. She was a good match for King Edward."

"And now?"

"Now she is unmarriageable," Osbern said matter-of-factly. "Edward was King of England, but he is no more. Edith was his wife, but she was also Harold's sister."

Fitz almost choked on the wine that had been brought to them straight warm and spiced from the fire. When he had managed to regain his ability to speak, he spluttered, "Harold's sister? The man that claimed the crown and was defeated by our King William in the invasion?"

Osbern nodded. "The very same. So you can see why she is no longer allowed to marry. Many do not realize that she is still in England – they assume that she travelled with her rebellious brothers to Ireland."

Fitz sighed. It was a desperate end to her life, this woman who had once had it all.

"What is to become of her?"

"She is living with the nuns here," Osbern said nonchalantly. "It is expected that she will take holy orders before too long."

Fitz nodded. That would certainly solve the problem for them. Anyone who married Edith now would have a claim to the throne...a claim that King William would never allow.

"So, brother," Osbern said, slapping down his goblet and giggling slightly as the wine slopped over the sides, "how is your wife?"

Fitz's stomach clenched. He had managed to forget the matter of his family for several days now.

"To tell you the truth, I know not," he confessed. "I have not been in Normandy these last two years, and it has been difficult to get letters safely across the sea."

Osbern raised an eyebrow. "Do you not miss them?"

Fitz opened his mouth, and closed it again.

"God's teeth, man, do you not even miss your children?"

"They are children no longer," Fitz said softly. "My eldest is married, and now my youngest two – "

"The girls?"

"Yes, the twins. They are nearing sixteen summers – they are almost due to be wed to young men themselves. They are not children anymore."

Osbern looked at his brother knowingly. "You do not mentioned your wife."

"Adeliza?" Fitz thought about the woman that he had been sharing his life with for so many years. "It is not that I do not miss her."

Osbern waited for Fitz to complete his sentence. "But?"

"But what?" Fitz took another large bit of the meat cooling in front of him.

"Surely you must have some tender feelings for her?" Osbern looked amazed.

Fitz smiled wearily. "Osbern, did you ever take a woman?"

Osbern looked outraged. "Brother, I am a man of God!"

"Yes, but that has not stopped many others."

"True," Osbern admitted, "but it has been enough to stop me."

"Then you do not understand what it is to be with a woman that you cannot love."

Fitz almost bit his tongue in shock that he had uttered those words aloud. His brother's jaw had fallen in shock.

"William FitzOsbern," he said angrily, "I cannot believe that you just said such a thing of your lady!"

"Forgive me," Fitz said quickly, "it was a sentiment stemming from tiredness and too much wine."

Osbern looked at his brother carefully, and then nodded curtly. But he did not speak to him again, and turned instead to speak to the chaplain sitting on the other side from him.

Fitz cursed himself silently. It had been many years since he had been able to speak so with his brother, and of course, he had managed to insult him. He sighed, he should not have spoken so about Adeliza, but the truth remained that the little affection that he had had for her when they were young had soon drifted away. It was like that, with important marriages, he counselled himself. No one expected a love match in these days.

Fitz was roused from his thoughts by the sound of something that he could not possibly be hearing. It sounded like horse's hooves – but there was no way that a horse could be this close to them.

The doors were flung open, and a man dressed in armour astride a horse was silhouetted in the darkness. Fitz smiled wanly. At least his ears were not giving out.

Gasps were made all around the room as the man on the horse gently nudged his steed forward. Heads turned to get a good look at the man, and Fitz saw that King William rose out of his seat.

Men all around the room, loyal to the Norman cause, slowly reached for their weapons. Fitz's heart was hammering – what kind of man rode into a feast of celebration completely armed? What did this man want?

"Hold!" A Norman shouted out, racing to stand in front of the horse. "Who goes?"

The man on the horse reached up, and pulled his helmet off.

"Oh, no," Fitz muttered under his breath.

It was Marmion.

"If anybody denies that our most gracious sovereign Lord William, and his wife Matilda, are King and Queen of England, he is a false-hearted traitor and liar, and here I do challenge him to single combat."

Marmion's words echoed around the room, and men looked at each other with smiles on their faces. A challenge! A challenge from an unknown rider! His arm was raised with a gleaming sword, but even Fitz could see that it was more for ceremony that for battle.

King William sat down again, a hint of a smile on his face, and put his hand over his wife's. She was staring, transfixed, at the strange man who had come to defend their honour.

Marion repeated his words. "I say again: if anybody denies that our most gracious sovereign Lord William, and his wife Matilda, are King and Queen of England, he is a false-hearted traitor and liar, and here I do challenge him to single combat."

Fitz could not help but grin. He had given little thought to what Marmion's brilliant idea had been, but even if he had spent the last week mulling over the variety of things that he could do, he would never have guessed this. This was incredible.

And yet there were Anglo-Saxons around the room that were shuffling on their feet, feeling the handles of knives, and muttering to their companions. King William was not popular with everyone, and Fitz could see that there were many men – and a few women – that would gladly accept the challenge.

"You do know," Osbern whispered, leaning over to his brother once more, "that they'll be talking about this for months. Your man should be well rewarded for this."

"He will be," answered Fitz, "but the shape of that reward will depend on whether anyone decides to take up his challenge."

"None would dare."

"You can never tell with these Anglo-Saxons," Fitz reminded his brother. "You, of all people, should know of their proud nature. Not everyone has taken so well to our presence here."

"I say thrice!" Marmion shouted over the hubbub of voices that now filled the hall. "If anybody denies that our most gracious sovereign Lord William, and his wife Matilda, are King and Queen of England, he is a false-hearted traitor and liar, and here I do challenge him to single combat."

He looked around the room, his eyes glaring. Fitz could not help but admit that he was doing a very good job of being frightening and impressive. Marmion's eyes flickered around the room, staring down the men with bitterness in their hearts. They would do nothing today.
But thankfully, none in the room stood to accept his challenge of combat.

"In that case," Marion said, with a sweep of his arm, "never again shall words of bitterness and anger be spoken against our lord King William and our lady Queen Matilda – for they have been acknowledged as our leaders here today!"

Without saying another word, announcing his name, or even dismounting from his own horse, Marmion turned his mount around and exited the room.

Excited murmurings bubbled up from the people in the room. Fitz noticed that the most intrigued people were the women, who began to collect into groups, and giggle.

"Well, I'll say it," Osbern said, slapping his brother on the back, "your Marmion did it. None shall forget this. I shall not be surprised if men and women will speak of this in hundreds of years to come!"

"Nonsense," Fitz pushed him away. "It is merely a trick to encourage our Queen Matilda. A successful one, I grant you – but nothing that cannot be forgotten within a fortnight."

His words were shortened by the sound of a goblet crashing onto the floor. Everyone turned to the source of the noise to see the King standing.

"That got your attention then," he said, in his deep voice.

There was nervous laughter around the room. William smiled.

"First," he said, "my thanks to the strange knight who just entered here to defend my honour, and the honour of my wife. It was well done, and let the man who has the genius of it to step forward and take my thanks."

Fitz sat where he was.

"Will you not rise?" Osbern hissed.

Fitz shook his head imperceptibly. "It was Marmion's cleverness, not mine," he whispered. "I shall take no credit for it, even if I should wish to."

King William's eyes roved around the room, but none stepped forward or raised themselves up.

"So be it," he shrugged. "The loss is his, and his alone. And I now continue to bestow honour and glory." As King William spoke, Matilda was gazing up at him, her crown balanced delicately on her head, and there was such love in her face that Fitz almost felt embarrassed watching her. It had been many years since he had felt such devotion from the face of his own wife.

"Firstly, I honour the people of England, who are now one with us." The King's words were now being heeded by all within the room, especially those of English birth. One of them, a tall man, much older than Fitz was but still enjoying the vigour of life, quietly walked around from his seat to just beside the King. As their monarch spoke, the man began to translate for those that had not yet learned the Norman tongue.

"I return this royal court to the old ways," King William continued, "and keep the English traditions that made it so noble and so just. I give you the old offices that were taken from you, and give them to you as a gift."

As the man translated, puzzled and openly confused looks covered the faces of those English that heard his words. Fitz bit his lip. What was the king up to?

"The office of grand pannetier, I return to this noble court. It has been long gone, and this court has been the lesser for it. I offer it to Roger de Beaumont, for his outstanding service, and in the hope that it shall bring honour to his sons."

King William's majestic words were now met, Fitz saw, with wary smiles. Could it be that he was only going to reward his own men? Were the two nations always to be divided?

"I also grant the office – "

"My lord?"

Fitz's sleeve was pulled, and he turned away from King William to see who so desperately wanted to catch his attention.

"Marmion?"

The man was sweating slightly, his hair pasted to his forehead, but he was smiling broadly.

"I must speak with you, my lord."

He was panting slightly. Fitz bit his lip.

"Now?"

"This very moment."

"Are you sure that you cannot wait a mere – "

"No, my lord." Marmion flushed at the impertinence of interrupting his lord. "Please accept my apologies, my lord, but I would not ask if it were not important."

Fitz sighed. Marmion was right – he had always trusted his judgement up until this point, and he had never given him any reason to doubt him. Rising, he put a hand on his brother's shoulder to let him know that he was departing. Osbern looked confused, but Fitz nodded at Marmion, and his brother relaxed.

"I will try to write to you," Osbern muttered underneath his breath, without taking his eyes off his King.

"And I shall try to write back."

CHAPTER TWELVE

Fitz followed Marmion outside the great chamber, and out into the dusky air. Evening had fallen without them realising, and everyone had nothing but good food and good company to keep them occupied. The day was almost over, and what a day it had been.

Marmion seemed to be full of energy, but he was nervous. He kept looking over his shoulder, and twisting his head quickly to look the other way.

"Peace, Marmion," Fitz said gently. "There can be surely nothing of great import that you must tell me this very night?"

"This very night – this very moment," Marmion said with a broad smile breaking out over his face.

"Marmion, please stop," Fitz said with almost a laugh as the young man twisted around once more to look in the opposite direction, and winced as he pulled at his shoulder blade. "You do no good by spinning around like a man half crazed. What has got into you?"

Marmion took a deep breath. "My apologies, my lord. It is just – I cannot quite keep my excitement."

"Then try," Fitz said kindly, "or I shall have to be forced to return to my seat, and leave your news for another day."

"Then I shall speak calmly and plainly," Marmion said slowly with a great effort. "King William has already discovered that it was I who rode in and challenged all to defend the honour of him, and his Queen."

Fitz's mouth opened. "He knows? But it has been only minutes since you left the room!"

Marmion nodded. "His servants are very knowledgeable."

"Call them what they are – call them spies," Fitz said quietly, "for they are nothing less. How do you know this?"

Marmion took another deep breath, and swallowed hard. "A man approached me. He wore the King's colours, and he carried a sword."

"And? What did he say?"

"He embraced me." Marmion's voice was full of awe. "He embraced me, and said that I had done the King and the Queen great honour. He said that I would not be forgotten, and that the King wanted me to know personally that he was watching me."

Fitz breathed outward, and realised that he had been holding his breath whilst the young man had been speaking. "He said all of that?"

"And more," Marmion said in hushed tones, as if forgetting that he needed to keep his words a secret. "He asked who my liege lord was, and I told him that it was you, and he said – "

"That the King wished to speak with him."

Fitz and Marmion both jumped, turning to face the tall man who swept silently out of the shadows.

"Word to the wise," King William said quietly. "If you wish to have a private conversation, alone surrounded by darkness is not the place to have it. You could be surrounded."

Marmion had turned a pale shade of white, and Fitz guessed that he looked similarly terrified. It would never do to be discovered discussing the King, especially in the dark, just after his wife's coronation! What danger had they brought upon their heads now – and just how much had King William heard?

"Marmion," William said, turning to him. "You did my wife and me great honour this night. I thank you. Know that soon I shall be calling you to my royal court to become a knight of my chamber."

"My…my lord King, the honour is too much, I cannot possibly – "

"Nonsense," said King William calmly. "If I say that it is so, then it shall be so."

"But – but my lord…"

"Are you defying me, boy?" King William's voice become sharper, more dangerous, and Fitz spoke up.

"My lord King William," he said hurriedly. The monarch's face turned towards him, and it had lost some of the smile that it had when it came out of the shadows. "Marmion I am sure feels the great honour that you are giving him, but he is a younger son. It would bring shame on his elder brother if he was to join your chamber before him."

Marmion's stutterings were silenced, and he looked up into the face of the most powerful man for hundreds of miles.

"I see," King William brought a hand to his mouth as he pondered. "The right of supersedence does certainly rest with your brother. Is he a good man?"

"As good a man as I am, and I think better," Marmion replied shakily. "I have not seen him these ten years, but I hear that he is a righteous man with a strong arm."

King William barked a laugh. "High praise indeed! Then write to this brother of yours, and tell him to come to me. Tell him to present himself at court, with your name as his standard, and he shall become a knight of my chamber. You can come yourself when Fitz is finished with you."

Marmion's mouth opened, but no words came out. Fitz smiled, and clapped a hand on his young friend's shoulders.

"I am sure Marmion feels all of the respect and joy for himself and his family that you no doubt intend, my lord King William."

"Thank you," Marmion stammered. "I shall write to my brother immediately – right now, my lord King, I shall write to him – "

"That suits me well, young man," the King interrupted, "because I have need to speak with Fitz. Go, write your letter."

Marmion bowed low, and then bowed to Fitz. He bowed to King William once more before Fitz muttered, and he almost fled.

King William chuckled. "He seems a good boy – very like one of my boys. Where did you find him?"

"He found me," Fitz said honestly. "And he has proved himself over and over to be a man of loyalty and integrity."

"You like him?"

Fitz was surprised by the question. He had not expected the King of England and the ruler of Normandy to be so interested in what his opinion was.

"If you do not find it offensive, my lord King, I would ask why you care so much about my thoughts? I had not considered myself one of your confidants."

"A reasonable question." William nodded. "It is true that we are not as close as we once were."

Fitz nodded. Having grown up in the same household, the two men could have been very close; but there was something that had always held them back. Although related, there was enough distinction to keep them wary throughout childhood, and that wariness had never quite dissipated. They trusted each other, but it was a trust based on distance.

"Fitz, I must speak to you about the attacks that we have been suffering."

William's boldness and brashness threw Fitz, but he recollected his senses quickly.

"I want to make sure that anything I tell you remains with you," William continued. "And that if it does escape you, that the few you would share it with are trustworthy."

"You offend me," Fitz said hotly, "if you suppose that anything you impart to me could be shared with another. I am your cousin, and your servant, and your subject."

The two men stared at each other, neither being sure exactly who should speak next. Eventually, Fitz dropped his gaze.

"I beg your pardon, my lord King William," he said stiffly, "if I gave offence with my rash words. But I stand by them."

"I would expect nothing less of you, and you were right to speak them." William smiled. "There should be trust between us."

"There is," Fitz assured him. "I know that I have little to trust you with, but I hope that you will be able to share with me anything that troubles you."

William nodded. "There is much to speak about, but I am…unwilling for all to know my thoughts at this time. It is vital that I trust this discussion to you completely."

Fitz bowed. "Then speak."

The King sighed. He shuffled his feet, almost as if he was not sure whether or not to continue. Fitz couldn't believe what he was seeing: William of Normandy, William the Conqueror of England, King William who had travelled across the sea to take the land that was his once his – unsure of himself?

"God's teeth, man," Fitz said eventually, "I am no mind reader!"

William barked out a laugh. "That you are not, my friend, and I apologise once more. You have, of course, kept receiving messengers about the unrest in this land?"

Fitz swallowed. "I have indeed, my lord, but I have not considered it serious enough to pay much of my attention to. I feel, now, that I have been in error."

"The error has been made by many, and I am included in that number. Hereford's rebellion was expected, but Exeter has surprised me. I did not think them so...ungrateful. I had considered the efforts that I had made with this country to be sufficient to gain their loyalty."

"You must remember," Fitz said softly, "that to many here, we are foreigners. The majority of the English have never heard of Normandy, let alone been there or known who we were. Our arrival was a shock to them, and a few years cannot undo the many that they have enjoyed owning their own land, running their own country!"

"And yet we are here now!" King William exploded, and then hushed his voice, realising that they could quite easily attract attention. The darkness, after all, did not cloak the noises that they made. "I am here now, and I am the King!"

"And yet their allegiance is not to you."

"I hope that the castles will do their work," William sighed. "Castles have always been the perfect way to control people, back in Normandy."

"And yet, the people here are so different," countered Fitz softly. "How are we to know, truly, what they are like?"

There was a moment of silence between them as both men considered the two peoples that they were now surrounded by. On the one hand, the Normans: their own people, the culture that they had been raised with. Their voices spoke with a Norman tongue, and they thought Norman thoughts. And here, the English: a foreign race of troublemakers, the people over the water. Their history was dark and mysterious, and their language a class in acrobatics for those Normans, like Fitz, who decided to learn it.

"Thankfully, no rebellions have succeeded," Fitz said quietly. "We should be grateful for that."

"Gratitude can only lead a country for so long."

"But what else can we do?"

"Whatever it is, it shall not be done by you."

Fitz blinked. "My lord King William?"

"It is not that I do not value you, my friend," said William heavily. "If anything, I have depended too much on you such the invasion of England. You must be tired. It has been months – nay, years since you have seen your homelands. How do your children?"

Fitz swallowed, and stammered. "Well, it – it has been almost a month since a letter from my family has reached me. We move about so much, my lord."

William clapped a large hand on Fitz's shoulder. "No man should go so long without seeing his wife. I found being away from Matilda torture, and I see no reason why I should detain you from your family any longer. I am sending you back to Normandy."

"My lord!" Fitz's cheeks burned red, although his companion could not see them in the dark of the night. "If I have offended you in any way, please tell me – do not send me home like a child who has forgotten his manners!"

"Peace, Fitz," William said calmly. "I commend you for the work that you have done for me. There could have been no one better to have within my council, and beside me through these troubled times. But you will become useless to me if you do not rest. Come now: you know this to be true."

"I wish…" Fitz's voice tailed off. "I wish it were not so," he said simply.

"And I," said William. "But there it is. I shall send word for your passage across the sea to be arranged."

Fitz inhaled, and slowly let the breath out. There was nothing for it then. He was going back home.

CHAPTER THIRTEEN

Her eyes were shut, and her face was warm. The sunshine was beating down on her aching old bones, and she was enjoying the last of the sunshine of the day. The skirts of her red dress were spread around her, and every muscle within her body was desperate to relax. The summer was truly upon them, and just like every summer before it, Catheryn was worshipping it. She would soon be brown, much to the disgust of her family – but then, her family were nowhere close to her now. She would have the disapproval of others to contend with this summer.

Catheryn sighed, and opened her eyes. It was no good: whatever she attempted to do, she could never completely forget her loneliness, and her longing to be home. As much as Catheryn was acclimatising to her new life, it was as if a flower had been planted in the shade when it loved the sun: it would live, but it would be but a half-life, and that life was worth very little.

The clouds that were moving across the sky did so lazily. There was barely a breeze in the air.

Catheryn raised a hand up, reaching for the white fluffy cloud that was currently wandering across the sky. Her hand moved higher than the grass that was surrounding her, and she chuckled slightly, imagining what a passer-by must think – an arm growing amongst the crops, grasping to catch the sky!

No matter how far she stretched, Catheryn could not quite reach the clouds that looked like they were just beyond her fingertips. Hand still in the air, Catheryn closed her eyes once more, and began to hum one of her favourite lullabies. She had sung it to quieten both of her children when they had been small, and the tune came to her easily.

Images passed before her eyes quickly, as if they were really open, and she had found some way of returning to that favourite country – the past. Her husband, Selwyn, smiled at her, and Annis ran about her, still a toddler, shrieking with delight at the world. Whether memories or imaginings, they brought a smile to Catheryn's face.

"By God, woman, what are you doing?"

Catheryn jumped up, eyes wide open in shock. Not far away stood one of the largest horses that she had ever seen – black, and huge, and panting wildly. It had obviously been on the move for a very long time; but Catheryn's expert eye guessed that it had not been moving fast. She had been so wrapped up in her own thoughts that she had not heard its approach. There was a man atop the horse, disbelief and anger in his eyes. He had spoken Norman, a Norman that was harsh and clipped in tone.

Catheryn bristled. "I am...at least, I was lying down on the ground," she said defiantly, with as much elegance as she could muster at such short notice. "Not that it is any concern of yours," she added.

"Everything here is my concern," he said curtly, casting a quick eye over the fields in all directions. "You are a fool, lying there with a hand in the air like an infant. What if I had ridden over you?"

"Then you would have been the fool, not I!" Catheryn said angrily. "I am quite obvious in this green field." She gestured to the red dress that she was wearing, and then turned a frustrated eye at the man who had so rudely addressed her. "If you cannot see me, then the fool is not the one in a dress."

The man snorted. "And what do you think you are doing here? I know everyone in this area, and you are not known to me. What right do you have to lounge in this field?"

Catheryn almost spluttered with irritation. "This field is not a holy site, and I may lie in it if I choose! I am the lady Catheryn of the South, a lady of England, and…and a prisoner of the FitzOsbern family."

The man stared at her. The eyes that Catheryn had taken to be black and brooding seemed clear, like an evening sky. She could now see some blue in them where before had been all darkness.

"The FitzOsbern family?"

Catheryn nodded slowly. She had acted rashly – the same hot temper that she had tried to curb in her daughter had just been unleashed on this poor unsuspecting man, who probably had never spoken to a woman of her birth before. She cast a delicate eye over him, but could discern nothing except that he had travelled a long way. His dark beard covering his face was flecked with grey.

He, in turn, was looking back. His eyes took in the ruffled hair, swept vaguely underneath a veil; an English custom. The dress that she wore was of a fine colour, but seemed slightly torn and unkempt at the edges. She was nearing the peak of womanhood, but there was something hovering around the surface of her eyes.

"You are a ward of the FitzOsbern family?"

Catheryn rolled her eyes. "How many times must I repeat myself? Yes, I am with the FitzOsbern family – although I am more prisoner than ward, more inconvenience than guest."

The man looked at her for a moment, and then with a heavy sigh that his horse echoed, he dismounted. Turning to face her, he did something that Catheryn could never have expected: he bowed.

"My apologies, my lady Catheryn. I must blame the long ride that I have had on my incivility, but that is no reason to treat a lady in such a disgraceful manner. I trust that I have your forgiveness?"

Catheryn was so confused by this very sudden change in demeanour that she did not reply audibly, but nodded. This man was strange indeed.

"I am William," the man continued.

Catheryn smiled wanly. "Greetings, William. Have you a longer name?"

The man returned her smile, but it was a lot warmer than her own. "William FitzOsbern. Fitz, to my friends, which I hope to count you as soon, my lady Catheryn."

"William – FitzOsbern? But then you – " Catheryn said quickly, "you must be Adeliza's husband…you are the lord here."

"And consequently, your jailor," Fitz smiled. "Although I must admit that I do not like the title at all, despite the fact that it is an incredibly new honour."

"New honour…you did not know?"

"My lady Adeliza must have forgotten to mention it in her letters," Fitz shrugged. "There is often not much point in writing much down anyway, very few of them reach me."

Catheryn stared at him, unable to take in what she was seeing. A closer inspection revealed that Fitz was not much older than she was, still in the vigour of life, and not at all as she had pictured Adeliza's husband. She had always supposed him to be much older.

"You look confused."

"I am sorry, my lord FitzOsbern," Catheryn said eventually, feeling very self-conscious about the way that she was standing now that she knew that she was in the presence of her new liege lord. "It is just…you are not what I had expected."

The man laughed, and Catheryn could not help but smile in return. His laugh was open, and deep. It reminded her of Selwyn.

"What had you thought of me, then, dare I ask?"

Catheryn swallowed. "All I knew of you was that you were a counsellor for the King. I had thought of you as much older than you are, my lord."

Fitz laughed again, and Catheryn nervously joined him with a chuckle. It did seem ridiculous, in a way, but there it was.

"I must apologise, my lady Catheryn, for disturbing your reverie in such a fashion," Fitz continued. "I have been so long from here, I had almost expected it to have remained exactly as I had left it. The landscape that I had pictured did not include a hand growing out of the ground."

"No doubt you think me very foolish," Catheryn said with a smile. "But I find that being on my own, surrounded by the natural world, gives me time to think. To be myself."

"Rather far from your prison, are you not?"

"It is probably the best prison that I could ever hope to have," Catheryn admitted. "Your wife, Adeliza, is most welcoming, and I adore your daughters. I am intent on marrying them off to very eligible young men as soon as possible."

"Married? Goodness, do they need to leave us so soon?"

Fitz smiled slightly, his eyes never leaving the woman in front of him. It had been strange, riding closer and closer towards his home. It had not felt as inviting as this conversation did now, and he had found himself drawing his horse closer and closer to him, slowing him down, delaying the inevitable. Now he almost wished that he had ridden harder, to meet this woman earlier. There was something about her. Something different.

"You – you did not know that your wife Adeliza has been planning this?" Catheryn looked surprised that a father could have such little interest in his children.

"Do not misunderstand me," Fitz said hastily. "I care greatly about my children – all four of them. It is just that I have not seen Isabella or Emma…nor any of my family for over two years. When I left, they had seen but twelve summers, and I was not ready to part with them. Adeliza rarely informs me of family matters."

Compassion washed over Catheryn. Without really thinking about what she was doing, she walked up to Fitz, and put a comforting hand over his heart.

"Here is someone who can understand what it is to love a child from afar."

Fitz's eyes widened, but he did not move away. It almost felt natural, being this close to this woman.

The moment lasted for another few heartbeats, until Catheryn realised that she could feel them underneath her fingertips, Fitz's heart, beating away in his chest. The intimacy of what she had just done finally hit her, and she quickly removed her hand, taking a step backwards and blushing furiously.

Fitz took a deep breath, but it was ragged.

"I think we should return," he said, in a calmer voice than he felt by far. "No doubt my lady Adeliza will be expecting me at any moment, and I do not wish to give her cause for concern."

Catheryn nodded quickly, and took her place beside her captor. They walked along, saying nothing – for what words could form around the emotions that they now felt?

CHAPTER FOURTEEN

The day was hot, and Adeliza was tired of it. Summer to her was not for lying in fields, and reaching for the sky, but for retreating indoors, trying to find a cool space. She sat stiffly in her favourite chair in the hall. The majority of the life and workings of her home occurred here, and she saw no point in remaining in her chamber, missing it.

With a loud shout and what sounded suspiciously like a curse, Isabella and Emma hurtled past her.

"Slowly, girls," Adeliza said automatically, not even expecting her words to be heeded in the slightest. "Please be careful."

Isabella shouted something back at her mother, but the exact words never quite reached Adeliza. The two girls continued running, and pushing open the door, almost fled into the sunshine.

Adeliza sighed, but she could not help but smile. It was always a cause of wonder to her that such girls should have come from her. They were so wild, so untameable. Everything was at its extreme for them – it was either the worst day ever, or the best that anyone had ever had. The middle ground that Adeliza was so fond of seemed to pass them by.

"My lady?"

Adeliza turned to see one of her servants hovering slightly to her left.

"Yes?"

"I bring word, my lady, from the village. It is said that our lord William has been sighted, riding here."

Adeliza stared at the servant blankly for a moment, before she realised that she was probably expected to speak.

"William?"

"Yes, my lady." The servant looked concerned. "He should be here at any moment."

Adeliza recollected herself. She was meant to be ecstatically happy, she supposed. She smiled.

"In that case, I will walk out to greet him," she said slowly. "Thank you for bringing these joyful tidings."

The servant's face relaxed, and Adeliza stood, shaking the creases out of her gown. In a way, she wished she was wearing one of greater beauty – but then, Fitz had never been particularly concerned with the clothes that she had worn, anyway. This dress was as good as another.

Adeliza strode to the door that had been left ajar by her two exuberant daughters, and delicately manoeuvred herself through it. The sunshine poured onto her, and Adeliza flinched. The heat always made her feel uncomfortable.

There was but one road between the village and their home, and so Adeliza saw no reason why Fitz would not have taken it. The path crossed a few of their fields, and as Adeliza looked out to them, she saw a man walking from those fields towards her. He was not alone: a woman that Adeliza immediately recognised as Catheryn was beside him, and the two of them were talking. The man laughed. Adeliza knew that laugh.

It was Fitz.

Bile immediately rose in her throat, and Adeliza's face flushed, independent of the sun. The two companions ahead of her had not looked up and seen her – they were too invested in their own conversation to look anywhere else. Panic flooded through Adeliza's veins. It had been two years – no, more than two years now – since she had seen her husband. She had waited patiently, always waiting for the next letter to know that he had not been killed by the English in the last month. And yet he was not riding fast to her, to her family, to the home that they had built together.

He was…there was no other word for it. He was meandering.

They were but moments away from her now. Adeliza realised with a start that she had stopped walking. She stood there, stupidly, waiting for her husband and her prisoner to reach her.

It was Fitz who noticed her first. Raising his eyes up to see exactly how far they had come, he saw a woman standing in the middle of the path, arms hanging listlessly at her sides. She was dressed in a grey dress, that could once have been a light blue. She was his wife.

"Adeliza!"

He called her name, and a slight smile crossed over her face.

"You must excuse me," Fitz said to Catheryn hurriedly.

Catheryn barely had time to nod her understanding before he quickened his pace and lengthened his stride. It did not take him long to reach his wife, and he greeted her formally: by dropping to his knees.

"Oh, my lady wife," Fitz said, head bowed. "It is both a blessing and an honour to see you again."

Adeliza reached out a hand, and lifted her husband's face so that she could look into his eyes.

"Greetings, my lord husband."

Her voice was soft.

Fitz rose, and the couple embraced. By this time, Catheryn and the horse that had been left in her care had reached them, and Adeliza pulled apart from the arms of her husband, a blush creeping over her face.

"Catheryn," Adeliza said stiffly. "This is my husband, William FitzOsbern."

Catheryn saw with dismay that all of the reticence, the distance and the antipathy that Adeliza had clothed herself with when she had first arrived there as a prisoner had returned.

But then Adeliza smiled. "It is a great day, the day of your return," she said quietly, keeping her eyes low and respectful.

"It is indeed," Fitz said, not quite understanding why the laughing chattering woman that he had been walking with had suddenly disappeared into the demur woman before him. But then, if his wife was anything to go by, most women were quiet. "But I am tired from my travels, and I would like to retire for a time, before the evening meal."

Catheryn nodded. "I am going to continue my...walk in the fields." She could not help but let a smile escape, though she dared not see if Fitz had kept walking with her. She looked at Adeliza. "Please go on ahead: I shall not be long, but I would love to enjoy the last of the light, before we lose it entirely."

"We shall see you at the feast tonight," Adeliza said quietly. "It will be in honour of my husband's return."
"I will look forward to it."

Adeliza watched the woman go, wandering back purposefully towards the place where she knew Catheryn spent much of her time. She had almost forgotten that there was another person there until Fitz spoke.

"Shall we?"

Adeliza did not reply, but instead merely turned to face the way that she had come.

Fitz and Adeliza did not speak during their short journey back. At their arrival, a servant quickly came to take Fitz's horse from him, and then the lord and the lady of the family retreated to their chamber, where they would not be disturbed.

It was not until Adeliza could be completely sure that they were alone, and would not be overheard, that she let out the breath that she had been holding in. She slumped onto a chair, whilst Fitz threw himself gracelessly on the bed.

Neither of them spoke for several moments.
"You look well."

"Thank you," Fitz replied. "You look just as beautiful as when I left."

Adeliza smiled, but the smile did not reach her eyes. "I am older. There are lines where there were no lines before."

Fitz snorted. "Wisdom comes at a price, Adeliza, and if you want the wisdom you cannot claim that the cost is too high."

"I claim no such thing." Adeliza's reply was quick, but without malice. "It is just strange. I am certain I shall grow accustomed to it."

Fitz did not reply. He closed his eyes, and allowed himself finally to feel the ache within his bones. Every muscle cried out in pain; it had been a long and tiring journey, and would have tired out a man half his age.

"I have not told you how proud we are of you."
"Proud?"

Adeliza nodded, but then realised that Fitz could not see her. "Yes. You have brought much honour to the FitzOsbern name, and to Normandy. Our children and I are very proud of you."

Fitz heard the words, but they were spoken with no feeling in them. He and Adeliza had never been close; theirs had been a melding of two families, rather than a marriage of two individuals. But they had learned to live together well enough. They had, over time, created four beautiful children, and had had the joy of seeing them grow to be passionate and clever people. And yet now, after all of that time, there was almost nothing that they wanted to say to one another.

Adeliza shifted uncomfortably in her seat. The sight of the man that she had married lying on their bed was slightly shocking. She was amazed at how little she had remembered of him. Despite the long twenty years that they had spent together, it had only taken twenty four months of distance to rob her of the memory of his face. There were lines around his eyes that she did not think had been there when he left – but then, she could not be sure.

"Any vital news?"

Adeliza shook herself from her reverie. "None of enough importance to disturb you on the day that you have returned to us."

Fitz smiled slightly. It was good to know that the land that he had loved and left had survived the lack of him. Perhaps his steward had enjoyed the chance to work without his lord hanging over his head, commentating on his every decision.

"Fitz?"

Adeliza's voice was delicate as usual, and the iron at the core of her being was lacking. Fitz sat up, and turned to look at her.

He did not reply, but Adeliza continued, her words tinged with nervousness.

"Tell me...what is happening in England?"

Fitz closed his eyes again, still sitting upright. Adeliza bit her lip.

"Fitz, is it true that many battles have occurred since the winter season?"

"I do not wish to talk of war." It was not anger that filled Fitz's words, but something slightly more harsh. A bitterness mixed with exhaustion. He was a man who had seen too much anger.

"I am sorry, my lord," Adeliza said quickly, returning to a more formal tone. Her eyes lowered themselves, leaving the man that was lying on the bed. "I just wondered – England is such a far off land."

There was a long gap before any further words were spoken, and then it was Adeliza once more.

"Tell me of England."

Fitz did not bother to open his eyes as he replied.

"I do not wish to speak of it."

"I wish to know more of it. Tell me – "

"God's teeth, Adeliza, will you not leave the subject alone?" Fitz exploded. "War is never a beautiful thing, and that is what I have been doing for the last years – waging a war on a country that will not lose!"

Adeliza cried out. "It was only a simple request, Fitz!"

"And I am only telling you that I do not want to speak of it!"

"Your letters contained nothing, and I have been waiting many months for proper news," Adeliza bit back. Fitz had not even bothered to open his eyes during the entire exchange. "I know that we never married for love, but I had hoped to always be able to respect you."

She knew that she had gone too far, said too much, as soon as the words poured out of her mouth. But there was nothing to be done now: they had been said.

Adeliza looked, terrified, at the man whose power she was under. He was her husband, and she had learned to like him, but this was the first moment that she had been truly afraid of him.

"My lady Adeliza, come and sit by me."

She did not move. Adeliza looked at her husband, with a wary look in her eye. He was acting strangely, even for Fitz, and she could not decipher the reason. Tiredness, yes, she had seen it in him many times. But this was something different. This was something much more.

"Adeliza, come here."

His tone was firm, but once again there was no anger there. Fitz's eyes were still shut.

Adeliza rose, and carefully sat on the bed. Her back rested against the headboard, alongside her husband's. As Fitz felt the bed move, he opened his eyes. Reaching an arm around his wife, he drew her close, and began to speak quietly.

"England is a country of wildness, and of magic, and of terror. It is the country beyond the water, and it is filled with a people that are proud and humble, both at the same time. Every word they speak is a blessing, and every look at us is a curse. The land of England is covered in forests, and within them wild beasts lurk. There are parts of England that no man has ever walked on, trees under which no maiden has wept for a loved one, and stones that no child will ever gather. You can try to ignore its calling, and try to pretend that you do not even hear it, but even I am starting to realise that it back home for me. England does not belong to anyone. It did not belong to the English, and it does not belong to us Normans now. England cannot be owned, and it cannot be possessed."

Adeliza sat, entranced.

"Why?"

"Because it possesses us."

CHAPTER FIFTEEN

As Fitz walked into the room, a loud cheer went up from all around.

"FitzOsbern! FitzOsbern!"

"Welcome home my lord!"

He smiled. It was good to see so many of the people that he cared about, after such a long time. Age had not been gentle, and death had taken a few from their number, but those that remained were very dear to him. He could see that his steward had lost a few more teeth since he had last spoken to him.

Someone took his hand, and looking down, he saw that his daughter Isabella was smiling up at him. She looked completely different from the last time that Fitz had seen her; the baby smile and the wild hair had given way, he saw, to a more refined look. It was almost as if a different child stood before him – but Fitz mentally corrected himself. Neither of his daughters could be described as children any longer.

"Papa?" Isabella said, slightly nervously, but her smile remaining. "Is it good to be home?"

Fitz did not reply at first, but bundled the girl into his arms for a hug. She laughed, and he could not help but join her merriment.

"Indeed, child," he breathed, "it is good to be home."

Laughter broke out amongst the gathering, and Adeliza's voice swept over them all.

"Food, I think, Pierre."

A man standing at the side of the room immediately bowed his head, and a stream of people entered the room, bearing platters of food heaped high. The scent emanating from each one caught Fitz's attention as his mouth watered. Good food had been in short supply throughout the long journey.

"I can see your appetite has not dampened, Father!" Emma called out with a broad smile on her face.

Fitz returned her smile. "And I may still enact that threat that I gave you once when you were a small child – that if you do not let me get to my meal, I shall eat you instead!"

Waving a casual arm towards the minstrel standing by the fireside, he beckoned everyone to take their places at the tables, and begin to eat.

He did not speak to an unwilling audience. Men and women, glad to see their master return after so many years, could not be held back from enjoying the luxurious fare that had been prepared in his honour.

Fitz sat down at the head of the table, with Adeliza on his right. A petulant Roger was on his other side, and Fitz saw that he would have much catching up to do with his second son. There was obviously something playing on his mind, but the contents of it danced just out of Fitz's sight. He would have to see to that tomorrow.

One woman caught his eye. It was a moment before he recognised her. The woman that he had so unceremoniously startled. The woman that was his prisoner.

Catheryn stood, desperately trying to decide where she should place herself. Over the last few months, she had become accustomed to seating herself by Adeliza – but that place was now rightfully taken by her husband and her daughter. Not a servant, not a guest, not a member of the family: there were few precedents for this. Prisoners were not typically allowed to participate in events such as this, and Catheryn had no idea what she was to do.

Fitz watched her. She was quite obviously confused, undecided about what she should do. He turned, and caught Adeliza's eye.

They looked at their prisoner, thrust upon them by a King, many hundreds of miles away.

"Catheryn?" Fitz hazarded. He was not entirely sure exactly how he was meant to address this woman – half prisoner, half noble.

Adeliza came to his rescue. She rose stately, and a hush fell across the room. Even the minstrel stopped playing to listen to his lady – who blushed.

"My lady Catheryn," she said, softly. "Will you do us the honour of taking your place by my youngest daughter? Emma, I am sure, will value your company."

Catheryn looked at Emma, who smiled.

"I would be honoured, my lady," Emma said shyly, "if you would sit by me. I am but to perform a small task, and I shall return directly."

It was now Catheryn's turn to burn, although her cheeks reached a deeper red than Adeliza's ever did. Was such an insult ever to be borne? The girl who she had comforted, removing herself from her own seat so that she would not become tainted by the presence of an Anglo-Saxon woman? Emma had needed her then, but now she was just dirt?

But then Isabella rose, and Roger too moved from the table.

"You are not..?" Fitz laughed. "Surely, you are all getting a little old for this?"

"Age should be no barrier to accomplishment," Isabella threw back at him as she wove her way through the tables to reach the fire, where the minstrel stood, confused. "You should know that by now, Father."

The room laughed, and Catheryn relaxed. She finally realised what was happening. Beside the minstrel, tucked out of the way and in unassuming plain leather cases, were two lutes. Emma and Isabella reached for these, and the three siblings positioned themselves as a trio, facing their audience.

Catheryn was so captured by their beautiful music – Roger's strong voice perfectly balanced by the interchanging harmonies of the twins – that she almost forgot to take her place at the family table. There was a divide of space between her and Adeliza that Catheryn knew she could no longer cross.

When the siblings finished their song, the room erupted with applause, and none was greater than that from their father.

"Marvellous!" he shouted over the din. "I can only assume that you have been practising – something that I could never get any of you to do whilst I was here!"

Emma beamed. "You are a much less frightening prospect when you are across the sea, Father, but in some ways, that made us want to make you all the more proud."

"Yes," Isabella added as the three young people took their places at the table once more. "And it even meant that Roger had to talk to us every now and again."

"Oh hush!" Adeliza hissed as the girls descended into giggles. Roger did not make any show that he had heard them, and it was still not enough to force a remark from his lips.

Emma dropped into her seat beside Catheryn, still giggling.

"Now you must tell us about England," Emma said, wildly reaching for any food that was within her reach, "and about the heathens that you met there!"

It was not until the words had left her mouth and resonated in the air before her that Emma realised what she had said. Every eye turned to her, and Fitz cast a glance at Catheryn.

"My lady, I am so – I do apologise!" Emma stuttered, barely able to get another word out.

Catheryn took in a deep breath, and let it out slowly. "Mind it not," she said quietly. "It was but a slip of the tongue. You would not be so embarrassed if you knew what was said about your kind over the water."

Emma laughed, but it was a strained laugh, and she looked down at her plate, evidently deciding not to say another word that evening.

"And yet, the beast of England does not have the manners of the men and women of Normandy. Do not you think that you are, in some ways, a different creature?"

The incendiary words had been spoken by a voice that Catheryn did not recognise. But by following the direction that each and every person was looking, she looked at Roger.

He was clutching his knife a little hard for a man of calm, but his gaze did not falter as it met hers.

"My lord Roger," Catheryn said slowly, "I would no more say that a man of Anglo-Saxon stock was a different creature than I would say a man of Normandy. I see little difference."

"You lie!" Roger shouted, flecks of spit covering his lips. "We all know the ravenous appetites of the Anglo-Saxons, their complete lack of control, their inability to learn more than a basic way of life. You are lucky we came to civilise you – "

"Civilise? Is that what it is called, when churches are burnt to the ground and honest men watch their cattle slaughtered because it can be done?" Catheryn realised that her arms were on the table, and then realised that she had balled her hands into fists. "I am trying not to raise my voice, my lord, because you are a son of this house and I have great affection for your mother, but you do not know of what you speak!"

"I know you died as cowards! I know none mourned the dead, because you Saxons are incapable of emotion that deep, whilst each and every drop of Norman blood will be remembered forever!"

The boy – for he looked like a boy now, all of his manhood washed out of him – stared at the woman that had been living in his home for months now, taking the food from their mouths.

Catheryn stood up. The room stared at her, torn in their attempt to both look at her, at Roger, and away from both. She seemed majestic in her power, in her presence in the room. She looked taller somehow.

"My husband is named Selwyn," Catheryn said slowly. "I say that he is called Selwyn – and yet none shall call him by that name now, for his bones lie on one of the greatest battle fields across the water. He died protecting his land for the people that he loved; loved with a passion. He said that he would die for them, and he was a man of his word. And yet it did not matter that his blood…his precious blood was spilt, for it made no difference to the horde that attacked my home. Every waking moment is a point at which I am without him. Every sleeping moment is a time when I long for his comfort. My children…my son is dead, and my daughter may be just as lost to me. Sometimes I pray that she is, so that she will never know the shame and dishonour that our enemies cast on us, simply because we lived in a place that they wanted to own. And so I defy you, Roger FitzOsbern, to call my people cowards; I defy you to say we do not mourn; and I defy you to say that our loved ones will not be remembered."

The glare from her eye was enough to force Roger to drop his head, but even if he had been blind, her words would have shamed him, once, twice, three times over.

Catheryn sat down, and there was still silence. No man or woman seemed willing to break it.

"Harsh words have been spoken here," Fitz said finally, "and passionate ones. I cannot speak for all of the Normans; nor can I even hope to speak the feelings of those that live across the water. But in this no bitterness is spoken, and so I would ask that whatever feelings are nursed in the breasts of the people around this table, that they would be kept there, hidden from sight. There is no use for them here."

Heads nodded around the room – men that had fought battles, and had seen the light of life leave men's eyes, and then wondered at it all. Women smiled, painfully, at the remembrance of a missing face.

"I am sorry, Father, if my words offend you." Roger's voice held strong, if it did waver.

"'Tis not my apology you should be seeking, son."

Roger looked at Catheryn, but did not speak again.

"Come now," Fitz said, with a touch of roughness in his tones. "I will not have discord."

Roger swallowed. The words were evidently difficult for him to say, but it was clear that he must say them.

"I apologise, my lady Catheryn."

Catheryn looked at the boy for a moment. In many ways, he was still a child – but she suddenly had a flash of what her boy may have been like had he had the opportunity to reach that age. He would probably have been wild, just like Roger: wild, and full of opinions that he did not yet quite fully understand. He would have followed his father in all but sense, and though she smiled, she knew that he would almost certainly have fallen into mischief. It seemed as though Adeliza's son was just a boy, like all other boys.

"I accept your apology, Roger," she said softly.

For several minutes, nothing could be heard above the clatter of knives to teeth, and the satisfied munching of people that had been waiting a long time for such a good meal as this.

But before long, Isabella's incessant mind had to speak.

"Father, tell us about Queen Edith."

"She is just my lady Edith now, Isabella," Fitz reminded her. "Our Queen is Matilda, and her coronation was most magnificent."

"I did not know that you had attended," Adeliza said, looking suspiciously at her husband.

Fitz shrugged. "It did not seem important to tell you at the time."

Emma laughed. "Father, how could you? I would have loved to be there – was Edith very beautiful?"

"I have heard that she was," added Isabella. "Does she still wear a crown?"

Fitz shook his head. "She no longer has that honour," he said, "and yet, despite the lack of finery, there was certainly something very regal about her. From all accounts, she was a very popular Queen."

"And her son – Harold – he is well?"

Adeliza's words, innocently spoken, were met with much laughter throughout the room. Even Catheryn could not help but smile at the strange question.

Adeliza looked about her, confused. Turning to her husband, who was chuckling, she whispered angrily to him.

"Why does everyone laugh?"

"My lady," Fitz said formally, "Queen Edith and King Harold were not mother and son, but sister and brother. She married King Edward the Confessor, and her brother took the throne after his death."

Adeliza's cheeks burned. She looked around the room – Pierre was laughing openly, and the minstrel missed a note, so broad was his smile.

She swept up her skirts, and within a moment, had left the room.

CHAPTER SIXTEEN

Catheryn could see her. She was smiling and laughing, running past her in a flash of blonde hair tightly kept underneath a veil. Her daughter, Annis.

Catheryn watched as her daughter ran across the field, and once the girl was lost from her view, she turned to her husband.

"Selwyn," she smiled.

"Did you miss me?" Selwyn said, moving towards her and clasping his arms around her.

Catheryn breathed in the deep scent that Selwyn always had; a rough sort of smell, a mixture of the land that they loved and an essence that was only him.

"Of course I did," Catheryn murmured, "but – "

She stopped, and pulling herself out of his arms, turned to look at her husband.

"Selwyn…how can you be here?"

"Why would I want to be anywhere else than with you, my love?"

His face looked hurt, and Catheryn smiled slowly.

"I just thought – were you not far from here?"

Selwyn smiled broadly. "My love, what are you saying? You know that I would always come back to you?"

Catheryn turned, looking over the fields and the woodland that she knew so well. This was her home, the place where she belonged. Where they all belonged. But it was not possible, she could not possibly be here.

"Catheryn?"

Catheryn turned back to look at her husband, but with a thrill of horror she took a hasty step backwards. Exactly where Selwyn had been standing was…

"Fitz!"

"Yes, my dear?"

Catheryn ignored his words in her confusion.

"What are you doing – where's Selwyn? This can't be happening!"

But it was: and the man that was her captor was stepping towards her, slowly, a smile on his face, and her feet were trapped, stuck somehow to the ground, and she could not move, and every moment he got closer –

Catheryn took in a huge breath as she sat up. The dawn was just breaking, and she was covered in sweat. The dream that had consumed her mind and brought her so much happiness had turned, turned into something dark and strange.

But it would not do to dwell on it; that would only give greater strength to the images flowing through her mind. That would only replace the image of Fitz where that of Selwyn should be, whole and well. But he was not.

Hauling herself out of bed, Catheryn paced. The last thing that she wanted to do was stay here, in this room, empty as it was of anything that could distract her frantic mind. Using the last of the water in the jug beside her bed to wipe her brow and wash her face, Catheryn dressed.

Anything but remaining here to think.

The rays of the sun were just peeking through the clouds as Catheryn unlatched the outer door, and wandered out into the open air. If she just walk, she could find some peace; if she could just stop herself from thinking, thinking anything at all, then she could forget everything, and just be.

"My lady?"

Catheryn did not exactly scream – she was too old for that sort of nonsense – but some sort of strangled cry did leave her throat.

"My apologies, for I did not mean to startle you," said Fitz, as he crept out of the shadows and stood before her. "You…did not expect to see me?" he hazarded, looking at Catheryn's face.

"To tell the truth, I did not think of seeing anyone," Catheryn confessed. "I have found the hours here to be much later than that I am accustomed to. I usually have this part of the day to myself."

Fitz smiled wanly. "Then it is my turn to apologise for interfering with your leisure time – though I am surprised. I had thought noblewomen did not arise until absolutely necessary."

Catheryn rolled her eyes, and began walking towards her favourite field, her treasured spot.

"I am hardly a lady of leisure, my lord," she said, not able to prevent the hint of bitterness escaping with her words, "I am a prisoner."

Fitz cursed underneath his breath, and began following the woman that had so far brought nothing but argument to his life.

"I apologise again," he said to her back as she kept walking. "I meant no disrespect, my lady, but I am still learning how you are to be treated here."

He received no reply, but he could not help but watch her and continue to follow her. There was a grace about her, a characteristic she seemed to hold of knowing absolutely where she was, that was alluring. He had never witnessed it in another before.

"Are you still following me?"

Fitz laughed. "I am afraid I am. I have another apology that I must deliver before I feel at ease."

The figure before him came to an abrupt stop, and then Catheryn turned to face him.

"Well?"

"I...I feel it necessary to apologise for the remarks that my son made to you last night. It was ill-advised, and ill-spoken, but it was done, and I regret it."

Catheryn stared at the man.

"Why do you look at me such?"

"Because," Catheryn said slowly, "I am trying to understand you. I currently am struggling to believe that you, a lord of Normandy, are attempting to make amends between an Anglo-Saxon noblewoman and a Norman boy not much older than her own daughter."

Fitz shrugged. "I am a strange breed, perhaps, but I still believe that it is important to be right with those that we dwell amongst. Cannot you see the merit in that?"

"Plenty of merit, but not much sense." Catheryn shook her head. "You are, in every way, my superior. You are a man, and I am but a woman. You are a Norman, and I am but an Anglo-Saxon. You are the key keeper, and I your prisoner."

"Are not we a little old for this war-mongering?" Fitz sighed. "I see no difference between my people and yours, save that we came to your table uninvited."

Catheryn stared at him. The dark eyes that had previously betrayed a kindness in him were full of tiredness, but also with compassion. This man was of a different breed.

In the end, it was Catheryn who broke the silence.

"Do not concern yourself," she said briskly. "I was affronted, but not surprised. He is not the first I have met like him, and he will not be the last."

"And yet it brings me sadness that is should happen under my roof," sighed Fitz. He started walking, and within a moment he knew that Catheryn had followed him. Within another, she was walking alongside him.

"I do not think that you shoulder any…blame for what Roger said," Catheryn said hesitantly. "After all, he has just lost his father for the best part of two years."

Fitz reflected. "I had not considered it like that. But then, I have returned – I am healthy and well, which is more than many children can boast."

"But you have not returned."

"What mean you by that, my lady?"

Catheryn smiled sadly. "Your boy is now approaching manhood: you will both need to learn how to be father and son again."

Fitz shook his head. "So many were not as fortunate, and he complains."

"Just be grateful that you get the chance."
Fitz looked at his companion. No tears fell from her eyes, but there was a look of devastating sadness within them.

"*His nama is?*"

"*Ic wæs Selwyn.*"

It was a full heartbeat before Catheryn realised what had just happened.

"*Þu cwiÞst seo tunge?*"

"Yes," Fitz returned to Norman, "I do speak your tongue – but I must apologise, your accent is most strong."

Catheryn grabbed his arm, causing him to tug against her as she brought him to a stop.

"How do you know the language of my people?" She said accusingly.

Fitz laughed. "How do you think I have survived? It is only by learning your language that I have been able to serve my people, and protect your own."

"Protect?"

"There are many people – men that I am ashamed to say that I know – that treat your kind like animals. They see little worth in caring for the people of your land, and even less on wasting food on them. It took my learning the language of the people across the water to be…a bridge, perhaps, between the two of us."

Catheryn was breathing heavily. "We are being mistreated, then? I had assumed as much, but…"

Fitz tried to reassure her, but he could not help but be aware of the burning feeling emanating from her fingers, still gripping onto his forearm.

"My lady Catheryn, I hate to admit that you are hurting me, but – "

Catheryn dropped her hand as if it had caught aflame. It felt as though it had, and the furnace spread to her face. There was a stirring sensation in her gut that had nothing to do with hunger, but Catheryn could not understand what it was. She had more pressing concerns.

"My people, are they being mistreated?"

Fitz sighed, and began to walk. He could not bear to look into the eyes of this beautiful woman with such sorry tales to relate.

"Yes," he said heavily. "And no. Those of noble blood that are willing to cooperate have found themselves unwelcome prisoners in their own homes, whilst Normans take their place at the table."

"And everyone else?"

"The poor starved for the first year – the crops were burned."

"I was there when they burned the fields."

Fitz berated himself internally. "I am sorry, my lady, you do not need to hear these things from me. You have already endured the pain of the invasion, let me not lead you down the paths of memories to gaze at it once more."

Catheryn tried to smile, but could not quite summon up the strength.

"The invasion I know: but I was taken across the water within days of that bloody time. I have had no news, no news at all of my people, or the country that I left behind."

"I am afraid I am a rather useless messenger," Fitz confessed. "I spent most of my time relaying orders and presiding over court decisions. William wanted to use my gifts – "

"King William?"

Fitz nodded. "My ability to speak to the people came in useful. I became valuable, and before long the people I saw were of the royal court, and those walls did not include many Anglo-Saxons. I am sorry," he said softly, "but I cannot give you the knowledge that you seek."

"You cannot know the knowledge that I seek," Catheryn said sadly.

"Word of your daughter?"

Catheryn gazed at him desperately. "I have heard nothing, nothing at all. Tell me: could you find out, if I gave you her name? Could you use the royal court to discover her?"

As she looked at him, Catheryn saw the answer in his eyes before he spoke it in words. He could not help her: whether because no news could ever be found of a dead girl, or because he simply would refuse to help her, it made no difference. Annis was gone.

"I do not want to give you…false hope," Fitz said softly. "There is every chance that your daughter is no more, and did not survive the night you were taken. There is even more chance that she fled, like so many others did, to the nunneries, where even the women of God could not find refuge from the sword. I think you must come to accept that your daughter is dead."

"No," Catheryn wrenched her arm from him, and turning away from the man that would tell her lies, started stomping back towards the castle. "I would know if she was gone, I would feel it."

Fitz made no reply, but simply walked with her. Reaching down, he pulled a long piece of grass from the earth, and fiddled with it.

Catheryn slowed down as her thumping heart told her that she could go no faster. Neither of them spoke, until Catheryn noticed the grass between his fingers.

Catheryn smiled sadly. "I used to walk with Selwyn like this."

CHAPTER SEVENTEEN

A week later, Catheryn had again escaped from the monotony of castle living, and, as she always did, made her way down to her favourite field. There was no denying it: that was where she always wanted to be, and if not in her own chamber, that was where she was. The calm of the ground beneath her feet, shoes removed, and the feel of the grass beneath her hair: that was really being alive, despite this living death that she was forced to dwell in.

A quiet breeze blew, and Catheryn's skirts rustled. They reminded her of a younger time, a time before she was a wife and a mother, and nothing really mattered. The sun beat down on her, and Catheryn smiled.

She shut her eyes. Nothing could disturb her here: she was as alone as she was ever going to be within this prison.

"Alone," she muttered.

Catheryn snapped open her eyes and sat up, looking around; but there was no one to be seen.

"Stupid woman," she said to herself, "there's no one to hear your mad ramblings."

Catheryn smiled. It was strange, this feeling of being totally alone. Although she was still certainly a prisoner, it was almost like being free.

"Completely free," she murmured, lying back down and closing her eyes against the beating sun. "And yet, not free at all. Completely trapped, just waiting here. Hoping that everyone that I love is safe – and yet…"

Catheryn swallowed. She must not think of Selwyn, it would do her no good to go over those raw emotions one more time.

"Some are just lucky, I suppose," she thought aloud. "Some go off to war and come back, and some go off to war, and become the soil for the next year's harvest. Selwyn will never return, and yet Fitz…Fitz came back to his family."

A twig cracked, but Catheryn paid it no attention.

"And yet what difference is there between them?" she wondered aloud, reaching out both of her hands to the grasses around her. The rough texture tickled her palms. "They both fought for their families, and their families depended on them. And Fitz – he is just as strong and courageous man as Selwyn ever was."

Catheryn thought back to their conversation in the field a week ago, to the many conversations that they had partaken in the time since then.

"He is a good man," she said finally.

No more was said. The calming breeze and the warming sun called to her, and Catheryn slept. And because she was asleep, she never saw the figure of Fitz smiling, and walking out of the shade of a tree, back to the Castle.

As summer rolled into autumn, it soon became clear that Catheryn, opposite as she was to him in so many ways, was falling in love with Fitz.

Catheryn knew it was ridiculous. She had had her time for romance: she had met and married and loved a good man, and she had borne children. All of that young innocence was something that she had left behind long ago; something that made her smile, but not a way of life anymore.

And yet each and every time she saw him, her stomach churned. Catheryn could feel herself growing warm, a warmth not emanating from the sun but from something deep inside her. His kindness towards his servants, the delicacy with which he treated his daughters – they seemed to be merely further proofs of his worth, and of his good character. But although Catheryn would never dare admit her feelings to anyone aloud (for who would she tell?) if she were to confess, she would not be able to hide the fact that Fitz's very masculinity called to her in an almost primal way. She was used to belonging to a man, and she missed that.

Each moment was torment, each moment was delight. There was nothing she could do but hope that she would see him that day – and then curse herself for her folly.

For what was to be done? Fitz was a married man: married, moreover, to a woman that Catheryn did not quite understand, but certainly liked. They had built a haphazard friendship over the months, based partially on politeness and fear, but it was a friendship. Adeliza was the only friend that Catheryn had within a hundred miles. Was she so foolish as to attempt to break the most sacred bond that friend had made with another man?

Each day Catheryn would wake from fitful dreams, full of confused images. Selwyn would sometimes appear in these dreams, but he would never speak. He would just stand there, gazing at her, and no matter how much Catheryn implored him to say something, not a word was uttered. Catheryn would awaken, terrified and panicked. The nights that she did not dream of her dead husband were, in some respects, worse. Fitz was there, and Catheryn blushed when she next saw him.

Every day was becoming a torment, each evening a rehearsal of self-control. Catheryn began to find refuge in her field, just simply lying there and enjoying the weather. Sunny days passed sunny days, and Catheryn began to feel that, although she could not banish away her feelings, she could at least control them.

Each and every time Fitz and Catheryn talked, smiled, laughed, Adeliza's smile became more and more brittle. Her friendship towards Catheryn weakened, and her conversations became quieter, shorter. She was no fool, and Catheryn blushed at times to see the way that she behaved.

Harvest was almost over, but the rains came too quickly. For Catheryn, standing by the door to the stables with dismay painted on her features, it was the end of a time that allowed her to escape the confines of the stone prison she had been brought to. But it was impossible for her to consider wandering around in the damp and the dirt.

"My lady?"

Catheryn turned quickly, and saw Emma standing behind her, a book in her hand.

"We have gathered in the Great Hall – Mother has brought us some books, and we are going to entertain ourselves there. Will you not join us?"

Catheryn hesitated. "I will not be intruding?"

"Not at all!" Emma replied with a smile. "Many of the household join us on a rainy day. After all, there is not much else to do."

Catheryn smiled, and followed Emma to the Great Hall. Despite imagining that the entire family would be there, however, Catheryn saw to her horror that Fitz was the only person in the room. He was sitting by the fire, and humming a tune as he perused a long letter, resting open on his knee.

"Only you here, Father?"

"Only me," Fitz said with a smile, not looking up from his letter. The parchment was thick, and the writing bold. "I think your brother is sulking, although I do not know why, and your sister is wandering around looking for a dress that she is convinced a servant has stolen."

"What about Adeliza?" Catheryn asked.

Fitz's head shot up as a voice that he had not expected to hear reached him.

"My lady Catheryn," he said smoothly, folding the letter and standing. "I did not realise that you were here."

"Emma invited me," Catheryn said, in her confusion. "It is no trouble for me to go to my chamber, I have no wish to – "

"Stay," said Fitz softly. He must have realised that his voice was a little quieter than it should have been, because he repeated the word, this time in a stronger tone. "Stay. If you would; there is no need for you to be uncomfortable."

Catheryn smiled: it was a nervous smile, and it was nervously returned. Thankfully, Emma was not a girl who noticed much beyond her own limbs, and so joyfully bounced into a chair, opposite her father's.

"My dear, my lady Catheryn may prefer a seat by the fire."

"Please," Catheryn said quietly, "do not trouble yourself, Emma. I am quite happy to sit here by the window."

She had been amazed, when she had first arrived at the home of the FitzOsberns, just how many windows they had – and the high quality of the glass. It was not common for such things to be found in England. Glass windows there were few and far between; although, Catheryn remembered with a pang, they had always made sure that Annis had a bed chamber with a glass window. It had overlooked the courtyard, and she had loved sitting there, gazing down at the busy world beneath her.

"…my lady?"

Both Fitz and his daughter were looking at her, concerned. Catheryn realised that she had probably been asked a question.

"I beg your pardons," she said quietly, twisting her hands together in a manner most unlike her. "I did not hear what you said."

Fitz smiled: and it was a smile that tore at the very heart strings within Catheryn's chest. It did not seem possible that they were standing there, him with a smile on his face and her with a desperation to return that smile. And yet Catheryn did not know what he felt when he looked at her; she could not assume that because her feelings were involved, that he must return them.

"I merely asked whether you think you will be warm enough by the window."

"I…I will be quite warm enough, thank you, my lord," was all that Catheryn could manage before she had to break eye contact with Fitz. She strode over to the window, where there was a small alcove. Tucking her feet underneath her skirts, Catheryn turned her face away from the other occupants in the room, and stared at the window. Although made of a high quality glass, there was little that she could make out save shapes and shadows. Nevertheless, it was better than facing the stares of the man whom she was coming to consider very important to her very existence.

Emma soon settled, and lost herself within her book. Her father, however, was having more difficulty concentrating on the words offered to him by the author of his letter. Marmion's updates on the temperaments of the Anglo-Saxon people and the various court intrigues was not enough, now, to capture his attention.

She sat there, face turned to the faint rays of sun like a flower welcoming the end of winter. Fitz could hardly believe that she was there, let alone remove his gaze from her. Beautiful blonde hair, turning to silver in parts, washing down her back, barely visible through the veil that she determinedly wore, despite the mockery and slurs she had received. It marked her out: Saxon, it said, and yet Fitz loved it.

Catheryn was a woman like no other he had ever met. Most of the females that he was forced to consort with during his time were very much like his wife: meaning well, but bred to be cold, born to duty and feeling no fire. Adeliza did not laugh, like Catheryn did; she did not take the time with their children, as Catheryn did; she did not make every part of him feel alive just by one look, as Catheryn could.

Fitz jerked his eyes away from her, and back to his letter. Nothing could come of this, nothing could be gained by such idle thoughts. Nay, treacherous thoughts – for had he not sworn an oath of marriage and of loyalty to Adeliza? Had he not promised to stand beside her until either his or her body was laid to rest in the warm earth?

He had done so, and now he had to live with that decision.

And yet what had he gained from his loyalty to Adeliza? There was no love in their marriage. The creation of their children had been from tradition, and a sense of carrying on his father's name: there had been little joy in it save the physical release...

Fitz shuffled uncomfortably in his chair. There was no way to turn back time, and alter the decisions that he – and Catheryn – had made all of those long years ago. Divorce was unthinkable, leaving Adeliza was incomprehensible: he would simply have to learn to live with these conflicting emotions.

The piece of parchment swam in front of his eyes, and Fitz looked up. Catheryn was staring at him, and it was within that moment that they both knew.

CHAPTER EIGHTEEN

Christmas in 1067 was bright and crisp. A deep frost lay across the land, but it was not impossible to travel, and soon many of Fitz and Adeliza's acquaintances had made their way to the feast that threatened to surpass all others within living memory.

Chicken and hogs, fruit that Catheryn thought impossible to get hold of in these dark depths of the season, and spices that enticed every nose in the room filled the air. Holly and ivy had been brought in to give the Great Hall the appearance of a forest, and Catheryn could not help but smile.

And yet it was not the Christmas that she had wanted, or hoped for. Another season celebrated far from her home, far from her family, far from the daughter that she felt in her heart must be living somewhere. There were no rousing choruses of her favourite songs, and the carols that were hummed by the men, and sang by the women, were foreign to her ear.

Catheryn had to endure the stares and pointed fingers of the FitzOsberns' guests. Many had heard tell of the strange Anglo-Saxon woman that was being held captive, of course, but few had had the chance to truly stare at her, laugh at her veil, or draw their children away from her in fear that she would curse them.

By the afternoon, Catheryn had grown tired of the charade, tired of being part of the entertainment. Even a beautiful and impressive musical performance by the younger FitzOsberns could not draw away the mutterings of the crowd – and she sighed with relief when Fitz stood to announce the end of the proceedings.

"My friends, my dear friends," he said with a smile, and a hand over his straining belly, "it has been another good year, and another good day to come together and feast. But, as is our custom, the evening is for the family. And so I wish you a good journey, and a good repast until we meet again."

"Until we meet again!"

The cry was taken up from all sides, and goblets and tankards were raised to the promise of another great occasion to feast and frolic. Catheryn closed her eyes in despair. Was she ever to escape, was she ever to see the sun rise on her home again?

Within minutes, the Great Hall had been cleared, and the only people remaining were the FitzOsberns. Isabella stared at their prisoner.

"My lady Catheryn, I do think that you are relieved that we are now left alone."

Catheryn laughed. "You are most observant, my lady Isabella. I must confess that such vast hordes of people intent on discovering all about me while cursing my very name is not the way that I had intended to spend this Christmastide."

Isabella stared at her, eyes all honesty and confusion. Then she said suddenly, "You must be very lonely."

"Sometimes I am," Catheryn said simply. Out of the corner of her eye, she could see Fitz pausing in the stoking of the fire. "And then I remember that I am surrounded by good and gracious people, even if they are not my family. And that is better than for many others."

A smile was the only reply that she received from Isabella, but Adeliza rose from her chair, breaking off a conversation with Roger. He looked at his mother, bewildered, but before he could say another word, she had already stalked out of the room.

Catheryn caught Fitz's eye: something that she had been attempting not to do these last few months. There seemed to be a mutual understanding between them now, never spoken of, never referred to, that despite their feelings, no action would be taken. They had far more to lose than to gain.

"I think your mother has some orders to give the servants before she truly relaxes for the evening," Fitz said hastily.

Emma sniffed. Her nose was red, and she had been suffering from a cold for many days. "We shall see her this evening, Roger," she said comfortingly.

Roger shrugged off the friendly arm that Emma had tried to put around his shoulders, and followed his mother's example by leaving the room without another word.

Fitz sighed heavily. "Girls, why do you not spend a little time away from here, so we can leave the servants time to clear up. My lady Catheryn, I offer you the chance to escape stares by returning to your own room."

Catheryn flushed with embarrassment. Was she to be sent to her room, like a naughty child, just because her presence made the lady of the house uncomfortable? And then she realised: yes, it was perfectly reasonable. She was, after all, merely an interloper into this woman's home. She had traversed Adeliza's domain, and become a trespasser on her marriage. No wonder the woman could barely speak to her now.

"We shall return later on," Isabella said quietly. "Come, Emma."

The two girls left, arm in arm – a rare sight in the days of their almost continuous arguments. And so

Catheryn was just left standing there, staring at Fitz, the man that she had come to love.

"As I said," Fitz moved towards her, and Catheryn was almost foolish enough to stretch an arm out, to catch him, to finally make physical contact with the man that she had wanted to embrace ever since she realised what a great man he was, "I would return to your chamber."

And the last member of the FitzOsbern family exited the room.

After a time, Catheryn returned to the Great Hall. She had seen no other members of the family, but desired to sit by a warm fire – and the Great Hall was one of the few places that anyone could always be found, regardless of the season or the hour.

When she entered, she realised that Adeliza was sitting by the fire, a fur covering her knees. She was staring at the flames, wrapped in thought.

Trying not to make a sound, Catheryn backed away.
"Stay."

The voice was quiet, but it was not hostile. Catheryn hesitated.

"I am quite happy to return to my chamber – "

"Catheryn," Adeliza inclined her head just enough to take in the visage of her prisoner. "I am asking you to stay."

There was nothing to be done, thought Catheryn, but to endure it until the other members of the family arrived. Of course, she did not dislike Adeliza: in many ways, she quite liked her. But Catheryn's new feelings – or infatuation, she reminded herself – for Adeliza's husband meant that she could never feel totally comfortable around her hostess. Not until she had these strange emotions under control.

Catheryn took a seat opposite Adeliza's, and both women observed the fire for several minutes before either one of them spoke again.

"You still have hope?"

"My lady?"

"You still have hope," Adeliza repeated, "that your child is living."

Neither woman looked at the other.

"I cannot help but hope," Catheryn said finally. "To lose hope would be to lose all sense of life, all reason for living. Without the possibility that I shall gaze on her face again, I do not think that I could rise each morning."

Catheryn shuddered, unconsciously, at the thought that she may never see Annis again in this life.

"And yet, you have no proof of that. Nothing tells you, positively, that she lives."

Catheryn dragged her eyes away from the intoxicating flames, and said angrily, "Do you want me to give up? Does it please you to hear of my hopes, hopes you believe I shall probably never realise?"

Adeliza refused to look at Catheryn as she spoke. "It is better to accept that she is dead, and live your own life. You are young. Your time has not yet come to dwell among the dead."

"And my own daughter may be amongst the living!" Catheryn cried. "There is nothing within me that dares give up on that hope."

Adeliza said nothing for a moment; when she did speak, it was almost a whisper that Catheryn could barely catch.

"Sometimes hope is not enough."

Catheryn was spared creating any sort of reply by a loud noise. Emma thrust open the door with a crash and hurtled in, hair unkempt, feet cold, and eyes wet.

"You must go after her!" She cried. "You simply must!"

Emma crumpled in a heap where she stood.

Both Adeliza and Catheryn rose in an instant, rushing towards the stricken girl now sobbing.

"Darling daughter, what is the matter?" Adeliza tried desperately to look at Emma's face, but she kept twisting it away, tears wetting her already matted hair. "Tell me!"

"Perhaps she is unwell," Catheryn murmured. She was kneeling next to the mother and daughter, watching the younger in her distress and the elder in her panic to relieve the suffering. "She should be taken to her bed chamber."

"No!" Emma almost screamed now, it was as if she was working herself into a fury. "Someone must be sent after her, we must get a horse – "

"Emma, we do not understand you," Catheryn said firmly. "You need to calm down."

But Emma seemed completely incapable of any semblance of calm.

Footsteps could be heard, rapid and heavy.

"Emma?"

Catheryn knew that voice: it was Roger.

"Mother!" He exclaimed as he entered the room and saw the three of them, one in hysterics, one near to panic, and one trying to keep everyone calm.

"Roger, what is happening?" Adeliza said quickly, her hands never ceasing to try and calm Emma down.

Catheryn realised that she had never seen Roger so pale, so unable or unwilling to look his mother in the eye. "She has…she has not told you?"

"She has told us nothing we understand," Catheryn said quietly. "Do you know of what she speaks? Who must we go after?"

Roger knelt down by his sister, and whispered to her. Catheryn could not hear the words which he uttered to make her relax, but within moments she was able to lift her head, and gave a wan smile to her mother.

"I apologise, Mother," she said, her voice raw. "I did not mean to alarm you – and yet we must make haste, we must hurry if we are to catch her!"

Something close to a hint of what could have occurred touched Catheryn's mind.

"What has happened?" Adeliza grasped her son's arm. "Is it your Father, is he ill?"

"My lady mother," Roger said formally, and Catheryn's heart sank. "I have to tell you that Isabella and Emma...they had a fight. A truly momentous argument –"

"Which was all my fault!" Emma interjected, tears threatening once more.

"Which was, like all arguments, a combination from two sides," Roger corrected. Catheryn saw him give a smile, a rare thing indeed, to his sister. "It is not your fault, Emma."

"A fight?" Adeliza said urgently, willing him to continue. "A quarrel, that is all?"

Roger shook his head. "Isabella does not like losing arguments, you know that. She has taken a horse. She has gone."

A horrified silence filled the room. Adeliza stared at her son, as if he had begun speaking a foreign tongue. Catheryn watched her, desperate to remove herself from this family tragedy, desperate not to impose, desperately hoping that Isabella had not gone far...

It was impossible to tell exactly how long that silence would have continued if not for the enormous crash that was Fitz's entrance.

"She's really gone?" he said wildly, cloak already fastened around his neck, and trying to pull on one glove onto the wrong hand. "Who saw her leave?"

Emma began to cry again. "All I know is that she threatened to run away, and then she did!"

"You must find her, Fitz," Adeliza's voice was sharp. "You must find her. There is no knowing what is out there: wolves, or men in the dark. She'll get cold, she'll get ill!"

Roger stood up, and took two steps towards his father, before stopping awkwardly. "She would have made for the village, Father, I would swear by it."

"And suddenly you know all about your sister? You, a boy that never has time for them and has not even found the time to become a man?"

Roger's face became paler, but he did not look away, and met the gaze of his father. Anger and panic could be seeing warring in Fitz's face.

"I wish to accompany you on your quest to find her." Fitz snorted. "Do you really think that you could be useful?"

"Let him help, Fitz." These words were spoken by Adeliza. Her arm was around Emma now, and she had raised her to a standing position. "Let him help, and let all that offer their services help. There is no point in denying him, and every pair of eyes is another blessing in the hunt to find our daughter."

Fitz opened his mouth, but no words came out. Never before could he remember his wife speaking to him so. Perhaps it was high time, a small voice in his mind said, that she did.

"Fine," he said curtly, finally pulling off the glove and throwing it on the floor. "If you wish to come, dress for the weather and saddle your horse. I leave within moments."

Roger swept out of the room, but a small muttering of thanks was heard by all.

Fitz stared at the three women, and suddenly realised who they were.

"My lady Catheryn, would you be so good as to help my wife take our daughter back to her bed chamber. She needs rest, and complete quiet."

Without waiting for an answer, Fitz strode out of the room, glove abandoned.

His absence brought a silence into the room that was only filled by a hearty sniff. Adeliza and Catheryn looked at Emma, as though just remembering that she was still there.

"Come now," Adeliza said softly. "We shall get you into bed, and before we know it your father and Roger will have found Isabella."

"And she will go to bed as well," continued Catheryn in a quiet voice, taking Emma's arm under hers, "and tomorrow we shall laugh about the scare that she gave us all."

Slowly, the two women managed to coerce Emma, partially by soft words and partially by gentle tugs, to get into her bed. It took a long time to quieten her, to see her off to sleep. As soon as her breathing had slowed to such a point that they were sure she was asleep, Adeliza and Catheryn exited her bed chamber, and stood together in the corridor.

Catheryn had no words in which to express her anxiety, but knew that she must say something.

"My lady Adeliza," she began awkwardly in a whisper, "I want you to know…how sorry I am that this misfortune has visited your family – but…but I know that Fitz and Roger will soon find her – "

"Do not speak to me." Adeliza's voice was dark and quiet, and seemed to have the weight of the sea behind it. "Do not talk to me of your sadness, do not mention my husband and son who are risking their own lives to find her, and do not think to repeat back my own words to me. Yes, I see the folly of the words that I spoke to you, only earlier this very evening."

Catheryn opened her mouth, but she could give no guidance to this woman before her that was almost spitting poison in her attempt to rid herself of the pain that she was feeling.

Adeliza breathed heavily, and yet no tear threatened to fall from her eyes.

"Come with me," Catheryn said quietly. "We can await the news from the Great Hall, where there is a fire, and we shall hear as soon as anything occurs."

"No need," Adeliza said dully. Her eyes were now focused on something Catheryn could not see, something directly behind her. Catheryn spun around.

CHAPTER NINETEEN

Fitz stood there, almost blue with cold: a bundle of humanity in his arms.

"Isabella!"

Adeliza rushed forward as Fitz half lowered, half dropped his daughter onto the ground. As he leaned down, Catheryn could see Roger behind him, pale.

"Isabella?" Adeliza shook her daughter, but her eyes were closed. She did not respond.

"Fire." Catheryn spoke in a calm voice, but her insides were shaking. Isabella was clearly in a bad way, and if they did not take action, then they were sure to lose her. To be so close to retrieving her, and then to watch her die in their arms…

"We need to get her warm," Catheryn said fervently. "Is there a fire in her room?"

"I had one lit," Roger's voice sounded otherworldly. "Before we left, I gave instructions that one should be lit for when we returned."

"You did well," Fitz said listlessly.

Adeliza had tears running down her face. "She needs nought but hot food and blankets, she will recover, she is just a little cold…"

"Nothing can be gained from standing here," Catheryn said agitatedly, "she must be moved, and quickly. Emma may hear at any moment – "

As if the pronouncement of her name was an invocation, the door beside them opened, and a sleepy figure appeared.

"Isabella?"

"Emma."

Adeliza almost jumped when her daughter, wet and cold, lying on the floor, responded to the gasp that her twin sister had just given.

"She is alive! My child, my daughter, she lives!"

Emma began to cry once more, unable to move from the spot. Isabella said nothing more, but then it would have been difficult to hear her over the sobs of her mother.

Catheryn cast a panicked look at the only person that she knew could take charge.

"Fitz, help me."

The great man hesitated for a moment, and then instinct took over.

"Adeliza, help Emma back to her bed. You may join us once she is settled. Roger, send word: we need Ursule. You know who she is, and you know that she may refuse to come. You must make her come. My lady Catheryn, would you help me take Isabella to her bed chamber?"

Fitz's forceful words, his commanding air, was all that kept the people in that corridor moving, kept them sane. Emma's sobs subsided slightly as she was enveloped by her mother's care, and Roger spun away, running towards the stable without another word.

"My lady?"

Catheryn nodded at Fitz's words, and reached down to the heap of shivering girl. Together, with much difficulty, they managed to half carry, half drag Isabella to her bed chamber. Thankfully it was but a few steps beyond

Emma's, but as soon as they were able to lie her on her bed, Catheryn breathed a sigh of relief.

"There," she said, glancing at the grate and seeing with joy that a steady fire was already inhabiting it, "she is safe. Now all we need to do is – "

Fitz collapsed. He had been out in the cold for hours. A man his age would have fallen sooner. The sound was terrible: his head hit the floor and there seemed to be an echo from the sound. His arm caught the side of Isabella's chair, and it crashed over him.

Catheryn screamed.

"Fitz! Fitz?"

Kneeling by the unconscious figure of the man that she had never believed could be beaten by anything, Catheryn did not know who to tend to first: the girl whose breathing had become more and more shallow with every passing moment, or the man that had a trickle of blood flowing out of his head.

"Fitz?"

Adeliza stood in the doorway, a large fur in her arms. She had evidently brought it to enwrap Isabella. A look of shock filled her features.

"What has – did he trip?"

"I think not," Catheryn leaned over him, and pulled an eyelid back. His eye roved, and his lips muttered something incomprehensible. "I think he has caught a chill. Isabella is almost the same way."

"A chill?" Adeliza said, stupefied. "But they can't be ill – all of the FitzOsberns are strong, they are never unwell."

"They are now," said Catheryn grimly. "Where does Isabella keep her dry clothes? We need to get her out of these wet ones as soon as possible. Can you fetch dry clothes for your husband?"

Catheryn had to say 'your husband': she could not say 'Fitz', or even 'him'. She had to remind herself, even in the depths of this tragedy, that he was not hers to care for.

"Dry clothes?" Adeliza laughed a laugh of disbelief. "You cannot think that I am going to step one foot further into that chamber? The sickness that he bares could come to me, I could die too!"

Catheryn had moved over to Isabella, and one hand on her forehead told the entire story.

"She has a fever," Catheryn said hurriedly. "Every moment counts, Adeliza, we must get her warm and dry."

Pulling first Isabella's shoes off, Catheryn began to remove her clothes. But then she stopped. Adeliza was still standing in the doorway.

"Will you not help me?" Catheryn asked testily. "This is your child, after all."

Adeliza's eyes did not leave Isabella as she spoke. "I cannot go in – what if I, too, caught the fever?"

"You may. But that is the risk that we take when we have children: we lay down all of our own fears and worries, and give everything for them."

"That is easy for you to say. Your child is beyond your help, and therefore you risk nothing."

Catheryn's anger, always so carefully kept underneath her skin, erupted. "And yet I risk illness and possible death to care for yours!"

Adeliza did not respond. Eyes still on her daughter, she shook her head slowly. "I cannot do it. I cannot risk the infection, I do not want to be sick…"

Catheryn could not believe what she was hearing. "No one wants to be sick, my lady Adeliza. Neither your husband nor your daughter chose this – but this is the situation. And if you are not going to move one foot to help me, you can at least raise a hand. Bring me dry clothes for your husband."

Adeliza did nothing, said nothing. Catheryn turned away from her, and continued to strip the shaking child from the icy vestments that was causing her temperature to drop rapidly.

The next time that Catheryn raised her head, Adeliza was gone.

It did not take Catheryn long to discover the location of Isabella's clothes, and she quickly dressed her in the warmest woollen dress that she could find. Rug after rug was placed over her, and Catheryn finished with pulling the fur from the floor by the fire over the top of them all. One quick glance at Isabella's face told Catheryn that it may be too late.

But her next problem was even more pressing: Fitz was still lying on the floor, unable to move. Catheryn bit her lip. There had been a man that had fallen at her own home: a villager, who had struck his head in much the same way that Fitz had just done. He had not lived.

"Mother?"

Roger's voice could just be heard from the corridor, and Catheryn almost did not have the strength to reply.

"In here, Roger."

His worried face soon appeared at the door, but it became a look of surprise when he realised that it was not his mother, but their prisoner that was beckoning him in. But she did not retain his attention for long.

"Father!"

Falling down to the ground, Roger desperately tried to speak to Fitz.

"Can you hear me? Father, do you understand."

"Leave him." The voice was old, and harsh, and it came from the elderly woman who was revealed when Roger knelt down. Catheryn had never seen such an old person before. Every wrinkle seemed to be carved into her face, and she could only have been about half of Roger's height. She had a strange fur wrapped around her shoulders, and her dark eyes blinked at Catheryn.

"You must be the Anglo-Saxon woman everyone keeps talking about."

Her voice was dark: there was a sort of merriment in it, and Catheryn guessed that she was laughing at her.

"I am, indeed," Catheryn replied over Roger's mutterings. "And you must be Ursule."

The woman nodded. The movement stirred the fur around her shoulders, and to Catheryn's amazement, it turned to face her. The cat jumped down from Ursule's shoulders — which was not a great distance — and stretched. Its face glared up at Catheryn, and she suddenly had the feeling that she was intruding on its territory. Without a second glance at its owner, the cat stalked over to the bed, leaped onto the covers that Catheryn had created to bring some warmth into Isabella's bones, and curled up on top of them.

"Don't mind Reginald," Ursule said in a low voice. "He never gets up to mischief, and he brings better medicine than I."

Catheryn simply stared at this strange woman. She had never met anyone like her, and was unlikely to ever again.

"Anything to say?" Ursule's raised an eyebrow.

Catheryn took a deep breath. It must almost be the middle of the night, and tiredness dragged at her eyes.

"Nothing except begging your help in this matter," she said softly. "Fitz said — my lord Fitz said that you may not come."

Ursule laughed, and Catheryn inexplicably felt her spirits lift.

"He told you that, did he?" Ursule continued to laugh, almost croaking with the effort. "Then he should know better. I brought him into the world, and if I am not left to my own devices, I may be seeing him out of it."

Roger was stirred by her words, and he stood up stiffly. Catheryn could see wildness in his eyes, but for once it was a wildness tamed.

"You will help us," he said to Ursule. "You will...won't you?" He sounded less certain.

Ursule took in the room with one glance, and seemed to think.

"You'll pay me double for this, being Christmas?"

Roger nodded vigorously. "Two barrels of ale will be taken to your…home…in the morning. They shall be waiting for you when you return."

"I'll be here much longer than one night, my boy."

Ursule pushed her sleeves up away from her thin wrists, and strode over to the man on the floor.

"There's sickness here, and it will be many days before we see the end of it. But if you leave me to them, I can help them back onto the path of the living."

Roger tried to make some sort of sound of gratitude, but it was lost in Ursule's shout.

"Out with you boy! Sleep is the best cure for you."

Roger was gone before Catheryn could blink.

"And you too, my lady. Off you go to your chamber, or palace, or whatever you call it."

Ursule's voice was still sharp, but she was now preoccupied. She was prodding Fitz, trying to see what reaction she could create. She tutted under her breath when she could gain no response.

"I will stay, and help you."

"Oh, will you?" Ursule said drily. "You are prepared to face death, for them – your captors."

Catheryn smiled wearily. "I am reaching the point, my good woman, where I do not feel that I have much more to lose. And these people have been kind to me, and I do not want to see their family diminished by such tragic losses."

A beady eye stared at her.

"And you know," Catheryn admitted, "she does remind me of my daughter."

Ursule nodded. "Annis."

CHAPTER TWENTY

"How do you know her name – do you know my daughter? Have you had word?"

Catheryn could almost not get the words out fast enough, and yet Ursule just smiled quietly.

"This man needs to stay exactly where he is," she pronounced, completely ignoring Catheryn's questions. "Moving him would bring him death, and I do not think that he is ready to depart from this world quite yet. Not quite yet."

"Answer me!" Catheryn almost shouted, but then remembered the sleeping girl on the bed. Out of the corner of her eye, Catheryn could make out the strange outline of Reginald, Ursule's assistant. He was still sleeping on Isabella.

She moved to see how the girl was doing, and could not believe her eyes. Colour had rushed back into her cheeks, and her breathing was deeper, more regular, calmer. She did not look unconscious now: merely sleeping.

"Ah, yes. Reginald is a great healer," Ursule stated whilst pulling the other rug from the floor over the figure of Fitz.

Catheryn shook her head slowly. "There is no reason to suppose...the warmth of the rugs, of the fire, that is what has brought her back to health."

Ursule straightened up, and put her hands on her hips. "You believe so?"

Catheryn nodded. "There is no reason why a cat should heal a person from a fever."

"Take him off then."

Catheryn reached out her hands, and then hesitated.

"Harder than it looks, isn't it?" Ursule laughed. "It is strange how little people believe when they are well, but how much they cling to half-truths and wishes when the Lord seeks to take them."

Catheryn knew that the cat could be doing Isabella no good; but then, he was certainly not doing her any harm either. And although Reginald was only just beyond her fingertips, she found it difficult to close the gap. Why should she remove anything, no matter how small the chance was, that seemed to be bringing Isabella back to health?

"Ursule," Catheryn said slowly. "I like you."

Ursule gave a mock curtsey, and then laughed again.

"I have no strong opinions on you, my lady – which are strong words in themselves, seeing as where you come from."

In another room, on another day, to a different person, Catheryn may have reacted. But in this room, during this night, to Ursule the healer that wore a cat like a muffler, Catheryn gave in.

"I leave you this evening, only," Catheryn said, "for I desperately need rest. But I shall join you in the morn, and together we will bring Isabella and Fitz back to life."

"Fitz, is it?" Ursule's eyebrow was once again raised.

Catheryn said nothing. She left the room, went to her own chamber, and collapsed onto her bed.

The next five days passed in a haze of tiredness and obedience. Ursule moved into Isabella's room, and it was only on the third day that she deemed Fitz to be strong enough to be moved to his own room. Adeliza had refused point blank to allow him back into their bed chamber: Catheryn had winced when she had heard the shouts as she had tended to Isabella's rising fever.

And so a second bed was placed opposite Isabella's, and father and daughter fought the fever together. Catheryn and Ursule spent days and nights moving from patient to patient, desperately tending to the fever that at once threatened to overcome, and then to disappear. It was like fighting sunlight in mist: you could see more the absence of it than the thing itself. And as the New Year beckoned, still no great change was seen in either Isabella or Fitz.

But no matter what the servants had whispered, the words of Ursule or the unnerving stare of Reginald, Adeliza did not change her mind. So great was her fear of infection that she did not even visit her husband, or Isabella. Twice Catheryn heard the girl cry out for her mother, and twice the message was sent to the lady of the house, and twice the same reply had been returned: she would not come.

"You look half dead," Ursule said quietly, returning from Fitz's sickroom to find Catheryn hunched in a chair beside Isabella's motionless figure.

Catheryn smiled wanly. "You looked half dead when you arrived here."

Ursule laughed, but much of the merriment had gone.

Stirring, Catheryn continued, "I have been told that your meal will be coming shortly. 'Tis almost night already, I cannot believe it."

"Believe it." Ursule took another step forward towards Catheryn. Catheryn saw that Reginald had already left Ursule and taken up his customary position by Isabella.

"And this night shall be the hardest, I warrant you nothing less."

Catheryn brought a hand to her head. It had been pounding ever since she had awoken, and the pain of it was threatening, even now, to force her to bed.

"You should go. You can do little good here tonight."

"I can do no worse by staying," Catheryn said wearily. "I would not feel right leaving them."

"There are some that would comment on that. Some would say that your affection is…too great."

"Any concern will seem too much compared to that of the lady of this house." Catheryn bit her tongue; she should not have said such hurtful words, but Ursule neither raised that familiar eyebrow, or laughed at the words that she should not have heard.

After a moment of silence, Catheryn spoke again, asking the question that had been burning her lips.

"How do you know of my daughter?"

"I do not." Ursule's reply was too quick for Catheryn's liking, and she stood, determined to wrestle the truth from this woman who was half nurse, half healer, half mystery.

"You must tell me," she said desperately, "you must help me reach her."

Ursule sat down in the chair that Catheryn had just left, and put the back of her hand on Isabella's forehead.

Then she looked at Catheryn.

"It is all around the village," she said heavily, "that you left a child behind. A girl, almost a young woman. Many say that you left her because you did not care for her. But I know you, Catheryn of England: you are a woman that would not leave anyone behind in a place like that."

Catheryn could feel her legs trembling, but she was determined to stay strong.

"And that is all they say?"

Ursule hesitated.

Catheryn dropped to her knees in front of the older woman.

"Please," she said, tears that had been threatening for days finally approaching the surface. "Please, you must tell me. You must help me."

"There has been talk," Ursule said softly, with a nervous glance at the outline of Fitz to her right, "that the lord of this place has not forgotten your child. Letters have gone out from here, with our lord William FitzOsbern's seal, to all parts of England." She leaned close towards Catheryn. "To find your child."

Catheryn stared. "Fitz – my lord has been trying to find my Annis?"

Ursule shrugged. "That is what they say. And now you must go to your bed chamber – no, I will brook no excuse. You are no good to me in the same state as they, and that is where you shall end up if you do not take rest."

Catheryn's head swam. "You are right," she said thickly, "though I wish it were not so. You will send for me if…if anything changes?"

Ursule smiled a bitter smile. "If either one of these dies this night, you shall know of it."

Catheryn was raised from her nightmare by a scream. For a moment, she thought it was her own; she had often had to muffle her own terror in the night for fear of waking the entire castle. But this time, it was not her mouth that was desperately shrieking: it was another.

The sun had not yet broken the night into day, and Catheryn bit her lip. There was no knowing what had happened, but if Ursule really needed her, then it would likely be impossible for her to come and fetch her.

Sighing, and wrapping a cloak around her shoulders for warmth, Catheryn rose from her bed. The hysterical screams had not ceased, and Catheryn opened the door to the corridor to hear them even louder.

Strangely, the screams did not seem to be emanating from the room where Fitz and Isabella were being nursed. Instead, Catheryn thought they were coming from much further away.

Hurrying, bare feet catching on the rushes that were laid down on the floor, Catheryn almost ran. She pushed open the door to the Great Hall, and a terrible sight lay before her eyes.

Adeliza.

The woman was lying prostrate by the fire. It was a miracle that her hair had not caught aflame – it was uncovered and perilously close to the flames licking at the ground. There was a servant beside her. Both of them were crying, and it was Adeliza that was screaming.

"Adeliza!"

Catheryn rushed over to the woman who was both captor and rival, and tried to pull her into an upright position. Adeliza was completely limp, a dead weight in Catheryn's arms, and she seemed unaware of where she was.

"Adeliza, can you hear me?"

Her eyes were closed, but her mouth continued to cry out. Catheryn turned in bewilderment to the servant. Panic flooded through her veins. This could only mean one thing.

"...dead," was all that the servant was able to say between hiccoughing tears.

Catheryn's mouth went dry. Her worst fears had been realised: the long journey in the snow, the darkness, the cold, the damp, had claimed from this family one of their own. Someone had been wrenched from life, and now lay lifeless in the chamber just down the corridor.

But which one?

"Tell me," Catheryn shook the servant, not caring whether it was seemly or not to lay hands on another person, "tell me who is dead."

The servant, an elderly woman with wisps of grey hair, took a deep breath, and managed to speak clearly.

"She is gone – Isabella has gone. The Lord took her not a moment ago, and my lady, my poor lady…"

The servant descended into sobs once more, and Catheryn swallowed, her mouth feeling like death.

Isabella was dead. The vibrant, lovely girl that continuously goaded her father, and mocked her brother. The twin sister that Emma could not live without had disappeared, and in her place there was but a body, with no life within it.

Catheryn's eyes overflowed with tears, but instead of allowing them to fall she tried to control her emotions. A tiny part of her that she would not own as herself was glad that it was not Fitz, glad that the man that she had learned to love had not disappeared down the same dark tunnel. But Catheryn hated that part of herself: she could not imagine how Adeliza was suffering.

A thought crossed her mind that, if she knew of her own daughter's fate, she too may be joining with Adeliza in her desperate screams and passionate crying.

It did not do to dwell on such things.

"Adeliza," Catheryn said thickly, her voice full of emotion. "Come. Let us get you to bed; you need to rest. Come with me."

Adeliza could not be persuaded, and she could not be goaded; she was beyond coercing, and beyond cajoling. Her child had died, and she did not want to live any more.

Catheryn and the servant eventually managed to carry Adeliza back to her chamber. Catheryn tried not to look around with curiosity at the place where Fitz spent much of his time; she attempted not to see the clothes lying across the floor, the intimacy of man and wife that was so evident in the room, and the pieces of parchment that

Catheryn could only assume were personal letters adorning the top of one chest. This was not her place to be.

"Get her on the bed," Catheryn panted. The weight of Adeliza was incredible, and Catheryn knew that she had not totally woken up yet.

The servant helped Catheryn to put Adeliza underneath the covers, but during all of this Adeliza refused to say anything. She merely continued to cry, her sobs punctuated with screams. Now Catheryn was close to her, she realised that each scream was the name of the daughter she had just lost.

The servant hurried out, and Catheryn did not have the heart to force her to stay. The entire household would mourn this tragic loss – and Fitz was certainly not free from death either. There was much to be fearful of still.

"Adeliza," Catheryn sat on the other side of the bed, and tried not to think that this was Fitz's side. "Look at me. You need to sleep."

Adeliza turned to look at her, but there was only a small fraction of recognition in her wild eyes.

"Sleep," said Catheryn, kindly. "Staying awake will bring you naught but pain, and your mind needs to escape. Sleep is the only place that you can go, and I am sending you there immediately, my lady."

Adeliza's tongue reached out, and wet her dry lips.

"She is really gone?"

The croak was nothing like Adeliza. It had none of her strength, none of her pride, none of her power. Catheryn was devastated to see all of the fight truly gone.

"Yes," she managed, finally. "Isabella is gone."

Adeliza's face crinkled up as she began to cry again, but they were quiet tears.

"You…you will stay with me?"

"Of course I will," Catheryn reassured her. "I will not leave your side all night. And in the morning, I will go with you to see your husband, and – "

"No." Strength had returned to Adeliza's voice, but it was not the word that Catheryn was expecting.

"No?"

Adeliza shook her head weakly. "I will not go to see Fitz. He is still unwell, he could still be contagious. I will not risk it – "

"Your own husband? You do not care to go and see him?"

Adeliza's eyes met Catheryn's, and they were hard as glass.

"I will not see him."

CHAPTER TWENTY ONE

Neither Catheryn nor Adeliza really slept that night. The wind howled, and it was often accompanied by Adeliza's moaning. Even as she slept, she wept.

Catheryn did not sleep at all. She could not drag her eyes away from the woman who had just lost one of the most precious things to her. Adeliza turned frequently underneath the covers where Catheryn had placed her, unable to settle, unable to rest.

Her mouth murmured, "Isabella."

Catheryn had to hold back tears. It did not seem possible, it did not seem fair that someone so young and so full of life had had it swept away from her. She shuddered to think of the possibility that her own child had received a similar fate. There was no way of knowing where Annis was living, where she had had to live after the Normans took their home. Perhaps she, too, had perished on a cold night, after attempting to sleep beneath the stars.

Dawn broke slowly. The light ebbed through the translucent glass, and Catheryn tried to think of what would happen that day. A judge would be called, to see the body. A priest, too. Emma would have to be told.

Despite not having eaten anything for many hours, Catheryn felt sick.

"Isabella?"

Adeliza was stirring, but the dream that she was surfacing from centred around her dearest concern.

"Isabella, is that you?"

"No, my lady Adeliza," Catheryn said gently. "It is Catheryn. Your…guest."

Adeliza's blinking eyes suddenly found their focus.

"Catheryn! What are you doing here – in my bed chamber?"

Catheryn said nothing, but watched as the remembrance of the night before filtered into Adeliza's mind.

"No," she said slowly, forcing herself up and looking desperately into Catheryn's face. "No. It cannot be – Isabella is alive?"

Catheryn would have given anything to be elsewhere at that moment; to allow someone else to tell a mother, again, that she had lost a child.

"No," she said gently. "The Lord took Isabella last night. She is at peace."

A tear blossomed in Adeliza's eye, but to Catheryn's surprise, she did not descend once more into the hysterical sobs that she had been expecting.

"I knew that," she said softly. "I know it, as a sleeper knows she is in a dream. And yet I was so convinced that *this* was the dream. That I would wake, and find no hand of death had touched my family."

Catheryn said nothing. There was nothing to say.

"I must rise," Adeliza said suddenly, clawing at the fur over her, "I must prepare to meet the priest – he has been summoned, of course?"

"I…I do not know," stammered Catheryn, "I expect that Ursule has sent for him. Shall we go down together, to see how your husband is coping with the news?"

Adeliza paused in her struggle to free herself from her bed, and looked at Catheryn with eyes of steel. The tear was gone.

"I thought that I made myself clear last night. I will not go and see Fitz. He may still carry the disease which has just killed my daughter! You would ask me to risk myself?"

"I would ask you to be with your husband. He has just lost his daughter."

Catheryn spoke calmly, but she did not feel it. Did this woman have no wifely feelings at all? Surely she would want to comfort her husband, and be comforted in turn after this tragedy? But no: Adeliza would rather be alone, and far from the danger of death, despite the fact that her husband was an unwilling victim.

Catheryn forced herself to take a deep, long breath. The chamber spun slightly, and she reminded herself that she would need to eat as soon as possible.

"I am going to see him," she said simply.

Catheryn found Ursule guarding the door.

"What do you want?" she said, disgruntled. Reginald was snoozing around her neck.

"I need to see Fitz," Catheryn said quietly. "How has he reacted to...to Isabella's death?"

Ursule shifted slightly, looking uncomfortable, and Catheryn realised why at once.

"You haven't told him."

"And how could I? Sick as he is, near death's door himself as he was last night, was I to give him a reason to give up? I am not to be the bringer of bad news, my lady, even if you think that I should be."

"She died within five steps of him!" Catheryn hissed angrily. "She died just beyond his reach, and he still does not know?"

"Be my guest if you want the honour," snapped Ursule. Reginald awoke with a start, and hissed.

Catheryn rolled her eyes to the heavens. Was she continuously going to be telling parents the most awful thing that they could possibly hear?

Pushing past Ursule and not even bothering to reply, Catheryn walked into the room. Fitz was lying in bed, dozing. His hair was greasy, and pushed back against his forehead. His skin was sallow, but his breathing was regular.

"He will live."

Catheryn spun around to look at his nurse. "Are you sure?"

"As sure as I can be. It will take him a month to completely recover, but he will live."

Tears filled Catheryn's eyes, and she berated herself silently for being so relieved that the man she loved would live. He would live as another's, she reminded herself, and his daughter had just died. This is not the time to dwell on your feelings. This is a time for grieving.

Catheryn knelt by the side of the bed, and gently put a hand on his arm.

"Fitz," she said softly.

At first it seemed that he had not heard her, but after a squeeze of his arm, his eyes opened.

"Adeliza?"

Catheryn winced. It seemed that she was doomed to be mistaken for many people that morning.

"No, my lord. It is Catheryn."

"Catheryn." Fitz's eyes were bright, but they seemed to struggle to focus on her. "I am afraid that I feel very weak."

"Do not concern yourself with that," Catheryn said with a smile that she forced onto her face. "You have battled against a great sickness, and you have won. It was certainly not the first battle you have faced, although I pray that it will be the last."

A smile flickered over Fitz's features.

"I know that you have aided Ursule in my care, and I am grateful."

"You know that I would do...much to ensure your happiness." Catheryn did not trust herself to continue, and had just decided to bring the subject around to Isabella, when Fitz turned his head.

"And how is my daughter doing? Already up and out of bed, I see?" Fitz smiled, and it was a glorious smile. "How the young do shame the old. I had no idea that it was possible to recover from such a sickness in that time."

Catheryn did not need to look around to know that Ursule had left the chamber. Strong as she was in many ways, she was unable to watch this.

"Fitz," she said softly. "Isabella has not recovered. She was very sick, and last night...she lost her own battle."

Fitz stared at her. The words that she was saying did not make sense; he must have misheard her. But as he gazed up at Catheryn's beautiful face, he saw within it the truth. Isabella had died. His daughter was dead.

Tears filled his eyes, but there was only one word on his lips.

"Adeliza," he croaked. "Where is my wife?"

"She is very upset. She barely slept last night; I was with her."

Fitz waved away those concerns with a weary hand.

"But why did she not come and tell me this, herself?"

Catheryn hesitated. How was she to tell this man, who had suffered so much, that his wife was so fearful of herself becoming ill that she had laid aside all concerns for any other?

"She needs to rest," Catheryn said finally. "My lady Adeliza is weak, and she did not want to upset you with her tears."

Fitz once more just stared at Catheryn. The room seemed small, and dark, and they were alone.

"So what you are telling me," Fitz said with a dark expression, "is that the person who came to tell me, whilst I lie here on my own sickbed, that my daughter is dead, is the only woman who truly loves me."

CHAPTER TWENTY TWO

The moment that followed his words seemed to Catheryn to be long. Longer than long: she didn't know where to look, and almost forgot to breathe.

"Say that again," she managed, voice shaking. She was only too aware that her hand was still on Fitz's arm, and it seemed to burn like fire.

"Let us pretend no longer. You love me – and I have certainly felt the love from your eyes every time you have looked at me."

Catheryn opened her mouth, but Fitz continued before she could say any more.

"Try to deny it."

"I cannot," breathed Catheryn, "and I will not. But I must admit that I find it incredible."

"That I should love you?" Fitz struggled to sit up. "That I should be attracted to such a wonderful and caring woman as you?"

Catheryn shook her head, trying not to smile. "More that it is finally spoken."

"I have felt it for months," confessed Fitz. "It has been ever dancing around my lips, and yet I never allowed it to be spoken."

Catheryn almost smiled, but the remembrance of the empty bed in the room caused it to disappear as swiftly as it had come.

"Catheryn?"

Catheryn swallowed. "It is tragic that it has taken this – circumstances such as these to allow us to finally speak the truth."

A sharp look of pain passed Fitz's face. "You mean my sickness, catching this fever that stole my daughter from me and almost robbed me of my life?"

Fitz reached for Catheryn's hand, and clasped it tightly. Neither of them spoke for a few moments. Hot tears flowed across Fitz's cheeks, and Catheryn tried to show through the way that she clutched at his hand just how she shared in his sorrow, how she felt for the terrible loss that he had suffered.

Eventually Fitz regained control once more.

"It is done," he said heavily, "and it is terribly done, but it is done and there is naught I can do to change it."

"I mourn for you," Catheryn said quietly.

"And I appreciate the companionship," said Fitz. "When her own mother will not join me in the sadness, it is good to have some company."

Catheryn knew that she should leave him; that Fitz needed to rest, to completely recover his strength; that Adeliza would need caring for as well. But nothing beyond her mind made any sort of move, because every nerve in her body wanted to stay where she was. It was as if there was nothing else for her beyond the four walls of that sick chamber.

"Catheryn," Fitz said hesitantly. "You must know…you cannot fail to realise that there is absolutely nothing that we can do about these feelings that we have."

His words were like iron fists into her stomach, and yet Catheryn could not help but admit that she had been expecting them.

"Despite the fact that we love each other?"

Fitz smiled wryly. "Because of that very reason. This love we have...it cannot leave these walls. We can never speak of it again, and we cannot change the way that our lives are."

"I have nothing else to live for."

It was not until Catheryn said the words that she realised just how true they were. Her husband – Selwyn, the man that had taught her so much about the world – was dead. He had been killed on a field and laid where no one knew until the ground reclaimed its own. Her son had been cut down beyond her reach; she had no knowledge of what his last words were, his last sights, and sounds. Her other child could be dead or alive: she had no way of telling. Home taken, friends killed, country ruled over by a foreign lord that she had sworn no oath to. Catheryn had no other reason to continue, except this brave and honest man that lay before her.

"I am married."

"I know," Catheryn said, a tear in her eye that she would not let fall. "And despite my feelings for you, I cannot dislike Adeliza. She is a good woman, despite her faults."

"She is a good woman," Fitz agreed, "and she has given me a family. I have three children still living, and I cannot wrench away from them."

"I would not ask you to!"

"I would be forced to if I chose to leave their mother, you must know that," said Fitz. "Divorce...it is not permitted unless there are extreme circumstances. I made vows to Adeliza a long time ago, but they were made until death, and I am not a man to break them."

Catheryn was very aware of just how close Fitz was. His breathing was deep, and his shirt was not closed at his neck. The silver strands of his hair were just beyond her fingertips – and yet it was a divide that she knew she would never cross.

"And even," Fitz pushed through, heart breaking that his words would cause Catheryn pain, "even if Adeliza did not even exist, even if I was a widower, alone in the world, I am too close to the King. You are a disgraced Anglo-Saxon and I am the King of England's cousin. There is just – there is nothing to be done."

Catheryn sighed. "If only I had land, and power, or wealth, and friends."

Fitz smiled. "Small recompense for my loss, I suppose, but – "

"Do not misunderstand me!" laughed Catheryn bitterly. "I do not suggest them as alternatives. I just thought – if I had but one of them, then I would certainly be a more interesting and suitable marriage prospect."

Fitz shrugged, and then winced as something in his shoulder gave him pain.

"And I suppose that is that," Catheryn said quietly.

Fitz pulled a hand out to brush against Catheryn's face. His fingers felt warm, and the comfort that they gave to Catheryn could not be put into words.

"My love," Fitz whispered, "and I will call you my love, even if it is for the first and last time – just because I do not say that I love you, show that I love you, marry you, that does not mean that I do not feel what I feel for you."

Catheryn smiled sadly. "That will have to be enough."

She rose, carefully putting Fitz's arm back underneath the covers so that he could keep warm. Walking to the door, she opened it, and was about to walk through it when Fitz spoke.

"Catheryn?"

She looked at him: the man that she wished she could pledge her heart to.

"What will you do now?"

There was real concern on his face, and Catheryn smiled to see it.

"Do?" she said lightly. "There's only one thing I can do. I am going to break out of here, and find my daughter."

CHAPTER TWENTY THREE

With Fitz still in his sick bed, and Adeliza refusing to stir from her bed chamber, the heavy task of preparing Isabella's body for burial fell to Catheryn and Ursule. It took every inch of her self-control to prevent Catheryn from weeping as she gently caressed the young body with warm water. Isabella was so young, had done so little, had seen so little of the world. She had never grown, or married, or had children of her own. She had never learned to love literature, as Catheryn had, and she would never sing with her siblings again.

All of that was over.

"Just pretend that I am not here," said the priest, sitting on a stool by one side of the bed. He had been brought by Roger, and had been watching over Isabella's body for the vigil. He had not left her side for a moment over the last day, and the tiredness on his face had drawn lines of sadness around his eyes.

Catheryn smiled at him. "It is good to see you here, Father. Thank you for coming."

The man raised his hands, and said, "My lady Catheryn, you honour me. I merely come to a part of my flock that needs tending."

Tending, Catheryn thought. That was an interesting way of describing the horror that had flooded through this family, leaving nothing but devastation in its wake.

Catheryn cast a worried look over to the other bed in the chamber. Fitz lay motionless, but his eyes were open. Despite all that she and Ursule had said, they had not managed to persuade him to leave the room, or for Isabella's body to be prepared elsewhere. They had brought it back, and Fitz had stared unblinking at the body that had once held the laughter and the life of his daughter. He was still too weak to move, and too weak to attend his own daughter's funeral; this was the least, in his mind, that he could do, to be near her.

Ursule did not say a word as they worked together to dry Isabella's body, but Catheryn could see that she was deeply affected. Without noticing where she was going, Ursule accidentally trod on Reginald's tail; something that he did not easily forgive. But Catheryn could not draw her eyes away from the girl lying on the bed. She looked so peaceful. She could easily have been sleeping – and yet no dreams would visit her now.

"What jewellery will be placed with her?" Catheryn said, as Ursule rummaged in a box that had been given to her by Emma.

Ursule sighed. "Her sister has given us what she wants to be placed with Isabella, but..."

Catheryn spoke. "Why the hesitation?"

The sigh that Ursule let out was even deeper now. "She gave me some of her own wedding jewellery."

Catheryn's mouth fell open. Each daughter was given a portion of her mother's jewellery, to wear on her wedding day. They were always very precious, handed down from mother to daughter to daughter.

"For Emma to give these up..." Catheryn said softly. "It is almost as though she is saying – "

"That she will never marry," Ursule finished. "Yes, I know. But this is what she has given us, and I am loath to go against her wishes."

Catheryn considered it. Adeliza was a wealthy woman; she would have many other jewels that could be given to Emma. She was the only daughter now, and Adeliza was unlikely to have another child.

"So be it," she said softly. "Was a lead cross included?"

Ursule did not reply, but instead drew one from the box. She placed it on Isabella's breast, and then, without speaking, both she and Catheryn put the jewellery given up by her twin sister on her fingers, wrist, and around her neck. The gold glittered in the candle light. And then it was done.

"Jewellery can be replaced."

Catheryn started; turning, she saw Fitz staring at her.

"Daughters cannot," he said, his voice hoarse with grief.

"I know that," Catheryn said bitterly. "If there is anyone else in the world other than you that knows that, it is I."

Fitz opened his mouth to reply, but instead a tear escaped from his eye. A heavy hand moved to wipe it away. Catheryn knew that the pain he felt could never be removed. She turned back to her companion.

"What linens have been sent us?" Ursule asked, her voice thick with emotion that she would not allow herself to indulge in.

Catheryn pointed wordlessly to the pile that lay by the door. The linens were pure white, and soft. Ursule stepped across the chamber, picked them up, and brought them over to the bed.

"You know how to prepare a body for the grave?" she said, the harshness in her tones masking the deep sadness.

Catheryn nodded. "I prepared both my mother and my father, when their time came."

Ursule nodded. "Good. Then this should not take too long."

The priest had to move back slightly as they began to wind the lines of linen around Isabella. Catheryn and Ursule worked fast, silently, their hands crossing as they passed the linen to each other. Soon, nothing of Isabella was visible save her face.

Ursule sighed, and sat down heavily. "It is done."

"I shall finish here," Catheryn said kindly, and began to wind the last portion of linen around Isabella's face.

"No!" Ursule put out a hand to stop her. "That is not how it is done."

"But…" Catheryn said, confused. "It is the way that it is done – at least, how we have always done it."

"You are not in England now," Ursule said quietly, "and here, we leave the face uncovered."

It made no sense to Catheryn, but she obligingly put the last piece of linen down. She did not want to upset Isabella's family, after all. She could not help but quickly glance over to Fitz's bed, but his eyes were closed. It seemed that he had succumbed, finally, to sleep.

"I will follow you," Catheryn said quietly.

Before Ursule could reply, the door to the chamber opened. Roger stood there, his brother William behind him. Two of Fitz's men, part of his retinue, stood behind them. They were all dressed in black.

"Is she ready?"

Catheryn had not spoken to William, and so was surprised to hear how deep his voice was. He was almost a copy of Fitz – a replica of a Fitz that she had never known, but had probably lived around twenty years ago. His beard was a little lighter, and not so coarse, and there was no tiredness in his eyes; but save those differences, they could be the same man.

"She is ready." Ursule obviously realised that Catheryn could not speak. "Bring it in."

Catheryn stood back as the wooden coffin was brought into the room, and placed on the floor between the two beds.

Without a sound, Catheryn and Ursule lifted what was once Isabella, and placed her in the coffin. It had been lined with rosemary.

Roger and William placed the lid on the top of the coffin. All at once, Isabella's face was obscured from view, and it would remain that way forever. That was the last glimpse that any living person would have of the eldest FitzOsbern daughter.

Roger turned to Catheryn. "If you wish to dress for the...I believe that you should do it now."

"I would agree," the priest, still sitting down, spoke up. "I believe that we should leave soon."

"I will be but a moment," Catheryn replied, gathering up the remaining piece of linen. "And then I shall join you."

The church was cold. Candles had been lit throughout, but that did not prevent the icy breath of those that gathered within it from rising above them.

Catheryn drew her cloak to her, and shivered. The church was full; so full, in fact, that many of the local villagers were standing in the porch, and outside the church. All had wanted to pay their last respects to a girl that had been so gentle, and yet so wild. The men, as was the custom, wore black, and the women wore white. That was how it was for a lady of such high birth as Isabella. Why, you could say that she was a cousin to the King.

One woman sobbed. Catheryn could see from her place near the right hand side of the altar that it was

Adeliza. Emma was by her side, draped in white, and she had a hand resting on her mother's, which shook.

The coffin that held Isabella's body had been brought in by her two brothers and the two men Catheryn had seen them with earlier, and been placed before the altar. A white covering had been placed over it. In Catheryn's eyes the coffin seemed to get larger and larger, the church smaller and smaller.

Catheryn could hear that the priest was speaking, but it was hard for her to really take in his words. It was difficult for her to take anything in; that Isabella could be dead, that she would not see the spring; it did not seem to make any sense.

The priest had finished the prayers, and was now speaking about Isabella as the Mass was sung behind him.

"An innocent girl," he was saying, "who knew no faults, and will be received pure and whole by our Creator…"

Knew no faults, Catheryn thought, and smiled despite herself. The priest may not have said that if he had heard the two sisters fighting. And yet, he was right in a way. She had never done anything truly terrible, and yet had never experienced anything truly wonderful. Before all that life held for her had approached, she had been snatched away from it.

The candles were being distributed, and Catheryn lit hers from Ursule, who stood beside her. Ursule wore white also, but it was obscured partly by the fur of Reginald, once again wrapped around her neck.

At last, the coffin rose onto the shoulders of the four men once more, and was carried around to the middle of the church. A grave had already been dug there, and a memorial stone already carved by a man in the village. Slowly, with great care, the coffin was lowered into it.

"Grant this mercy, O Lord, we beseech thee…" The priest began to speak again, and many of those that had attended too many services like this one, began to speak along with him. Catheryn joined them.

"...so may thy mercy unite her above to the choirs of angels, through Jesus Christ our Lord. Amen."

CHAPTER TWENTY FOUR

Fitz's recovery was long, and hard. Catheryn spent so much of her time sending word to Ursule, begging her to come back to the castle and treat Fitz when he descended once more into a fever, that Ursule eventually demanded her own chambers in the castle.

"And don't forget my payment!" she would mutter, wandering down a corridor with Reginald weaving in and out of her tiny legs. "I won't do naught without my payment."

Roger disliked her, but could not help but admire the way that she managed to keep Fitz away from death, month after month.

"Whether it is witchcraft, or the power of God, or some other female power," Catheryn once heard him say to Emma, "there is something strange about that woman."

And yet despite his mistrust, Roger was always true to his word; each and every week, a new barrel of ale would be rolled by a servant into Ursule's chamber.

"Why do you think she wants so much ale?" Roger would ask Emma.

But Emma would invariably not reply. The loss of her twin sister had hit her harder than Catheryn had thought it was possible. For one so young, to be grieving in such a way – there was, Catheryn supposed, no telling exactly how long it would be before she would recover. If she ever would.

Adeliza spent another six months refusing to take a step closer to her husband. Catheryn moved through the motions of anger, disbelief, and finally pity at the way that Adeliza would be desperate for news of her husband, but not take the leap of walking into his sick chamber. Her fear of sickness grew after Isabella's death, and there was nothing that Catheryn could do to persuade her that the danger – for others – had passed.

Fitz's own danger did not disappear until just before Christmas in 1068. After three months without a single worrying turn, Ursule took Catheryn aside.

"That's finally done it," she said, smiling wearily.

Catheryn blinked.

"What do you mean?"

"He will live, and live strong."

Catheryn breathed a sigh of relief. "You are sure?"

Ursule shrugged her shoulders, made heavy again by the weight of a sleeping Reginald. "As sure as a body can be, my lady. He will not sink again until he is sunk into the grave, and I do not believe that will be for a good many years yet."

Christmas that year was taken slowly. Unlike the year when Fitz had remained, tossing and turning in his sick bed, unsure who the people attending to his needs even were, this year the entire family sat at the table. A space was left for Isabella. Her absence was like a weighty cloud, pressing on them heavily. They could not ignore it, and yet there was nothing to say, nothing to cry out at.

It was just…absence.

In the New Year, Catheryn realised that their lives had returned to what could only be described as normal. A sort of normality that seemed to belie the tension that was now present. She and Adeliza could never be friends again. By the time that February arrived Catheryn was sure of it.

"I was to sit there," Adeliza said curtly, as Catheryn gently lowered herself into a chair by the fire in the Great Hall. "You will not mind if I take it."

Without waiting for an answer, Adeliza reached out, grabbed Catheryn's arm, and physically pulled her away from the chair.

Catheryn stared with an open mouth as the lady of the house almost fell into the chair. Fitz was sitting opposite them. He looked up. Catheryn caught his eye.

Fitz shook his head, almost too slowly for Catheryn to see – but she did see, and she knew what he meant. He was telling her that it was simply not worth the aggravation to say anything.

Taking a deep breath, Catheryn managed to speak.

"My apologies, my lady Adeliza, I did not realise. I will happily sit elsewhere."

But after taking a quick look around the Great Hall, Catheryn realised that there was nowhere she could be that would not make her feel awkward. Adeliza's presence was like a poison, slowly turning Catheryn against her.

Adeliza, tragically, was not aware of this. She had been moving in a mist of pain ever since her child had departed this life, and there was nothing that could be done to reach her. The idea of losing her husband, of course, had marked upon her the awful loss that it could have been.

It could be said of Adeliza that she had never learned to truly love her husband until she thought that he had been taken from her. In the dark moments in the night, when she could hear him wailing, and yet could not stir a step to go to him, she clutched at her pillow. She knew that if she lost him now then she would never be able to forgive herself.

But she had not. Adeliza woke every morning happy in the knowledge that Fitz had been saved, that the sickness that had possessed his body for so long had finally decided to offer him a chance of life. But then the day wore on, and she saw it.

Adeliza could not help it. She could not help looking at them, her husband and the woman that had intruded into their lives for so long. Nothing was said, and no move was made, but it was plain to her that there was something between them. Suspicion was not a part of Adeliza's character, but now it was difficult for her to ignore the tension between them. Something had happened in that sick chamber, and it made Adeliza curse the decision that she had made to abandon her husband in his hour of need. And that she did abandon him, Adeliza knew. She could feel it in the very depths of her soul.

"A letter for you, my lord."

Both Adeliza and Catheryn started, so intense had been the glance that they had shared. A servant was standing quietly behind Fitz, and there was a heavy piece of parchment in his hands. Catheryn could see that there was a large seal pressed into the opening of the parchment, but from where she was standing, she could not see what it was.

Adeliza could, and she cursed the man who had sent it.

"A letter?" Fitz reached an arm upwards carelessly, and the servant, after a pause, placed it into his hand.

Bowing, the servant left the room. Catheryn had been about to return to her own chambers, but nothing could move her feet now. She was too intrigued by the letter; Adeliza's colour had altered so rapidly, there must be something terrible within its pages.

Flicking the letter over in his hands, Fitz's face fell when he saw the seal. He cursed inwardly, and then reminded himself that he should have expected this. He should have expected it for many months now – if anything he was surprised it had taken them this long to send word.

Breaking the seal with his thumb, he pulled open the parchment, and read the florid handwriting of the clerk to the King.

"Fitz?" Adeliza could not contain herself, and despite promising herself that she would say nothing, she immediately broke that promise. "Fitz, what does it say?"

Fitz sighed, and Adeliza's heart fell.

"It is him, then?" She said dully. "I knew that he would call you eventually, but now seems too soon."

"Him?" Catheryn interrupted.

"This does not concern you!" Adeliza snapped.

Catheryn coloured. "I apologise – my natural curiosity has got the better of me."

"Peace," Fitz said quietly. "Catheryn, you need not apologise. It is no secret." Looking at his wife, he nodded. "It is indeed a letter from King William. He has given me the charge of the city of York."

"York?" Adeliza tried the foreign word on her tongue. "What is it, a small village?"

Catheryn smiled. "It is a great place, a great city. My cousin Gospatrick has the power of Copmanthorpe, just South of there."

Fitz flinched, and hated the words that he spoke.

"Gospatrick has been...replaced."

Catheryn blushed once more, only this time it was with anger, not embarrassment.

"Replaced? Is it so easy to get rid of a man? Are people so insignificant now that they can be replaced without even his own family knowing his whereabouts?"

"You do not know the whereabouts of your own daughter," Adeliza remarked bitterly. "And you would think that was the closest bond imaginable."

It took all of Catheryn's resolve and strength not to move against the woman that taunted her about her daughter.

"Annis aside," Catheryn said through gritted teeth, "I would have thought I would receive word on this."

"It happened many months ago," Fitz said, waving a hand, "and I did not realise that you and he were kin."

"But the letter," Adeliza said before Catheryn could speak, leaning forward eagerly. "Does it demand your return?"

The two women that loved him turned to hear his answer. Fitz sighed heavily.

"It does."

Adeliza fell back in her chair, head falling down with the disappointment.

"And you will not refuse him."

"My lady wife, I cannot refuse him. He is the King."

Fitz rose with heaviness in his heart, and weakness in his legs.

"I must go to prepare," he said to Catheryn. "You must excuse me. And Adeliza.." Fitz's voice broke off; the cough that had dogged him for many seasons taking over his throat for a moment. "Adeliza," he said when he had regained control, "you must be strong."

He kissed her on the cheek, and for a moment Adeliza really believed that he had come back to her, that they could be made whole again. But then he pulled away, and she saw the smile he gave Catheryn as he left.

CHAPTER TWENTY FIVE

The journey was long, but finally it was over. Fitz spat on the ground as he dismounted awkwardly from his horse.

"My lord!"

A young man rushed towards him, and helped him descend the last foot towards the ground. Every part of Fitz ached, and he could feel the tiredness that had so wrecked his bones since his illness flowing back into every sore muscle. He would need to rest before he could re-join the royal court.

Months of travelling around England had continuously brought him back to his bed, and yet he had never fully succumbed to the illness that had threatened his life. It had been a long summer – longer than Fitz had ever thought possible or ever imagined. When he had left his home in Normandy at the beginning of the year, it had been with little thought to his return. And yet now here he was, with the winter approaching once more, and the last of the autumn warmth disappearing day by day.

"May I be of any assistance, my lord?"

Fitz looked hazily at the Anglo-Saxon man that was waiting patiently to hear his response. A matt of blond hair covered his head, as it did on so many of the native people, but there was a look of kindness and of gentleness on his face.

"My name is Orvin," the man said in a strong voice, "and I offer the assistance and hospitality that my people are known for."

His eyes seemed to challenge Fitz to dispute this, but Fitz was too tired to start another battle when it seemed as though his own body was fighting one.

"I thank you, Orvin...?" Fitz knew that using the full name of an Anglo-Saxon was a great show of respect, and he saw no reason to forego the pleasantries.

Orvin was evidently pleased. "Orvin, son of Ulfwulf, of the South," he said. "You do me much honour, my lord."

"And you me," Fitz said stiffly, "and yet I fear I shall show much dishonour to a good friend of mine if I accept your services. Would you be so good as to fetch Marmion from inside? I had hoped that he would be here to greet me, but – "

"You have been sorely disappointed?"

Fitz smiled at the familiar voice. He needed familiarity, here in the evening of a long day while he waited outside the tents that contained the knowledge of his future. Whatever King William had planned for him, it had not been contained in that letter.

"Marmion," Fitz's smile broadened as the man who had spoken came into view, "you are older but probably not much wiser."

Marmion did not hold back – he pulled Fitz into a hug that he probably would have been afraid to do when they had last met. Fitz saw Orvin slip away.

"It is so good to see you," Marmion said. "In truth, it warms my heart to see you standing so strong. We had heard that you were knocking on Death's door."

"He did not want me," Fitz shrugged. "And so I have returned. Thank you for your letters: they have kept me sane for many months."

Marmion laughed. "I hoped that the gossip would entertain you."

Fitz joined him in his laughter. "It was more the certainty that there was a world outside of my sick chamber. To know that other people were living normal lives, far away from the smell of vomit and the nightmare of fever…it was very comforting."

Marmion's face fell slightly to see his lord so serious, and he clasped a comforting hand on his shoulder.

"The sick chamber is put behind you," he said quietly, "and now you have reached the King's camp. He has been looking for you these four days."

"Then perhaps someone should remind our King just how long it takes to cross the small sea," Fitz said drily. "Normandy is a long way from here."

Marmion nodded, and beckoned that Fitz should walk with him towards the encampment. "I think our lord King has more pressing concerns on these shores at present."

Marmion's voice was dark, and Fitz suddenly felt cold.

"What has happened?"

"Nothing, nothing," Marmion said hastily.

"Ah," said Fitz. He knew politics. "So it has not happened yet, then?"

"Nothing can escape you, can it, my lord?"

"I was figuring out court intrigues before you were born, Marmion," Fitz said heavily.

Marmion did not reply, but pushed open the huge door of the castle that seemed to have appeared in front of Fitz like a sorcerer had put it there.

His companion laughed at the expression on his face.

"The gully disguises it well, do you not think?"

Fitz's mouth was still open.

"Come."

The older man followed the younger into warmth, and light. The entrance hall was full of men in red robes, many of them talking hurriedly in hushed tones. Fitz's stomach turned: this was the opening of war, his mind told him. This is exactly how it started, what seemed like years ago, back in Normandy. This was how we decided to go conquering.

"Sit, my lord," Marmion beckoned Fitz towards a large chair, rich with furs, and right next to the fire. "If you will rest, I shall bring you food. You must be starving."

Faces around the room turned to stare at him, the newcomer. Many of them were unrecognisable to Fitz. Had he really been gone that long?

"I must admit, my appetite is not what it was," Fitz said quietly. "But I would be happy to sit and rest. The journey has robbed me of what little strength I had when I left Normandy."

Marmion nodded silently. It was plain just by looking at Fitz that he had greatly suffered. There were lines of exhaustion on his face, and he limped slightly, wincing when he put his left leg down to the ground.

"Then sit," Marmion said gently. "And I will leave you to relax."

Fitz lowered himself gingerly into a chair, and then relaxed his aching muscles. The seat felt good.

Marmion began to walk away, but Fitz called him back.

"Wait – Marmion?"

"My lord?"

Fitz waited until his old servant was close to him, and then spoke in a lowered tone.

"The man that greeted me when I first arrived…Orvin?"

"Orvin, yes my lord."

Fitz hesitated, but then continued. "What do you know of him?"

Marmion thought for a moment, and then spoke slowly.

"I think he is of good family – Anglo-Saxon family, that is. His father accepted King William's rule, and thus his name and house was protected. Orvin is currently looking for patronage – he is the second son."

"That would explain it," Fitz murmured. Without another word, he waved Marmion away, and started concentrating on the most important thing to him at that moment; resting.

In fact, he rested so well that he was dozing within moments. It was some time later that a loud crash caused him to wake.

Fitz stared round the room with nervous eyes, trying to work out where the noise had come from. The sun had really set now; more candles had been lit, and the room was glowing. But there were now only a few others in the room, and none of them had made any noise. They were, however, all staring at the outer door.

Someone had knocked.

The door opened without anyone replying, and the first man that walked through was wearing the same red robes that Fitz had seen adorning many a man within the castle. Following him was a tall dark man, splattered with rain and mud. His hair was wet, and was smeared across his forehead. Several men followed him, each one just as wet and just as tired.

The tall, dark man looked hastily around the room. His eyes could obviously not discover what he was searching for, and he gripped one hand into a fist.

The inhabitants of the castle could not help but smirk at the motley band, but Fitz stared at them. Whoever they were, they had obviously come a long way, and on a matter of great importance.

One of the servants in red stepped towards them. Fitz saw with disgust that he was not going to treat the visitors with honour – and Fitz was right.

"And?" The servant had a sneer on his face as he spoke.

The tall man did not seem to notice it. "I would see your lord. If convenient."

Fitz could barely catch the words, so quiet was the newcomer's voice.

"It is not convenient. What makes you think that he will see you?"

The servant's reply was just in the vein that Fitz had expected, but it still shocked him. How could a servant speak to a man like that? Despite the dirt of the stranger, it was quite clear that he was of noble birth. You could see it in his carriage, the way that he held himself, and the way that his men stared at him, just waiting for any signal to act.

Fitz would have challenged the servant on his rudeness, but it did not seem to bother the tall man. Instead, he smiled. Before Fitz realised exactly what had happened, the tall man's followers had encircled the servant, and twitching hands were reaching for sword handles, appearing from under cloaks.

The tall man spoke again, and his voice was just as quiet as before – but there was a depth and a passion in it that Fitz had not heard before.

"Because I have travelled far to see him. Because I am a lord of this realm. And because I'm asking nicely."

The man smiled, but the smile never reached his eyes. Fitz did not blame the servant for swallowing nervously, and backing away from the reach of the itching fingers, ready for a fight.

The servant muttered, "I will speak to my lord."

The servant started walking towards a different doorway at the back of the room, Fitz thought that would be the end of it – but just before the man passed through the doorway into the corridor, he threw a shout over his shoulder.

"Though don't hold your breath!"

He was gone before anything could be done. One of the men that had come with the stranger stepped forward as if to follow, but his lord stopped him.

"I've been holding my breath ever since I left home," Fitz heard the tall man mutter, as if to himself. "I've been holding my breath for the last three years."

Fitz stared. The man stood, tall and proud, and yet there was a brokenness about him. Fitz did not recognise him; despite his title of a 'lord of this realm', Fitz did not remember seeing him at the royal court, nor at the coronation of the Queen. Who was this man, and why did he come here to the King's court in such a way?

The servant by this time had returned, and one of the men clutched at his lord's arm. They both looked towards the man in the red robes.

"My lord will see you now."

And Fitz could see that the servant was not happy about it, and so he tried to hide his grin, in case it was spotted.

The tall man spoke briefly. "Thank you."

However, it was not to be so easy. As he and his men started to walk towards the corridor, the servant put up his hand.

"No. Just you, my lord Melville," said the servant. "Your men may remain here and warm their hands. They are not to come also."

Melville, thought Fitz as the two men argued it out. It was not a name that he knew. Of course, it would be foolish for him to suppose that he would know each and every man that roamed these lands – but to come at such a time, in such a way. It must be important news for the King.

Eventually the man called Melville capitulated, and he followed the servant out of the room alone. The men that he left behind stood awkwardly. They all looked tired, and one looked particularly exhausted. Fitz watched him as he swayed.

Fitz stood up. Enough was enough.

"My brother Normans," he said gently. "Will you not rest by this fireside with me? Like you, I have travelled far, and have just stopped to allow my feet to recover." He saw their hesitation. "You are most welcome."

The men all looked at one – the man that had placed his hand on his lord's arm to tell of the servant's return.

He nodded. "I am grateful, my lord. You do us much kindness by your welcome."

They came towards the fire, and stood around it, trying to dry off their soaking wet clothes.

"Please," Fitz said, still standing. "Have my chair."

But one of the men smiled. "Peace, my lord father," he said formally. "I thank you for your offer, and return it to you. Sit, and we shall enjoy the fire together."

Fitz smiled with gratitude, and collapsed back into the chair. In truth, he was not entirely sure whether he would have been able to stand for much longer, but he hated the way that these men had been treated. Had they not any entitlement to respect?

The moments passed, and still this Melville did not return. The servant that had led Melville out of the room returned, and after spying Fitz, walked towards him hurriedly.

"My lord FitzOsbern," he said in a gracious voice full of deference. "I did not see you there – permit me to offer you welcome."

Fitz looked up at him in disgust. "And what have I done to afford such a welcome?"

The servant was confused. "My lord?"

"These men are guests here just as much as I," Fitz said. "And yet you treated them like dogs. What is your name?"

The servant's eyes flickered over Melville's men, warming themselves by the fire.

"William," he said bitterly. "William of Bologne."

"Thank you," Fitz said harshly. "I shall remember that. Now leave us."

After the servant had left, the man that the others seemed to follow spoke quietly to Fitz.

"You did not have to do that, my lord FitzOsbern."

Fitz smiled. "I am called Fitz by those I respect."

The man met his gaze, and smiled. "And those I respect call me Robert."

Time passed, and still Melville did not return. All save Robert stood by the fire; Fitz watched Robert as he paced up and down, unable to stay still, despite the obvious tiredness that he felt. He was worried.

Fitz closed his eyes. Then opened them again. Whenever they were closed, his treacherous eyes only showed him the form of the woman he loved: Catheryn's face danced before him, her beauty radiating from his memory.

He must not think on her, he must remember that he was married.

Loud footsteps caused the men around the fire to look up, and then visibly relax when Melville strode back into the room.

"We return home," he called to them.

"What, immediately?" Robert looked disappointed.

"This very moment," Melville replied, reaching his men and smiling at them wearily.

The man that Fitz had thought the most tired started to speak.

"My lord, we are exhausted."

Melville nodded. "And so is every single person that we left behind. Exhausted of not knowing whether they are to live or die." Fitz stared in astonishment as Melville's companions all nodded sadly. "We must ride to give them the news."

There was a moment of uncomfortable silence that Robert eventually broke.

"News?"

Melville's smile told the story before his words did.

"The King will not be taking Ulleskelf. We are saved."

Robert nodded. "Then home. The sooner the better."

Fitz watched them gather their cloaks around them, readying themselves for what he assumed was a long ride. He had never heard of Ulleskelf; it could not be a Norman holding. But why on earth would King William want to take another place in England – why were these people living under the sentence of death?

Suddenly, as one man, Melville's companions threw themselves onto the floor, kneeling. Fitz looked up, and saw King William stride into the room, bitter anger on his face.

"Did I not tell you to take *all* your men?"

Melville looked as confused as Fitz felt. "I...*Jean!*" Fitz could just about see another figure standing behind the King. This figure rushed towards Melville, and the two men embraced.

"My King – you told me that you had Jean killed."

Fitz stared. This was not the King William that he knew, not the King William that he had left all those years ago.

"I told you that I could not allow such a man to remain amongst my retinue," smiled King William. "I told you that I had disposed of him. Consider him at your disposal."

Without waiting to hear any response from Melville, King William turned away and left the room, shouting out, "*all* of your men, Melville."

Fitz watched. The men were tired, and they were hungry, and from what he could tell all they wanted to do was sleep. And yet they turned to Melville, waiting for his command.

"Onward."

It was only one word, but it was enough to take them striding outside once more, Jean amongst them. Fitz smiled. It heartened him to see such loyalty and such friendship; many had thought it lost within the invasion several years ago, but it was still blossoming in the strangest of places.

"My lord FitzOsbern?"

Fitz looked up. The rude servant, William, was standing before him, a smile on his face that was evidently there to please.

"My lord, the King will gladly see you now."

CHAPTER TWENTY SIX

The King did not look happy.

"Fitz."

Fitz bowed low. "My lord King William. It is good to see you again after so much time."

"We had heard...troubling reports on your sickness," the King said.

Fitz did not immediately reply. Looking around the room, full of red and gold decorations, his eyes found what they were looking for.

"May I sit, my lord King? I must admit that I have had a long journey, and I would not say no to the chance of a rest."

King William spread an arm out wide.

"Thank you, my lord King."

Fitz sat down, and his back thanked him for it. He could not go on much longer without sleep, he knew, but King William wanted to talk to him, and so they would talk. It was a little unnerving for Fitz, being alone with his monarch. But here, in this room full of gold and silver, there was just the two of them.

Thankfully, the King seemed just as preoccupied as Fitz felt. The great man now had tints of grey in his hair, which Fitz had never seen before. There were slightly more scars on his hands, and one across his face that Fitz did not remember. It seemed as though King William had been fighting just as many battles as Fitz had in the time that they had been apart – although Fitz's had been against sickness, and William's had been against the people of this realm.

"Would you like an apple, Fitz?"

Fitz started at the strange question, but his stomach answered for him. It gave a loud rumble, and King William laughed. He took one from a bowl, and handed it to Fitz before he sat in the chair opposite him.

Fitz bit into the apple, and the juices ran out of his mouth. It was delicious.

"I thank you, my lord King," he said after satiating his appetite. "But I must ask if I can speak freely to you."

The King looked at him intensely. "Have I ever given you cause to hide the truth from me?"

"Not at all," Fitz said quickly. His brain was not ready for this. "I merely wanted to remind myself of that truth. It has been many months since I have had the good fortune to sit with you, my lord King."

"Too long."

"You honour me," Fitz smiled. "I must ask you, my lord King, why you have summoned me here? Here, in so strange a place, and so quickly too. Your letter gave no indication, and I have heard nothing worrying whilst being in Normandy."

King William sighed, and it was only then that Fitz suddenly realised. William was old. He had not been old when Fitz last seen him – he had hardly seemed to approach middle age. But now, looking at the tired man before him, with the cares and concerns of two nations sitting on his shoulders, Fitz knew that he had not been summoned here for an idle task. King William needed his help.

"I will be as honest with you as you are with me," King William sighed. He picked up an apple from the bowl by his side, but instead of eating it, merely fiddling around with it in his fingers. All of his attention seemed to be wrapped up in the fruit. Fitz watched him uneasily. This was not the King William that he knew.

"My rule is being challenged."

The voice was quiet, but Fitz could detect the same power, and the same determination within its syllables. He relaxed. King William may be older, but that probably meant that he was wiser.

"Challenged? I was not aware that any were so foolish as to challenge you, my lord King."

King William snorted. "You would not be, out in Normandy amongst people that love this family. But here, in the North, it is quite a different matter."

"What shape has this challenge taken?"

"Did you hear of the York march?"

Fitz shook his head. "Little accurate news ever managed to reach me in Normandy. As far as we knew, all was well."

"Well it is not," King William said heavily. "In the summer just passed, I found it necessary to go to York to put down an uprising against my rule. Many fled, rather than face the wrath of my sword, and yet I was glad to see little bloodshed. And so I left."

Fitz knew the pattern. "And they rebelled again."

King William nodded. "I wrote to you just after that second uprising in York. They had taken York, and in the end there was no choice but to destroy all within it that defied me."

Fitz sighed. His King was not a brutal man, but he did not forgive. You were given but one chance, and if you decided to ignore that one occasion of forgiveness, you would not see another. You would be destroyed.

"And now?"

"And now," said King William, "the Danes have got involved. Their King – Sweyn – he has come over the frozen water, and helped this Edgar to take back York."

"They would not dare!" Fitz said angrily. "What right have they to interfere in your lands?"

"No right, but right of power, and that right they have all too much."

Fitz stared at his King. "Why York?"

"Have you ever been?"

"This is as far North as I have ever travelled," Fitz confessed, "and a cold, weary land it is too. What passions can be stirred by this cold city of York?"

King William smiled. "It is, to tell you the truth, a beautiful city. It is almost Norman in its buildings. The river flows through it quietly, and it is surrounded by the landscape of this country in a way that gives it much splendour."

"...and that is it?" Fitz said disbelievingly. "It is a beautiful place, and so blood is shed time and time again to keep it?"

"York is so much more than that," King William reminded him, finally taking a bite from the apple in his hands. "It has been a centre for learning for hundreds of years. Its archbishop is one of the most powerful men in the land. The nobles of the North congregate there, they make law there, justice in the North is served here in the courts. If you have York, you have the North."

Fitz sighed. "What is to be done?"

King William stared at the flames in the large stone grate. "I will destroy them."

Fitz shook his head. "It has been done before – twice – and neither time has encouraged people to peace."

"This time there will be no people left."

"My...my lord King?" Fitz looked confused.

King William's gaze flickered over to him. "I will destroy them," he said quietly. "I will kill every man, woman, and child that comes into my path from here to

York. And I will burn every dwelling, and I will slaughter all cattle. I will bring death to these people, and they shall learn that to defy me is to die."

Fitz stared at his King in horror.

"You think me too harsh, no doubt."

Fitz found his voice, though he felt at any moment it could break. "My lord King, what you are suggesting is…it is not battle, it is murder! To kill everyone, every Anglo-Saxon that you meet with – "

"And Norman," King William said quietly, still staring into the fire.

"Every Norman!"

"And why not?" challenged King William. "They did not support me, they have not been fighting the rebels. They are just as much traitors as the rest of them. Anglo-Saxons!"

He spat into the fire, and the flames sizzled. Smoke rose.

"My lord King," Fitz began again, "surely you can see that this is madness – the sheer scale of it, the number of deaths!"

King William smiled, and threw the remainder of his apple back into the bowl.

"I will say to you what I said to young Melville. He had come here to plead for his life; for his life, for the life of his Saxon bride, and the lives of those that lived under his protection."

Fitz stared, confused. "You granted it."

"Oh, you know that, do you?" King William scowled. "Then it will be through the royal court already. I had hoped to keep it…quiet."

"But if you can change your mind in that quarter –"

"My lord Melville and I have a special understanding," King William said curtly. "He has not managed to change my mind on this course of action, and you will be just as unsuccessful."

"But why?" Fitz exploded. He could not take it anymore. "My lord King, I lost my daughter to sickness. It was cruel, and it was painful, and it took her from me. You have not lost a child – you cannot know the agony of a parent staring into the unseeing eyes of one that they loved. But your actions will give that pain to hundreds, perhaps thousands across this land! Can you not see the suffering that you will cause?"

King William was silent for a moment, and then he spoke. His words were weighty, and Fitz saw that he chose them carefully.

"As I told Melville: I have only reached this position by making difficult decisions such as these. It is the remit of Kings, and Kings only, to make choices whether a man will live or die. You cannot think that I make them lightly, you cannot think that I make them with joy in my heart? But this burden – for it is a burden – is one that I shoulder myself, rather than give to lesser men."

"But – "

"God man, do you think I like this!" It was now King William's turn to show his anger, and Fitz flinched. No matter his age, King William was still a powerful man. "Do you think I seek destruction? But if I do not act, if I cannot stamp out these flames of rebellion, they will not be content to remain where they are – the flames will spread across the entirety of England, and perhaps even to Normandy. We would return to war, and countless would die. It could go on for years, do you not see?"

Fitz saw. He imagined the devastation that a war would bring them; he thought of their enemies close to them in Normandy, and how they would relish the chance to disband what King William had created.

"I do not like this," Fitz spoke frankly. "I do not like this at all."

King William leaned back in his chair, and sighed. "Neither do I."

"And the Queen?"

King William smiled. "You think that she approves in any way? She does not. In many ways, I am grateful that this pregnancy has prevented her from taking more of a role. But like me, she sees the use that this destruction can bring. Those that rise up from the ashes of this time will be strong, and most importantly, loyal."

Fitz smiled. "Queen Matilda is pregnant?"

King William returned his smile. "You did not know?"

"As I said, news rarely reaches us."

"Well, it is good news. Welcome news, to distract me in dark moments. And now," King William said with a sigh, "I must demand that you join me."

For a moment, Fitz did not quite understand. "Join you?"

"In this campaign," King William said irritably, annoyed that Fitz was not following his meaning. "You are a good fighter, Fitz, and you're loyal. You may have been away, but there are many men here that would name you friend, and follow you into the fight. There are few others that I can trust. The Harcourts, of course – but then they will follow me anywhere. I need you."

Fitz's mouth opened. "My lord King, I have been very ill – "

"You came here. You are well enough."

"My recovery continues my lord," Fitz tried to explain. "The strength that you remember…it is gone."

King William shook his head. "I do not believe that."

"I must refuse."

"And I must ask again," King William said quietly. "As your friend, and as your cousin, and as your liege."

The two men looked at each other.

Fitz swallowed. "My lord King William, I will follow you."

CHAPTER TWENTY SEVEN

Catheryn sat and watched, from the middle of her favourite field, another summer come and go without getting one single step closer to her daughter.

She had thought, when she first arrived here, that the pain would lessen as time went on. And in many ways, it had. Every moment of her day was not wrapped in concern over Annis; she did not start every time she thought she saw a blonde girl wander past her; she no longer cried out in the night as she watched her daughter be taken away from her, again, and again, and again.

But Catheryn, watching one of the last golden leaves fall from the trees before her, could not pretend that the pain was gone. This grief, if grief it was, did not leave her alone, but was instead a constant companion. Sometimes silent, sometimes vocal, there was never any doubt that it was there.

Fitz had been gone for several months now. His leaving had been sudden, hurried. The contents of the letter that he had received, the night before he had left, had clearly troubled him. Catheryn could see that they troubled Adeliza still, but the two women had not spoken of it. They had barely spoken to each other at all.

Adeliza had wrapped herself in her children. They were her fortress, and her strength. They were the only things worthy of her attention, and Catheryn left them together.

After the death of Isabella, the family had closed within itself, like a creature that had suffered pain and wanted to retreat. Catheryn was not unwelcome, but she was more like a remembrance of a former life than a guest, and more of a servant than a prisoner. To be sure, she was not treated unkindly: but she was barely noticed at all.

Catheryn fell back onto the autumn grass with a sigh. She closed her eyes. She could remember when William, the eldest son, had come to visit his mother.

He had been a gentle man, but Catheryn had seen no love in his eyes. She was sad to see that he understood his mother very well – too well. Oh, young William was still quite clearly grieving at the loss of his sister. Catheryn had been told that his first child had just been born, and they had named it Isabella, after the beloved sister that had been lost. But none of the children – not William, nor Roger, and especially not Emma – could forgive their mother for refusing to comfort and console Isabella in her final hours.

It was this lack of forgiveness that Catheryn was trying to escape. Once again, she was lying on her back in the middle of a field, trying to put as much distance between herself and the awkwardness of the castle as she could.

But she could not avoid it for long, and she could certainly not avoid it for ever: not if she wanted to eat. Groaning slightly at the resistance put up to the movement she made by her bones, Catheryn rose, and stretched. Parts of her ached that had never ached before. By the position of the sun, Catheryn guessed that it was around midday. Time for her to break her fast.

Catheryn spent the entire day without seeing a single soul after breaking her fast, and she was glad of it. It was easier, not speaking to anyone, not being given the chance to offend. That evening, however, she resigned herself to the fact that she would have to spend some time with the household. Despite being a prisoner, she was still a noble woman.

Roger and Emma looked up when she entered. They were eating in silence, whilst the servants ate further down the table, murmuring quietly as so not to intrude.

Catheryn followed Roger and Emma's example, and finished her meal quickly. After a brief smile to Emma, she returned to her chambers.

This pattern was followed by Catheryn for three days – until she realised that there was something amiss. Although she spent almost no time at all with the family, she still *saw* Emma and Roger at least once each day: but the same could not be said of their mother. Catheryn calculated that she had not seen Adeliza for over four days.

"Emma," she said quietly one evening, "how is your mother?"

Emma smiled wanly. She had still not totally accepted that Isabella was gone.

"My mother?"

Catheryn nodded. "I have not seen her for many days."

"You know, neither have I," Emma confessed. "But I know that Roger has been keeping an eye on her."

"My apologies, sister," said Roger. Catheryn smiled to see him; his sister's death and the removal of his father once more had really brought out the man in him. "But I have not seen our lady mother for five days. I had assumed that you were reading with her each of these afternoons."

"And I had supposed that you were." The siblings stared at each other in confusion.

"Are you saying," Catheryn said quietly, "that no one has seen your mother in over three days?"

Both Emma and Roger nodded.

Catheryn stood up. "I must go and see her. There must be – although, I am sure that she just prefers her own company. I will, however, take her some fruit. She must be hungry."

The worried faces of Emma and Roger stuck in Catheryn's mind as she hurried down the corridor towards Adeliza's chamber. She had never been back there, not since that dreadful night. It felt wrong, in a way, trespassing on Adeliza's privacy. Catheryn bit her lip.

She was standing outside the door to Adeliza's chamber. Should she go in? Was it really her place to be so inquisitive?

For a moment, Catheryn started to go back. Emma was Adeliza's daughter, surely she should be the one to go to her mother.

But then she stopped, and shook herself. There was nothing to be afraid of. She should check that nothing had happened to Adeliza.

With a trembling hand, Catheryn knocked on the door.

"My lady?"

There was no answer. Catheryn knocked again, slightly harder now, and three times.

"My lady Adeliza? It is Catheryn. I have brought you some fruit. Can I come in?"

Catheryn listened at the door for any sort of reply, but she did not receive one.

She opened the door.

Then Catheryn screamed. There, lying on the bed, was Adeliza. Her face was pale, almost white, and there was a sheen of perspiration across her forehead. Her hair was greasy and lank, and she was shivering.

Catheryn rushed over to her.

"Adeliza!" Her skin was boiling, like a fire. Adeliza opened her eyes, and murmured, but the words that she uttered did not make sense.

"Adeliza?" Catheryn put her hand on Adeliza's forehead, and felt the fever burn within her.
Adeliza was sick. She had the same illness that had claimed her daughter.

CHAPTER TWENTY EIGHT

The dark had crept in without Catheryn realising it.

Evening had come, and she had not stirred from the bedside of her patient. Adeliza lay motionless, unable to even draw the energy to turn over. Catheryn's hair was damp, pushed against her forehead. The heat of the evening had been unexpected, and she had removed her veil when she simply could stand it no more.

Ursule tutted. "She doesn't want to get well."

Catheryn smiled, and turned to see the old nurse once more back in the castle.

"It is good to see you, Ursule. I was worried that I may be alone."

"Children not want to help her?" Ursule shook her head sadly. "It is a sad occasion when a family rips itself apart."

"Oh, no," Catheryn hastened to correct her. "I would not allow them near. This sickness has already claimed a life – I will not let my lady Adeliza and my lord FitzOsbern lose another child."

Ursule moved closer to the candlelight that was by Adeliza's bedside, and Catheryn saw that, despite the heat, Reginald had already taken his place around Ursule's neck.

"You are a wise one, you know," Ursule said slowly, casting her gaze over Catheryn's face, "and yet it will bring you no happiness."

A chill went up and down Catheryn's spine, but she smiled. "You do not scare me, Ursule. I know you too well. And because I know you, I know that you will help her."

She did not need to elaborate on who she referred to.

Ursule shrugged off the cat, who complained bitterly, but leapt onto the bed. Slowly, lifting his paws gingerly, Reginald crept to the head of the bed, and curled up next to Adeliza.

"And what good could I do?" Ursule said tartly. "I am but an old woman."

"This is true. But then, there is no one this side of the water that I would trust with a patient as I would trust you."

Ursule tried to look unconvinced, but Catheryn could see that she was flattered. After all, did not all those who had lived for many years secretly worry that they will eventually lose the respect of those that had more recently arrived in this life?

"My fees will be doubled," Ursule demanded, in a soft yet forceful voice. "Now that we know the sickness takes life, it will be twice as dangerous for me."

"And for me."

"You are here by choice," Ursule reminded her.

Catheryn smiled. "And so are you. I did not send for you, and I do not believe that Roger has either."

Ursule could not look her in the eye.

Catheryn laughed, and tried not to disturb Adeliza. "How did you know?"

Ursule shrugged. "How does anyone know anything? The gossip has already reached the village. All I had to do was listen."

Ursule leaned over the patient. She put her hand on Adeliza's forehead, and then paused to feel the lifeblood pumping through her wrist. She shook her head.

"I do not like this," Ursule mumbled.

Catheryn's mouth went dry. "You think she is in some danger, then? Just her daughter?"

Ursule shook her head once more. "I do not think that she is in some danger: she is in the worst danger imaginable. The chance for her to live is slowly ebbing away, I can feel it."

Catheryn's mouth fell open. She had no idea that the situation was so serious.

"You cannot mean – she may die?"

Ursule nodded. "This sickness is a dark one, a deadly one. How long has it been since that poor child ran out into the snow? Months, and months, and months: and yet here it is, trying to take another victim with it into the cold lands."

Catheryn moved the fur over Adeliza, trying to keep her warm.

"She should be getting better, not worse," she murmured. "She has so much to live for."

Ursule sighed. "Sometimes, that just is not enough."

Days passed. Catheryn sometimes could not tell just how long she had been with Adeliza in her bed chamber – her sick chamber, now, full of herbs and strange smells, remnants of Ursule's latest offerings. The nurse had decided to move into the castle once more, but she took a chamber close by. It was Catheryn that never left Adeliza's side.

There were times when Adeliza was conscious, able to talk, and to understand. It was in those times that Catheryn became convinced that Adeliza would live. How could a woman so full of life, so far from old age, so concerned with her children, die?

"Roger is well?" she would ask of Catheryn, her thin hands clutching at Catheryn's in desperation to have news of her son. "And William's Isabella, you have news of her?"

Catheryn would give her all the information that she could, but she was almost as isolated as Adeliza was.

Yes, in those times Catheryn rejoiced, for the sickness seemed to pass. And then within moments, Adeliza would sink once more into the deathly state that the illness drew over her like a shroud, and she was silent. Her breathing would quieten, and it was all Catheryn could do to keep her warm.

In those moments, Catheryn wondered when, not if, she would die.

About a month after the sickness first descended, Ursule sat opposite Catheryn, the two of them keeping the bed between them. Adeliza had managed to eat a full meal that morning, and she was sleeping now. As far as Catheryn could tell, it was a restful sleep. Adeliza was on the mend.

"My lady?"

Catheryn looked up. "You do not have to call me that, you know."

Ursule smiled. "Are not manners in short supply lately? I thought that I would share them about. No use in old women like me keeping a hold of them when the young may require them."

"That is true," Catheryn smiled. Ursule was knitting what seemed to be a very large blanket. Reginald kept playing in the parts that she had finished, and every time she attempted to shoo him away, she dropped a stitch. "And I appreciate the courtesy."

Ursule rolled her eyes, and continued, "I was going to ask, my lady, whether or not you had sent it."

Catheryn furrowed her brow. "Sent it?"

"Yes. Whether or not it had already gone."

"I'm sorry, Ursule, but I have absolutely no idea what you are talking about."

Ursule's face fell. "Then, you did not get my message?"

"Was it sent by cat?"

Ursule scowled. She did not take well to people mocking her beloved cat Reginald.

"I apologise, Ursule," Catheryn said hastily, "but I did not receive any message from you."

Ursule sighed. "Then I hope that we are not too late."

Catheryn was confused. "Too late for what?"

"To contact Fitz, of course."

The two women looked down at Adeliza. She slept with a smile on her face.

"Do you really believe that to be necessary?" Catheryn whispered. "Do you really think that she is in such danger?"

Ursule looked at Adeliza sadly. "Do you not recall that this was exactly how Isabella looked?"

Catheryn tried to recall that hazy time of pain and confusion.

"I...think so," she said slowly. "But she looks so well!"

"So did her daughter."

Catheryn's heart turned to ice. "I must send word to him immediately. He must come back!"

"I think we may be too late."

"No," Catheryn shook her head. "I will find a fast servant, and we will get to Fitz in time."

"What shall you write?" Ursule asked curiously, dropping another stitch as Reginald pounced on the ball of wool.

Catheryn shrugged sadly. "I shall tell him that Adeliza may be about to die."

The letter was written, and entrusted to one of the stable boys. He was, according to the family, the fastest on a horse that they had ever seen. Along with a bag of food, and a small purse full of gold to get him to his master, the boy left.

Catheryn did not watch him go. She was tending to Adeliza. Ursule had been right: the momentary healing had passed, and she had never seen a person so unwell. Adeliza seemed barely aware of where she was; eyes open, she cried out for Fitz, for her daughters, and in the depths of the night when Catheryn was desperate for sleep, she cried out for her mother. Tears fell down her face as imagined nightmares tried to take her away from her family, and it was all Catheryn could do to calm her.

Adeliza certainly did not recognise Catheryn, but a calming voice seemed to be all that she needed to settle. And so it continued for three days, until one morning when both dawn and the fever broke.

"Catheryn?"

The voice was faint, and it carried much sadness with it, but it stirred Catheryn from the careful slumber that she had managed.

"Catheryn!"

She awoke, and saw Adeliza's eyes open – and know her.

"Adeliza," she said sleepily, moving from the chair against the wall to the stool beside the bed. "You are awake."

"Yes," Adeliza smiled weakly. "And it feels as though I have been asleep for a very long time. What day is it?"

"It is Sunday," confessed Catheryn. "The family have just departed for early morning Mass at church, but I wanted to stay behind, to see if you would awaken. You certainly have been…away from us for some time."

Adeliza nodded, but stopped quickly.

"Does your head hurt?" Catheryn rose quickly, walking towards the little table where Ursule had laid out her concoctions. "I have something here for that if you wish."

"Catheryn," Adeliza said softly. "Sit with me."

Catheryn obeyed, and took the hand that the sick woman held out for her.

"May I ask you…a delicate question?"

Catheryn nodded. "Of course you can, my lady."

Adeliza blushed slightly before she spoke. "Do you still think of Selwyn? Your husband?"

Catheryn paused before she answered, but she could not deny the truth.

"I do. He was the love of my life, and I cannot go through one day without remembering something bittersweet about the time that we had together."

Adeliza was staring at her with eager eyes, hungry eyes.

"But then," Catheryn hesitated, but continued. "I know that Selwyn would not want me to stop living, just because he died. There is so much more that I can do, that I can be. He would not want me to give up on life."

Adeliza smiled wanly. "I think that you are a wise woman, Catheryn."

"No," sighed Catheryn, "but I have had these things to think on for some time."

They sat in silence for a moment, and then Adeliza broke it once more.

"My marriage to Fitz – it was arranged for us, you know. Our parents wanted us to be together, and neither of us put up any fight."

"It is common," Catheryn smiled. "For both my people, and yours. I was rare in that I was given the choice."

"You were lucky. And yet, I do not think that our marriage has been bad. He has never loved me, but he has been good to me."

"You have taken good care of each other."

Adeliza smiled a tired smile. It seemed like a great effort to move. "Love is not necessarily the answer – and yet, it would have been wonderful to truly earn Fitz's love."

Catheryn looked at her. Adeliza stared right back. The smile was gone.

Adeliza closed her eyes. The smile slackened. The breathing halted.

Adeliza was dead.

CHAPTER TWENTY NINE

The wind was cold, and Fitz hated it. It was the one thing about this country that he believed he could never quite grow to love: the weather. Always cold, always harsh, it seemed to get worse with every passing day that he spent here.

Admittedly, his bad temper was not solely due to the weather. Despite the many conversations that Fitz had had with the King since their first, he had not been able to change his mind about attacking the North. Fitz shuddered at the thought of just how many people would die in the next few months. Hundreds. Thousands even. It would be the most devastating thing to happen to these people since…

Well. Since the Normans had first arrived.

Fitz blew onto his cold hands. Dawn was still being waited for, but most of King William's army was already awake. It did not do to be unprepared for the call to leave, especially when they were about to depart on such a solemn journey.

Catheryn would probably be asleep now, Fitz thought. She had no idea the terror that he and his people were about to unleash onto her people, and she would be devastated if she did know. Fitz hoped fervently that her daughter had remained in the South. It would break Catheryn to know that she was here, in the North, in danger.

And yet so many daughters were, and sons, and mothers, and husbands. And their world was about to end in blood and fire.

Fitz shook his head, and began to stomp to the hastily constructed shacks where his horse had been stabled. It was none of his business, what Catheryn may think and feel. He should not even be thinking of her at all – and yet it was hard, in this her very own country, to pull his thoughts away from her. They liked to dwell on her, and it was almost impossible for him to forget her.

Sometimes, when Fitz was low in spirits and cold under the blanket that he had been given, he thought of the beautiful woman that had made him realise just how precious his life was. He had never given it much thought before: his life had been something that had belonged to other people. He swore it to his betters, he pledged it to his wife, he played dangerously with it in battle – but it was never something that he valued. Now he had been shown what a world of love could be like, and he mourned its death before it had even taken a breath of life.

But enough. Fitz began to saddle his horse, pushing any thoughts of the blonde haired woman out of his mind.

As much as he could.

"Fitz!"

He turned around, and saw Marmion walking towards him, wiping the sleep from his eyes.

"You are up early," Marmion remarked. "And if you don't mind my saying so, my lord…you look terrible."

Fitz laughed, in spite of himself. "Always one for compliments, you were."

"No, I mean no disrespect," Marmion said hastily. "But I am worried about you. You have not been the same since your sickness."

Fitz shook his head. "Nothing has been the same since my sickness, but I thank you for your concern. Am I to look forward to your company today?"

Marmion smiled, awkwardly. "Well, actually Fitz…King William has given me some men of my own. He has been impressed with me, ever since the coronation of Queen Matilda. You do not mind, do you?" he rushed, looking fearfully at his old master.

"Not a bit," Fitz said, "I smile on your good fortune. It was high time that someone noticed what a fine man you are, and now the finest among us finally has."

Marmion's smile turned to one of relief. "Then truly, you are not angry?"

Fitz shrugged. "What am I to be angry about? The only problem that I can see for me is that I will have to grow accustomed to seeing your face infrequently. I know that we shall remain friends."

The two men embraced, and Fitz was reminded strongly of Roger. Here was another young man that sought for his approval.

"Now be off with you," Fitz said kindly. "I imagine your men will need pushing out of their beds."

"Much like I did," Marmion winked. "Now I know how it feels to be the one pulling off the rug!"

Fitz chuckled as he watched the impetuous young man stride away from him. Rays of light had begun to fall from the sky since their conversation began. Morning had come.

A scuffle caught his attention, and Fitz turned to see another young man walk into the stable, hesitate, and then bow deeply.

"My lord."

Fitz knew the boy, but it was a while before he could put a name to that face. In fact, he had finished preparing his steed before the name came to him.

"Orvin."

The young man turned, a frightened look on his face. "My lord? I apologise, I was not aware that you wanted to be alone – I can return…"

"Peace," Fitz said kindly, and the features of the young man relaxed. "Orvin, son of Ulfwulf, of the South, it is good to meet with you again."

Orvin smiled, and pushed some of his blond hair back from his eyes. "And you are well met, William FitzOsbern, son of Osbern, of Normandy."

"I did not know that you were to accompany us."

"I follow King William," Orvin's Norman was good, but his Anglo-Saxon accent was strong despite himself. "Where he goes, I go."

"And where he kills, you kill?"

Fitz cursed his tongue as soon as the words were spoken, but they could not be taken back.

"Forgive me," he said quickly, noting the wide eyes of the Anglo-Saxon man. "I spoke hastily, I spoke without thought. Please forget it."

"It is of no matter," Orvin said smoothly, but a heightened colour filled his cheeks. "You are not the only man that despairs at this action, and yet follows his King with loyalty in his heart."

Orvin was finished with his horse, and began to lead it out of the stable. Fitz watched him go, and then a thought struck him.

"Orvin?"

The man paused, and looked back at Fitz.

"I know that you seek patronage, a lord," Fitz said quickly, "and I seek a young man to ride beside me. Will you join me?"

A smile broke out on Orvin's face, and Fitz was amazed to see just how dramatically it changed him. He seemed older, and more certain of himself, of who he was.

"It would be my honour, my lord."

Orvin walked up to Fitz, dropped to his knees, and with his head lowered offered up his clasped hands. Fitz brought them between his own palms, and began the ritual.

"Will you, Orvin, son of Ulfwulf, of the South, swear yourself to me?"

"I will."

"In times of battle and times of peace?"

"I will."

"When times are hard and when joy reigns?"

"I will."

"Then rise, Orvin, son of Ulfwulf, of the South, for you are sworn to me."

He rose with a smile on his face.

"I am honoured to be a part of your company, my lord."

Fitz smiled but there was no happiness within it. "Do not be too hasty, my friend. The day is just beginning, and if I am any judge, it will contain much sadness."

The two men, with their horses saddled and ready for the day ahead, walked out into the dawn.

"To horses, to horses!"

The cry came from one man wearing a costume of deep red, but it was soon taken up by the men surrounding the camp.

"To horses!"

"This is it," muttered Fitz, sure that no one would be able to hear him under the din of the rattling of swords and the neighing of awakening horses. "This is the moment where I truly lose my soul."

Orvin did not seem to have heard him. Fitz could not help but see parts of Catheryn in him: the blond hair seemed to be an Anglo-Saxon trait that many had, but there was also a softness in him, an acceptance that this was his life now – another feature that Anglo-Saxons up and down the land had acquired, as it became clear that King William and the Normans were not leaving.

"Orvin," he said quietly, and the young man was immediately at his side. "I have a few last things that I have not packed in my tent. Could you fetch them for me?"

Orvin did not even reply – he was already running towards Fitz's tent. Fitz smiled. He already knew which tent was Fitz's out of the hundreds that had been put up around the castle as more and more men amassed here, ready to destroy the North.

It did not take Orvin long to bring the last of Fitz's belongings to him, and the two of them began to stow them safely within the various leather bags that were attached to their horses. As they worked, a voice behind Fitz coughed. He coughed again.

Fitz rolled his eyes – reminding him painfully of Catheryn – and turned around.

"Can I help you?"

The man before him was small, and slight, and holding out a letter. The parchment was slightly soggy, as if it had been accidentally dropped in a puddle, and picked up again hastily. It had not dried out well.

"Letter for you, my lord FitzOsbern," the man panted slightly, but managed to keep his breath. "From Normandy."

"From Normandy?" Fitz took the letter, but did not recognise the hand. "Thank you." A small coin was passed to the man, who then vanished into the crowd of men milling about, shouting orders and laughing at a man who had slipped in the mud.

Orvin looked at the letter curiously. "Will you not open it, my lord?"

Fitz shook his head. "Whatever news it contains can wait."

"But what if it is urgent?"

"It will not be."

Orvin looked at him, confused. "How will you know, if you do not read it, my lord? There are plenty of men here who are just staggering from their beds; their horses are not ready. We have some time yet before we must leave."

Fitz looked around. He was right, of course: but in truth, he did not want to read the letter. Although it did not look like it, it could only be from Adeliza's hand, and any word that he read from her would only remind him more painfully that the affection that he felt for her...just wasn't enough.

But he sighed. He could not ignore it for ever, and Orvin was right. There was time.

"All hail the King!"

Once again, the cry that was begun by one was raised by many. Fitz saw King William stride amongst his men, commenting every now and again to raucous laughter. Fitz's heart was sore, tired of battle, and yet this man, this King that he followed seemed ready once more to slaughter innocents.

Faced with two evils – the letter, or talking to King William once more about the terrible acts that they were about to commit – he chose the former. Breaking open the seal, the parchment unfolded to reveal only a few lines.

Fitz put out a hand for his horse, and put most of his weight on the bridle. Adeliza was sick; she had the same illness that had tormented him, that had dragged away their Isabella from life. And in the lines that Catheryn wrote, it seemed that Adeliza was about to be dragged away too. Suddenly all of the emotions that had seemed lacking in his marriage, all of the times that he had smiled with his wife, laughed with her, cried over their children's hurts, planned for their future – they filled his head so quickly that he almost clutched it as if in pain. Perhaps the love that he had been looking for...what he thought he could have with Catheryn...maybe that was not the only love that there was. Perhaps what he and Adeliza had was love, after all. And now he could lose her.

"Fitz?"

And to think that the news should come in the words of the woman that he had loved, that he did love, that he could not love. That Catheryn should be the one to write to him.

"Fitz, can you hear me?"

Where was Roger? He had left his son in charge. Why had he not contacted him before now?

"Fitz, if you don't answer me, I shall call a doctor!"

Fitz blinked. King William was standing before him, and a look of – was that concern?

"I am sorry, my lord King William." Fitz spoke briefly and quietly, and then turned away to mount his horse. Out of the corner of his eye he could see that Orvin had done the same.

"Fitz, what is going on?"

"Which way South?" Fitz's question was to the entire crowd that had gathered to stare at him. Several men pointed in the same direction.

Fitz spurred his horse on, and Orvin followed him.

"Damn it, Fitz!"

But the cry of King William was falling fast behind them, and the wind caught at most of it. All Fitz could think of was going South, getting to the water, crossing the water – and getting to Adeliza.

"My lord?" Orvin was riding beside him, and although he raced along with him at the same speed, there was a look of shock on his face. "Where are we going?"

"Normandy."

"Fitz!"

His name was called out by a voice that he knew well. Fitz slowed down, and allowed King William to catch up with him.

"What the devil is going on, Fitz?" King William panted slightly at the effort. He was not a young man anymore.

Fitz thrust the letter into his hands, without stopping. Nothing would stop him.

King William leaned back in his saddle while he read the short letter, and the colour drained from his face.

"Have I your leave to go?" Fitz had not meant his words to sound so sarcastic, but King William nodded, his face grim.

"If I had received such news, of my Matilda, I would not have slowed for the King."

Fitz smiled briefly at his liege and friend, and then spurred on his horse. He must return, before it was too late.

CHAPTER THIRTY

Fitz was not quite aware of the days passing. The only reason he knew that days had passed was because Orvin insisted that he ate something three times a day. The food tasted like ashes in his mouth.

The first day brought them to London, and instead of allowing themselves rest, Fitz demanded that they continue. The streets of the capital city were a maze, especially to Orvin who had never been there. It had taken the entire night to get through it, and when dawn rose again, it rose on two men riding hard towards the coast.

When they arrived, Fitz was bitterly angry. They had missed a boat, and another would not leave until that evening. The captain claimed that a smooth wind was coming in, and he would delay the departure until then.

No amount of anger, shouting, or bribery could bring the man to change his mind, and so Fitz and Orvin had no choice but to wait. It was torturous, waiting there on the beach. When the clouds moved, Fitz could even see Normandy, see the coast. And yet it was so far.

The night brought movement, and Fitz and Orvin boarded the ship. The crossing was fair, and yet although they arrived just as night had settled, Fitz refused to stay in an inn. No: they must continue. His home was deep within the bosom of Normandy, and it would take much riding to get there.

And so they rode.

It was three days, and Fitz and Orvin galloped across the Norman countryside. Orvin had been violently sick that morning; not sleeping for three days would do that to you. It was a test of loyalty, this march into a land where Orvin knew only hatred and fear – but he had followed. He had sworn loyalty to Fitz, and he had followed.

The trees and the villages that they were now passing seemed familiar to Fitz. Curves of mountains started to remind him that he was almost there. Almost home.

"Not long now," he called out to Orvin, who was sitting uncomfortably in his saddle. "You can rest soon."

"I can continue for as long as you need, my lord," Orvin said, his usually strong voice slightly wobbling.

Fitz smiled, despite the desperation coursing through his veins. Orvin was a good man, and he was lucky to have him. The ride alone would probably have killed Fitz, his mind unable to prevent him from despairing.

Within moments, he realised where he was. It would take only a little longer before he would be able to see his home.

The moment came, and no view had felt so sweet. Never before had Fitz felt so wonderful that his home was visible – but then, never before had he been so ready to return. It is strange, he thought, how death makes us realise what we truly value. Ever since they had been married, there had been nothing but graciousness and politeness between him and his wife. Now Adeliza was near death, he suddenly realised how vibrant she made his life. He did not love her in the way that a man should love his wife; but there was tenderness there.

"Who is that?"

Orvin's voice forced him to concentrate. Fitz squinted: it did certainly look like there was someone standing by the door of the castle. As they continued, horses increasing their pace at the sight of rest, Fitz smiled. It was a woman. His heart leapt. Adeliza had survived.

But it was not to be.

As he and Orvin grew closer, everything within him cried out in pain.

It was Catheryn.

By the time that they reached her, Fitz's body was shaking with exhaustion, and pain, and confusion. His horse pulled up by the castle walls, and Fitz fell off his horse into Catheryn's arms.

"Adeliza?" he croaked.

Catheryn looked down at him.

"She is gone."

CHAPTER THIRTY ONE

Catheryn had never felt more awkward in her entire life. It was intolerable, this feeling of sinking underneath the weight of her sadness.

It had been but one day since Adeliza had passed on, but the entire household was still reeling. Roger had immediately ridden out, desperate to give the news to his brother William in person. Emma was not answering any knocks on her chamber door, but it was possible none the less to hear her sobs through the wood.

Catheryn had even spotted Ursule wiping away a tear, although she had stared back at Catheryn defiantly, daring her to mention it.

Catheryn did not. She had been too busy trying to organise what was to be done for Adeliza's body. The priest had been called; he had come; and he had openly wept before her. Catheryn realised with a bolt of surprise that Adeliza, despite her strange animosity to her since she had arrived, was a beloved woman. There would be many mourning at her graveside.

But Fitz – she had not expected him to arrive so soon, and yet so late. Mere hours would have given him the chance to speak one last time to his wife. It tore at

Catheryn, that lost moment. She had been at Adeliza's side, but once again it was not she that was wanted.

The Great Hall was full of people, and of silence. Few were able to eat, staring at their plates, appetites destroyed by the sorrow that had descended on the castle.

Neither Emma nor Roger had come for the evening meal, and so Catheryn and Fitz were alone at the top family table.

Catheryn had never felt more alone, and more intrusive. The bread and chicken that sat on her plate were untouched.

She should not be here. Once again she was intruding on a family's grief, a grief that surely no person should be a part of. She was not wanted.

Catheryn cast a quick glance to her left, where Fitz sat. His eyes were empty, and no food had been placed before him. Not even his wine had been touched. His hair hung as his head was slightly lowered, and he said not a word.

Catheryn sighed. The loss of a spouse, even one that you did not completely love, was not something that you recovered from easily. There were still times that she woke in the night, sweating, screaming, fingertips stretched out in the hope of catching one last touch from the man she loved.

And yet...a small part of her that she despised, but could not ignore, was smiling. Fitz was free. He was a free man, and he could marry again.

Of course, it would be many months before he would ever be able to consider himself free. She knew better than most that he would need the time and space to grieve – but after that... When Adeliza's touch had been forgotten from his skin, and he had to remind himself to be sad, perhaps they...

"My lord," she said softly to him, reaching out a hand to gently touch his arm. "Can I get you nothing to eat?"

Fitz shook his head. He did not even turn to look at her, but a flinch of his arm told her that her touch was not wanted.

She removed her hand. "I want you to know…that it was peaceful."

There was no response.

Catheryn knew that he would want to know these things, that they must be said; and the sooner the better.

"I was there," she continued, "and she spoke of you, with much love."

At this, she caught Fitz's attention. He inclined his head slightly, and blinked, very slowly. There was no moisture in his eyes, but as Catheryn could see them more clearly, she saw that they were red and raw.

"Her passing was not painful, and at the end she…she seemed ready to go – "

"Ready?" Catheryn winced at the pain in his voice. "How can you say that – how could she have been ready to go?"

"I only meant," Catheryn said quietly, "that she had accepted that it was her time."

"Her time, her time," muttered Fitz, a hint of madness in his voice. "Who are you to say when her time was? Was it Selwyn's time, when he was slaughtered on a battlefield for a country that he could not protect?"

Catheryn gasped, but quickly regained her composure. "I know you are lashing out in grief, and so I shall not take offence at your words. I want to give you peace, that is all."

"She took my peace with her," Fitz's voice cracked, "and left me in this world alone."

"You are not alone. I am with you."

As soon as the words were said, Catheryn realised that she had made a mistake: she had moved too soon.

"You?" Fitz stared at her in amazement. "Who are you? *What* are you? You are just a woman, my lady Catheryn. A noble woman, maybe, and a beautiful woman,

I must admit: but you are a prisoner here. You are not my sister, or my friend, to tell me what to do and what to think and how to feel."

"That is not my intention!" Catheryn said forcefully. "I only – "

"What?" Fitz stood up, unable to contain his anger and pain any longer. Every muscle within him was strained, almost at breaking point. "I have ridden day and night three times over to be here, foregoing rest, ignoring food, challenging God in order to be here as my wife lay dying, and what do I find?"

His voice was so loud now that servants and other members of the household were turning their heads to see what was happening. Ursule was stroking Reginald slowly, staring at Catheryn.

Catheryn grew hot, and she could feel the blush on her cheeks.

"Fitz, you are suffering from a great loss, it is natural that you are angry – "

"Angry?" Fitz's voice boomed. Orvin, sitting alone and nervous amongst the household that he barely knew, could not believe that his new master could speak so loudly. "Yes, I am angry! I am angry because the woman that I have gone through life with has been taken from me, and no one did anything to stop it!"

Catheryn could not believe what she was hearing. "Ursule and I did everything that we could!" she cried. "Sometimes the sickness is stronger than we are!"

"Did you?" Fitz stared at her, something indescribable in his eyes. "Did you really do everything that you could for Adeliza? Despite the fact that you were jealous of her, that you did not like her?"

"That's ridiculous, I had great affection for my lady Adeliza – "

"But more for me."

Catheryn's mouth fell open. A gasp went around the room, but she did not turn to look at them. Her eyes were transfixed on Fitz. The man that he was, the man that she knew, the man that she had grown to love, was completely gone. In his place stood a skeleton of that man, a mere shadow of his former self. Instead of calm, there was panic. Instead of mercy, there was accusation. And instead of love, there was hate.

"You wanted me," Fitz said quietly, but forcefully, "and I told you that we could not be together because I was married. From that moment, Adeliza was merely an obstacle – "

"That is not true!"

"An obstacle preventing you from getting what you wanted. And so – what did you do?" Fitz's eyes were wide now, as though he was trying to see the truth through a dark mist. "Did you not help her, when she fell sick? Did you give her something, something that would prevent her from getting well? Or," Fitz took a step backwards, away from her, "are the depths of your malice even deeper? Did you…did you make sure that she became sick?"

"My lord."

Catheryn and Fitz turned to look at a young man, with blond hair, who was standing at the opposite end of the room.

"My lord, perhaps we should retire. We have had a long journey," said Orvin, a gentle smile on his face.

"Quiet!" shouted Fitz. "Who asked for your opinion?"

Orvin went red, and sat back down. No one else stirred.

"Fitz," Catheryn spoke quietly. "I know how you are feeling."

"You can't – "

"Yes. Yes I can," Catheryn smiled sadly. "You are not the only one here who has lost a loved one, a husband, a wife, when they least expected it. You are not alone in looking back and wishing that the last farewell had been a warmer one. You are not the first, nor the last, to bemoan

God for taking someone so precious. You feel broken now, but you will heal – "

"I will not." Fitz's words had a finality in them that shook Catheryn. "I will never love again, now that you have killed my wife."

CHAPTER THIRTY TWO

Fitz sat in his bed chamber – the room that had held so much depth of sorrow over the years. Losing a child at birth had been terrible; but he and Adeliza had borne it. Losing Isabella had been terrible; but he and Adeliza had learned to bear it. But losing Adeliza...

He dragged a shaking hand through his hair, and flinched as one of his nails caught at his scalp.

It still did not feel real, this loss. At any moment, he expected Adeliza to walk into the chamber, and berate him for not completing a task that she had asked him to do. Fitz tried to smile at the memories, but they brought nothing but pain. Sharp jagged edges of pain shearing down into his very memories.

There were few parts of his life that did not contain death – but this, this was beyond anything that he could have expected. Fitz rose heavily, and stared out of the window. The cracked glass needed replacing, but it was still possible to see through it.

Catheryn was pacing. He had noticed that she always paced when she was angry, or upset. A careful flick of her head kept a tendril of hair out of her eyes.

Fitz stared at her. Catheryn was beautiful, and gentle, and probably everything that Adeliza was not. But had Fitz ever really noticed the deficiencies of his marriage until Catheryn had wandered into their lives, ordered here by a far off King because a nameless lord could not stand her presence? Before she had entered their lives, had Fitz ever really realised that Adeliza needed to be more, so much more, in order to make him happy?

Happy. A state that Fitz had not been for a long time.

Something warm and wet trickled down by his right ear. Fitz put up his hand, and when he brought it back in front of his eyes, he saw that he was bleeding. The nick in his scalp must have been deeper than he thought.

Then suddenly, Fitz started. Catheryn had stopped pacing, and was staring up at him. Her eyes were full, and even through the misted glass he could see that tears had fallen down her cheeks.

He turned away from the window, and sat back down on the bed, in the centre of the room, the room where Adeliza died.

The moon had waxed and waned, and four weeks had passed: and yet nothing within the home of the FitzOsberns had changed.

Roger had returned, and brought with him his brother and family. Baby Isabella was now smiling, and yet she received very little attention from her aunt and uncle. Neither could look at her, speak her name, without recalling her namesake. It was painful for them.

The three siblings were brought together by death, once again, and it was just as painful. When Adeliza was laid to rest, beside her daughter, no person bothered to wipe away their tears. They fell, unhindered, onto their garments and onto ground.

William had not stayed long. He had attempted to speak to his father, but Fitz had taken to shutting himself away, seeing no one, eating barely enough to keep a child alive. After trying, desperately, to speak with his father about some problems he was having with the local village, William realised that it did not interest Fitz. He had no time for the concerns of the world now: his whole world had been his duty to his family, and now his daughter and his wife had been taken from him.

The parting of the siblings had been watched by Catheryn, and she watched it with sadness. Their words of sorrow barely explained the concerns of their hearts, and in the end, embraces were all that they could manage.

They reminded Catheryn of her own daughter. An only child now, an orphan, for all the good that her mother was to her. Annis was just as alone in the world as they were, although they did not know it. Why were parents so often ineffectual, Catheryn wondered. Why do we let our children down?

Catheryn and Ursule had gone through Adeliza's bed chamber, removing the debris of the sick room to leave it clean, perfect, whole. Fitz had not slept the room since his return; he had been sleeping in a guest chamber.

"It is an ill time," Ursule muttered, and nodded sagely, Reginald wrapped once more around her neck. "He shall not recover from this, mark me."

Catheryn's eyes widened. "He won't – he won't die, will he? Do you mean that he will die?"

"Oh, yes," Ursule nodded, and then her face broke out into a smile with no warmth in it. "We shall all die at some point, my lady. But Fitz; something inside him, that brings us all life, and joy, and happiness – that part of him is dead. It cannot be brought back to life, and he shall never feel those things again. He lives, yes: but he is not alive."

Catheryn shook her head sadly. "It feels like such a waste."

"Because you wanted him to feel those things for you?"

Catheryn stared at her in horror. "What – how could you...?" she stuttered.

Ursule waved a nonchalant hand. "There is more that I know besides healing the sick."

The blush that never seemed far away from Catheryn had blossomed once more on her cheeks.

"You would never...you would not say anything, would you?" Catheryn had not meant her words to sound so much like a plea, but they did.

Ursule smiled. "It is not my place to say anything, my lady. What you feel, and decide to do about those feelings, is up to you."

The old lady swept out in a flurry of fur, and Catheryn was left alone, standing in the marriage room of the man that she loved, and the woman that she had been publicly accused of killing.

Catheryn sighed. Her status as a prisoner had not changed, despite the force of death that had passed through the castle. There was nothing for her to do here, except wait for release: to England, or to a much sweeter kingdom.

Catheryn could not stand there for long, and she soon made her way to the Great Hall. It was empty, and Catheryn breathed easy. The last thing that she wanted was to be amongst people now. Silence, and rest, were all she craved. Settling herself by the window, she shut her eyes, and breathed out deeply.

"Éadesburg – éadesburg Catheryn, æðelflæde Theoryn, supa?"

Catheryn's eyes snapped open. The blond man, only a few years older than her own daughter, the man that had tried to get Fitz to rest that dreadful evening when he had returned, was staring at her. She had not even heard him come in.

"Thank you," she said quietly in her native tongue. It was almost a relief to be able to wrap her tongue around familiar sounds. "It has been a while since anyone has greeted me by my proper name."

The boy – for he was a boy in many ways – turned red, but smiled. He then kneeled, and bowed his head.

"It is an honour to speak with you, my lady Catheryn," he said to the rushes on the floor. "I have wished to speak to you many times, and yet it is only now that I have been able to."

Catheryn stared at the man, but no spark of recognition hit her.

"I must apologise," she said softly, "for I do not believe that I know you. Come closer, and speak with me a while."

Although he hesitated, the man did approach her.

"My name is Orvin, son of Ulfwulf, of the South."

"Of the South?" Catheryn's eyes lit up. "Then in that case – "

"I knew your husband," Orvin interrupted. "Or at least, my family did. I am the second son of the eldest daughter of the family where your husband served, before you married him."

Catheryn smiled. "It is always good to hear from people of my own country, and you are doubly welcome as a friend of my husband."

"He was a good man."

Catheryn nodded. "He was one of the best men I ever knew, and he may never truly recover from his terrible loss."

Orvin hesitated, and then continued. "My lady, it is not my place to…to pry into the affairs of those that are above me. Yet I am sworn to my lord Fitz, and I cannot help but see that he is unhappy."

"Yes, he is," Catheryn said softly. "But then, losing someone as important as our lady Adeliza, after losing your own child…it is a terrible thing. It is understandable that he is…upset."

"I know," Orvin said quickly. "At least," he amended, "I have never been married, so I cannot know what it is to lose one's life companion. But I did lose my mother when I was very young, and the pain of that remains with me. I know what it is to lose someone precious."

"Too many of us do."

"And yet," Orvin continued, "I am sworn to my lord Fitz, and as you know him so well, I would ask of you: is there anything you can think of that I can do to bring him relief?"

Catheryn stared at him. "You…want to know what would make Fitz happy?"

"He is my lord," repeated Orvin. "I serve him, but in this case, I do not know how to serve him."

Catheryn gazed at him; this young man who had already known such suffering, such pain. He was in a foreign land, with no friends or elders to guide him – and yet his thoughts did not run on how terrible his life had been, but rather how he could make the life of another less terrible.

"You are a rare breed, Orvin, son of Ulfwulf," she said slowly, "and if I think of anything that can bring Fitz back to the land of the living, I will tell you."

Orvin barely had a chance to reply, mouth open, before a loud knock was sounded on the Great Hall door.

"Enter!" Catheryn spoke loudly, unsure as to who it could be. Why would anyone knock on the door?

A man entered, dressed in thick leather. He had obviously been riding, from the spurs on his boots, and he seemed grateful for the warmth that the castle provided.

"Welcome, stranger," Catheryn said, standing up. Orvin rose beside her, but took a humble step backwards. "You are welcome within these walls if you bring peace."

"I bring peace," said the man. His voice was strange; Norman, yes, but with an accent that Catheryn could barely recognise. "I am the bearer of a message, intended for the ears of my lord William FitzOsbern. Is he within?"

Catheryn turned and smiled at Orvin. "Would you be so good as to fetch my lord Fitz here, Orvin?"

Her voice was soft, but he heard her. Orvin walked out of the room, leaving Catheryn and the messenger alone.

"Orvin will fetch my lord FitzOsbern," Catheryn said formally. "Until he returns, I bid you wait here."

"My thanks," said the messenger, relaxing. "It has been a long journey, and I would welcome a rest."

"Have you come far?"

The messenger stared at her, and hesitated. "What is your name, my lady? My patron is...I do not want all to know that I am here."

Catheryn tried not to become irritated. Back home, amongst her own people, all knew her that saw her. Orvin was living proof of that. And yet even messengers questioned her very right to be there.

"I am lady Catheryn, daughter of Theoryn, of the South," she said, much more haughtily than she was happy with, "and I have no wish to pry into the business of your patron."

"Ah, the prisoner," the man smiled. There was no malice there, but he clearly did not consider her important enough to fear any longer. "I have heard of you."

Catheryn was spared the indelicacy of replying with rudeness by the door slamming open. Fitz stood in the doorway, and he looked awful.

He was still wearing the clothes that Catheryn had seen him wear over a week ago, and if the smell was anything to go by, he had not removed them since that time. His hair was greasy, and there was a stain of something by one corner of his mouth.

"My lord William FitzOsbern," the messenger bowed low, his face not betraying the surprise that he felt. "I have come far to deliver a message to you."

"Then deliver it." Fitz walked into the room, and stood by the fire. He had ignored Catheryn completely.

The messenger hesitated. "I would prefer to deliver it in private, my lord."

Fitz shrugged. "We are alone. Deliver your message."

The man cast a nervous glance at Catheryn, who smiled wearily. Of course, Fitz no longer counted her as worth paying any attention to.

"Well...in that case..." said the messenger awkwardly. "I bring you greetings and warm words of friendship from Richilde, daughter of Robert, widow of Baldwin VI of Flanders. Since the sad loss of her husband, which she is sure you will appreciate, she has been protecting the rights of her son, Arnulf, whose uncle has cruelly attacked his succession to Flanders. She knows of your greatness, both of character and with the blade, and she asks that you join her side as her husband in this fight for justice."

Catheryn gasped. Fitz did not look round at her. He did not even look at the messenger. He just continued to gaze into the fire.

"And my lady Richilde's terms are?"

Catheryn could not help herself. "Fitz you cannot seriously be considering – "

"Quiet!" he barked. "What I consider to do is no business of yours."

Fitz turned now to look at the messenger, who looked slightly confused.

"I repeat," Fitz said quietly. "What are her terms?"

"Her terms are but few," the messenger said quickly. "She asks that the marriage take place within a fortnight, and that you commit yourself and ten men to her son's cause. She asks that you will fight for him, and for her, and that you will ask King William of England for assistance. She also says that there will be..." Here the messenger coloured slightly, but continued on, "no need to consider any potential children."

Fitz nodded slowly. "Then I accept. I will go to her in twelve days from today, and we shall be wed two days later. Tell your lady that I thank her for her generous offer, and I look forward to being a good sword for her son's cause."

The messenger bowed; understanding the dismissal for what it was, he left the room quietly, leaving Catheryn and Fitz alone.

"Marriage?" Catheryn whispered. "You are going to be married?"

"What of it?" Fitz said harshly. "I am a man, and a man needs a wife. Is that not what we are told?"

Fitz went back to the fireplace, and continued his watch of the flames. Catheryn shook her head, and moved towards him.

"No," she said, "you do not have to marry again, if you do not want to."

"Just because no one wants to marry you that does not mean that I am in the same boat."

Catheryn gasped. "Do you think your cruelty to me makes your viewpoint valid?"

Fitz sighed, and turned to face her. They were but fingertips apart from each other, but Catheryn dared not breach the gap.

"I can never trust you again," Fitz said softly, his eyes full of pain staring directly into hers. "Living with you like this…it is a torment. Perhaps God is punishing us for the words that we spoke, one night when I lay on a sick bed. We should never have revealed those feelings for each other, and now they are killed, dead in my heart. I will not remain here, and I will marry my lady Richilde. Anything is better than staying here with you."

CHAPTER THIRTY THREE

"I cannot believe what I am hearing!"

"Believe it," Fitz said with an air of finality. "Do you think that we can pretend that what we have done is not wrong?"

"We did nothing!" Catheryn said heatedly. "Our very inaction says more about our... friendship, if that is what you want to call it, than anything else! Yes, we had feelings for each other, but surely the fact that we did nothing – "

"Did we do nothing?" Fitz broke the intense gaze between them, and began to pace in the Great Hall. "We did not betray Adeliza directly, but who knows what you said to her, what you did to her, when I was absent."

Catheryn laughed. "You really think that I am the sort of person that could be so cruel? Perhaps you do not know me as well as you think."

"And perhaps I know you better than you do!" Fitz cried. "I know all about your first marriage – you chose your own husband? What kind of girl were you, what kind of family was yours that permitted the rash decisions of a young woman to decide her fate?"

Catheryn bristled at the accusation. "Just because you and Adeliza were chosen for each other – "

"And is not that the way that it should be?" Fitz glared at her. "My father chose my bride, and I have chosen the bride for my son. If God be good, I shall choose another bride for Roger and a husband for my daughter. But you...you go against what is natural. You thought that you could just choose your life companion when you were young, and what is to say that you did not feel the same way when you met me. Adeliza was inconvenient, and look!" Fitz looked around the room in mock surprise. "Where is she?"

Catheryn stared at him. "It is as though grief has completely slain the man that I knew," she said slowly. "You are a stranger to me."

Fitz sighed. "I cared for you, once," he said softly. "But you must see – you must see that I cannot now. My feelings for you are too entangled in the loss of Adeliza. With every passing moment, you become more repellent to me than before."

Anger coursed through Catheryn's veins. "In that case," she said bitterly, "you should return me to England!"

"Perhaps I will!"

"Good!" Catheryn said heavily. "It is something that I have been asking for these last four years, and it would bring you joy to be rid of me. Let us combine the two together."

They stared at each other, anger and bitterness and resentment lying thick between them. The combination of all three made it impossible for them to take a step forward, impossible for them to meet. The way was blocked, and neither attempted to remove the emotions that barred their way.

"Orvin!"

Fitz's shout made Catheryn jump. Within moments, Orvin stepped through the door, nervously. He had clearly heard some, but not all, of the shouting.

"My lord?"

Fitz forced his face into a smile. "Orvin, this is – "

"He knows who I am," Catheryn interrupted bitterly, "and better than you."

Fitz glared at her, but then turned back to Orvin.

"Orvin, you swore yourself to me," said Fitz. "You swore yourself to me when times are hard."

Orvin nodded.

"Orvin, times indeed are hard. This woman needs to be returned to her country, and I never want her to return here again. I have a task for you that is long, and arduous, and I feel you should have the right to refuse."

Orvin looked nervously from the lady who was clearly attempting not to let tears overcome her, and the man who looked as though he would never cry again.

"Tell me the task, my lord, and I shall decide," he said finally.

Fitz breathed deeply, and then spoke. "It is this: I would ask that you go with her, and that you stay with her. That you swear yourself to her, and obey her. That you remain with her until the end of her days, or yours. And that during your years of service, you ensure that she never takes one step onto Norman soil."

Catheryn gasped. "But what if my daughter is here – what if Annis has been taken to Normandy, just as I have?"

"I care not," Fitz said with a wave of his hand. "You are not my problem, nor my responsibility any longer."

"But the King..." Fitz stared at Catheryn, and her voice trailed away.

"The King placed you into my hands. I could have killed you: your very life is mine to command. And now I command that you return to your homeland, and never venture here again."

Fitz's gaze was piercing, and Catheryn could not help but drop her own under the weight of it. He turned to the only other person in the room.

"Well, Orvin? What say you?"

Orvin swallowed. This was probably the biggest decision that he would ever have to make.

"I swore to obey you, my lord," he said slowly, "and so that is what I will do. I will swear myself to my lady Catheryn, and ensure that she is returned safely."

Fitz nodded. "It is a wise choice, and I honour you for it."

Orvin bowed low, and then left the room quietly.

"And so this is goodbye." Catheryn stared at the man who she had once believed could heal her heart from the brokenness that it felt, shattered after Selwyn's death.

Fitz stared at her. "Both bitter and bittersweet, is it not?"

Catheryn nodded. Her feet did not seem to want to obey her. She knew that if she did not leave the room as soon as possible, she would start to cry.

Without any warning, Fitz rushed towards her. Catheryn raised her arms up instinctively having lived too long in the world to expect comfort, but she had no reason to fear. Fitz swept her into his arms, and crushed her to him. For a moment, Catheryn thought that he had changed his mind; that all of the anger and resentment had disappeared, and he had realised that they had to be together.

But it was over almost before it had begun.

"Leave." Fitz pulled away from her, and took a step backwards. "Leave as soon as possible."

"You'll never see me again," Catheryn said quietly.

Fitz nodded. "So be it."

CHAPTER THIRTY FOUR

The sky was dark, and the waves were high.

Catheryn had hoped for a morning crossing, but just like many of her plans to return back to England, this one also had gone awry. Fitz had wanted her and Orvin to be gone by sundown, that fateful day when he accepted Richilde's marriage proposal. But it was many weeks before she was able to leave: King William had demanded news of Adeliza, and her death had brought Catheryn's own rights into question.

The King had not liked it, but Fitz had been correct. Her life had been placed into Fitz's hands, and it was up to him to dispose of it. Had Catheryn been a man, of course, she would never have been allowed back into her country. But she was merely a woman, and so after Christmas had come and gone, and January's winds disappeared, it was finally in February that she was allowed to step onto a boat bound for England. Fitz had left almost as soon as his marriage had been decided, and had joined his new bride. Catheryn had spent months wandering around an empty castle that held nothing but memories of sadness and death.

England. As soon as Catheryn stepped down from the ship that had brought her and Orvin across from Normandy, Catheryn knew that she was home. It smelt right, the paths seemed firmer under her feet.

"My lady?"

Orvin was staring at her, a look of concern on his face.

"Yes, Orvin?"

Orvin smiled nervously. He was still not used to accompanying a woman, especially a woman whom he had heard much of as a child.

"You have been very quiet on our journey, my lady," he said awkwardly. "Are you unwell? Do you require more rest?"

Catheryn smiled. Such a caring boy. He made her think of what her son may have been like, if he had been permitted to live.

"I am quite well," Catheryn lied. "But I would appreciate the chance to stay somewhere tonight."

"I shall make enquiries."

Orvin rushed off into the darkness, leaving Catheryn standing by the horse that Fitz had reluctantly given her. It snuffled at her hand, looking for a treat.

Within moments, Orvin had returned.

"I have found an inn," he said quickly, "and secured two rooms for this night. I did not know whether you wanted to remain here longer – "

"Decisions can be made in daylight," Catheryn said with a smile. "Right now, I want warmth, and food, and then a bed."

She left Orvin to rest the horse and put him in the stable, while she found a table inside the busy inn. Voices of Normans surrounded her from every side. In many ways, it was as though she had never left in Normandy.

Food was brought to them, and while she and Orvin ate, not a word was spoken. It was not until they had finished that Orvin opened his mouth once more.

"My lady," he said quietly, so that they would not be overheard, "I know that it is not my business to pry into your affairs, but now that we are in England I feel that I must ask you: what are your plans? The country that you left four years ago barely exists."

Catheryn nodded wearily. "I will be honest with you Orvin: I have no plans at all. My husband is dead, my son is dead, and my daughter Annis is almost certainly dead. Where would I look for her body, all these years later? I know not whether any of my family or kin are living; I have had no word from England since I was taken."

"No word at all?"

"None. But you have been here – you must have some knowledge of what happened to them," Catheryn said eagerly. She had forbidden herself from asking before, but she could no longer hold the question in, no matter what the answer was.

Orvin turned red, and shuffled uncomfortably in his seat.

"My family...my father knew that our King..."

Orvin looked around the room at the sheer number of Normans around them. Many of them carried swords, and a few wore the deep red of King William. Catheryn watched his gaze, and understood. You never knew when you could be overheard.

"My father knew that the usurper, Harold, would not prevail over King William," Orvin continued slowly. "Harold may have been the brother-in-law of the previous King, but that did not mean that he could sit on the throne himself. My father did not ride out against King William, and he accepted his rule when it came. We have not heard much from the Anglo-Saxon families that we were once close with, before the Conquest."

He glanced up at Catheryn nervously.

"You are worried," she said slowly, "that I would judge you – that I would think ill of you because of your decision to accept King William."

"Your husband died attempting to defeat him," Orvin said quietly. "Can you blame me?"

Catheryn sighed, and shook her head. "You are right to be wary."

"I think that it is best if we rest, and then, as you say, make decisions in daylight."

"You are right," Catheryn smiled. "Nothing can be gained from running away from the past in darkness."

Catheryn spent the night in bitter dreams of men without faces that would not stay with her. Each time, she begged them not to go to battle, and each time, they would leave her. When she awoke, sunlight was streaming through into her room, and her head hurt.

She went downstairs to break her fast, and saw Orvin, the only person in the room, sitting at a table, looking as though he was about to vomit.

"Orvin," she said, rushing up to him. "What is wrong?"

When she got closer, she could see that he was holding a piece of parchment. Norman words were scrawled over it.

"You have news? News from whom?"

It was only then that it struck her who the news could be from. The only one that they could be about.

"Fitz. Is he – "

"He is dead." Orvin's words struck like dull weights into her chest.

Catheryn sat down. "Dead?"

Orvin nodded. "In a battle near Cassel. Richilde's son Arnulf died also. Roger has written to me, to let me know that my vow to him is now broken, and I am free to go where I choose."

Fitz was dead. Yet another person that was precious to her, wrenched away from life. She could barely breathe; every movement seemed to be difficult, like wading through sand. The man that had seemed so vibrant, so full of life…just like Selwyn, Fitz had gone. But she had to be strong: she had to be strong for the one that could be waiting here, somewhere in these English shores.

"And...and what do you want to do?" Orvin asked nervously. A tear fell from Catheryn's eye, but she made no motion to wipe it away. She would have time to properly grieve later.

Orvin made his decision. "We need to eat. Let us break our fast, then we can decide."

Catheryn nodded, and Orvin gestured that food should be brought to their table.

They were still trying to eat when three Norman men strode into the room, laughing loudly.

"And she really stood up to them?" bellowed one, tall and dark.

"She did!" another replied. The three of them sat at a table close to Catheryn and Orvin, and thumped the table. Food was brought to them immediately, and all payment offered was declined with a fearful look. The woman, an Anglo-Saxon, darted away from them nervously after she had brought them their food.

"I still cannot believe it," said the third. "King William fills me with such fear, I could never go to him and ask for protection."

"Oh, it wasn't her," said the first. "It was Melville that went to the King – but while he was away, his wife made sure that the entire village was brought into their home! She didn't want any of them to die, apparently – Anglo-Saxon scum. But then, she's a Saxon too."

Catheryn smiled, despite herself. That sounded like something that her own child would do. Annis could never bear for an innocent to be hurt.

"Well, I suppose a couple more Anglo-Saxons walking around won't make much difference," one of the men muttered. "After all, enough were killed in the Harrying of the North."

The three men laughed darkly.

The tall man spoke again. "What was her name, anyway?"

Catheryn looked up. This woman sounded like someone powerful – perhaps she would recognise the name.

"I'm not sure," the third man said dismissively. "It began with an 'A', that's all I know."

Catheryn's heart leapt. Could it be – it could not be Annis?

"I know what it was," the second man spoke up again. "Heard it when I was serving the Queen. Her name is Avis."

CHAPTER THIRTY FIVE

Catheryn breathed out a deep sigh. It was too much, of course it was too much, to hope that the woman that the men had been talking about was her daughter. Another tear escaped her, and this one she did brush away. No matter how hard she tried to forget the man that she had left behind, Fitz kept forcing himself into her thoughts, and it was heartbreaking to believe that he was no longer alive.

"Ah," said Orvin, with a tired smile. "It is not your daughter."

"No." Catheryn's voice was dull. "It never could have been, I suppose. Life is not that simple."

"Your daughter's name is Annis. Is there anything else that we have to aid us in the search for her?"

Catheryn picked at the last morsel of food before her. "There is little, I suppose, that would mark her out from others, the countless other motherless girls that were left here after the invasion."

Orvin smiled again, but his smile was dark. "I think your daughter had a little more on her side than that, with you as her mother."

Catheryn laughed. "I suppose you could say that. A wild temper, however, is not always the greatest tool during a time of war."

Orvin nodded, but did not speak.

"She has long blonde hair," Catheryn said dismissively, "and she wears...she used to wear it behind a veil."

"My mother always wore a veil."

"We all did," Catheryn said quietly. "That was the way."

The three men that had been chatting loudly by them finished their meal, and left. Catheryn did not realise how tense and uncomfortable she was until they had stepped through the door and out into the street. Every muscle in her back relaxed, and she breathed freely once more.

"You will get used to it," said Orvin under his breath. "We have all had to. The Normans are everywhere now, you cannot avoid them. It is not something that you can accustom yourself to overnight, but with time, you will."

"I had thought myself used to Norman ways, after my years spent in their own lands," admitted Catheryn, "but to see them so close, some of the men that could have fought my husband, my friends...how do you all live like this?"

"We have no choice."

Catheryn started: it was not Orvin who had spoken, but the woman who had served the three Norman men. Catheryn had not heard her approach their table.

"I am sorry," she said defensively, "I know that I should not have spoken. And you are a lady – you could know the King – please forget that I said anything. Please forget that you met me."

"Wait!" But before Catheryn had even got the word out, the woman had fled. Catheryn turned to Orvin, but he answered her query before she had even made it.

"Yes, we are all like that. The last few years have taught us to be careful of who we speak to, who we speak before. That is our life here."

Catheryn sighed. The England that she had left had clearly gone, and she would have to learn all of the new rules to this new England.

She looked at Orvin. He was young, but he was blunt. He would never lie to her.

"Do you think that my daughter is dead?"

Orvin hesitated. "I do not know for sure – no one does. But I...I would be surprised if we found her alive and well."

"Thank you for your honesty," Catheryn said softly. "Do you think that she is still in England?"

This time Orvin looked a little brighter. "They had little reason to take her to Normandy. You could have been a useful hostage; she had no title, no lands. If Annis lives, she lives in England."

Catheryn breathed out a sigh of relief. "It's not much, but it's something."

"My lady," Orvin said gently. "Where do you think you are going to start your search? Annis could be anywhere on the island."

Catheryn shrugged her shoulders. "We have to start somewhere. Why do we not travel to my home – my former home, I assume it is now."

"Is it far?"

Catheryn thought for a moment. "On horseback...two days, maybe three days ride?"

Orvin rose, brushing the crumbs from his tunic. "Then that is where we shall go. After all, you may like to see your home."

"Full of Normans?" Catheryn laughed as she followed him out to the stables. "I think not. I have no idea what – or who – I will find there."

CHAPTER THIRTY SIX

Catheryn and Orvin managed to acquire the services of two horses – although at a price dearer than Catheryn had ever thought possible. The man that sold them the horses stared at her strangely, and Catheryn found herself blushing under his gaze. When she had last been in England, no man would ever have dared look at her like that; but now she was merely a traveller on the road. He could look as he wanted.

As they departed, Orvin began humming a tune under his breath. The sun had risen, and the clouds had parted, leaving the March air cool and crisp. Catheryn pulled her cloak tighter around her, and listened to Orvin's humming. It was not a tune that she recognised, but it was so similar to a lullaby that she had sung to her children that it brought a smile to her face.

"What is that tune called, Orvin?" she asked quietly.

Orvin smiled, and drew his horse alongside her own.

"It has no name that I know of," he said gently. "My mother used to sing it to me when I was growing up, and it has always comforted me. She called it the song of coming home."

"I like that."

They rode on, following the crowds that were making for Canterbury.

"It will be easy to travel from Canterbury," Orvin said. "And it is safer to keep to the busier roads. The Normans have tried to keep the number of bandits down, but during this winter months, when darkness comes early, travellers are easy prey."

Once again, Catheryn shivered. She looked around her at the other people making for the great city of the South. Most of them were walking by foot, carrying loads and baskets that seemed destined for market. An elderly couple just in front of them were on horseback, but moving slowly. Behind them a group of Norman soldiers bickered about the food rations that they had been given. It was a motley crew, certainly, but every moment that she spent here, in her own country, surrounded by the people that she was born with, raised her spirits. Even the groups of Normans passing them could not diminish her spirits. Surely here there will be the chance to find her daughter. Surely she will be reunited with Annis soon.

Orvin moved his horse close to hers once more, and began to talk in a lowered voice. "My lady Catheryn, I think it would be safer for you if you were not to give your real name when you make enquiries."

Catheryn raised an eyebrow. "You do?"

Orvin nodded. "Your husband's name is still spoken of with great reverence here, and there are some fears amongst the Normans that an uprising under his banner could occur during the cold months, when food is scarce."

"I see," Catheryn said slowly, but with some pride. "I had not realised that Selwyn's loyalty had created such devoted followers. And you are right: it would not do to raise concerns and suspicions. But then how are we to search? We are, after all, seeking for Selwyn's daughter."

"If you announced yourself as her nurse," Orvin suggested, with a blush over his face, "and I know the dishonour that may cause you, but I think it would be safest. My lord Fitz…he asked me to keep you safe. And I intend to honour that."

Catheryn did not reply. The mere mention of Fitz broke her heart once again. That a man such as he should be forced to go back to war again, fighting for the rights of a boy that was not his own – that he should lay down his life for that! – it was too much to bear. Selwyn, her first love, died for the sake of his children and for his land: but what did Fitz die for? For the child of another, in a strange and foreign land.

A voice was speaking, and she forced herself to concentrate on it.

"I am sorry, my lady, to bring you pain," Orvin was saying. "I intend only to protect you."

Catheryn smiled, despite the pain. "And I honour that intent, Orvin. And I thank you for it."

They did not speak again until the sun had reached its peak in the sky, and the sight of Canterbury met their eyes. Snug in its little dip, it was a welcome sight. Catheryn had not ridden this long for many years, and her aching bones needed a rest.

"We shall stop here," she told Orvin. "If you could purchase provisions, we shall eat on the road. I wish to reach Essetesford by nightfall, and we should be able to stay with William, son of Osmund, of the South."

"My lady," Orvin said quietly. "William, son of Osmund, is no longer the holder of Esstesford."

Catheryn turned in shock to look at the young man accompanying her. He nodded.

"He was…replaced. Hugh de Montfort now lives there."

Catheryn could barely speak. "What – William…where is he? He was my cousin. I had expected him to still be there, still waiting for me, still able to help me…"

Orvin cast her a warning glance, and then dismounted from his horse.

"My lady, whilst you are here, you must learn not to ask questions." His voice was low, but Catheryn could still hear every word that he was saying. "Naught but ill comes of it."

"But a man cannot simply disappear!"

"You know nothing!" Orvin spat. His face was red. "I apologise my lady if those words seem harsh, but that does not prevent them from being true! Your time in Normandy may have been difficult, but you have generally been treated with respect. For us Anglo-Saxons that stayed here, it is has been dangerous. People disappeared. Some were executed. Some just…never returned. Men and women that you thought you could trust spoke out against you, told Norman soldiers of old wrong-doings, old grievances. This country – unless we can build it anew – it will rot."

Catheryn looked around her. Children were pouring out of small homes, barefoot despite the cold. Women stuck their heads out of their homes, and looked fearfully at the great lady that they saw on a horse. Some lowered their heads, and some scuttled inside.

"Is it really so?" whispered Catheryn. "Do the people of England really fear for their lives in this way – is every day a struggle not only to survive, but to be left alone?"

Orvin smiled sadly. "It is: and not for many, but for most. There are few here that live comfortably under this new rule, save those that have married them."

A bitter bile crept into Catheryn's throat. "And how many of these marriages are chosen by our Anglo-Saxon women?"

"To my knowledge, not one." Orvin's reply was dark and bitter. A shadow of sadness crossed over his face, and Catheryn could see that an unpleasant memory had passed through his mind.

"And so I could have been the first," murmured Catheryn. It was a strange thought, but one that she should not dwell on. There was much to do, and darkness would be here soon.

"I shall meet you at the West Gate," she said to Orvin. "Bring as much food as you can carry. I have the feeling that we may not eat well tonight."

CHAPTER THIRTY SEVEN

During their ride to Essetesford, Catheryn was silent. Although she had no proof, she was now convinced that her daughter Annis was dead. Why else had Stigand had no word from her? She had known him, and trusted him, ever since she was a child. If she had needed help, then he would have been an excellent man to turn to. And yet he had heard nothing from her. No hope could be found at her old home.

Orvin kept looking over at his travelling companion with a worried face. He had not asked her who she had met with in Canterbury, leaving her personal affairs to her own thoughts. And yet the meeting clearly had not gone well; he could see it in her eyes. The light that usually lit them had been extinguished, and she merely stared sullenly at the road before them.

The evening drew close as they arrived at Essetesford, and they secured two rooms in the local inn. They ate without speaking, and after they were finished, Catheryn rose without a word and departed for her chamber.

Catheryn lay on the bed. What was the point in continuing, she thought. She was the last member of her family to survive this terrible conquest, and by the sounds of it, many of her relatives and friends were dead; killed in battle, taken by force, executed for not supporting this new King. What sort of land had this become?

A dark part of her almost hoped that Annis was no longer living. Catheryn shuddered to think what sort of state she would be in after these four years, without any protection.

It felt as though Catheryn had just shut her eyes, but within moments a hand was shaking her shoulder.

"My lady?"

The voice was timid, and female. Catheryn opened her eyes. A servant girl hovered uncomfortably above her.

"I am sorry, my lady, for waking you," she said in a rush, "but a young man asked me to, and I dare not disobey him…"

She looked anxiously at Catheryn, who smiled.

"You did right." Catheryn pulled herself up, and winced as her bones creaked. "Tell him I will join him soon."

Orvin's face was dark when she saw it.

"We must leave," he said curtly. Catheryn saw that he had already placed his cloak around his shoulders, and his right hand sat heavily on the hilt of his sword.

"Now?"

"This very moment." Orvin dropped his voice as he spoke. "It is not safe here. Too many Normans."

Catheryn nodded, and sent a servant girl to bring her belongings down from her chamber. The horses were sent for, and in the dark of dawn, they rode out.

"Home," Catheryn said softly. "I never thought that I would see it again."

The sight of the place where she had been born, grown, married, and borne her own children brought such joy into her heart that for a moment she thought it would burst.

"It is beautiful," Orvin said softly. "But I am afraid that it is not your home any longer."

Catheryn rolled her eyes. "I am fully aware of that, Orvin. But this was my home for so many years, the fact that another has dwelt here for the last four really makes no difference. It is as though they have been caring for it. For me."

"I hate to disillusion you, my lady," Orvin said, "but it has not been kept for you. I made enquiries at Essetesford; the lord here now is a lord Richard. He has no wife, and no children."

Catheryn and Orvin stood next to their horses, about a mile from her home. The wind rustled through their cloaks, and Orvin shivered.

"Do you intend to enter there?"

"I am not sure," Catheryn said slowly, "and yet I cannot see what other choice we have. If we are to discover what happened to Annis, then our search truly begins here."

"What happened to her?" Orvin said, confused. "You...you think she is dead then?"

Catheryn sighed heavily. "What other conclusion can I draw? You have lived here, you have seen the way that we have been treated – and our women surely have suffered terrible fates. Four years...it is a very long time. It is too much to suppose that she has lived that long. She would have waited for me," and here Orvin heard a catch in her voice, "but she would have waited in vain. I did not return in time."

"Until we see a grave," Orvin said stoically, "I shall not believe it. If your daughter has half of your determination, my lady, she lives."

Catheryn laughed, despite herself. "I suppose that is true. Come: nothing can be gained by standing here. Onwards."

They mounted their steeds, and made for Catheryn's home.

"Halt!" A voice called out. The door of the Hall opened up, and a man in dark blue stepped out. "You have approached the home of Richard, lord of this area. State your business."

Catheryn and Orvin exchanged looks, and Orvin dismounted slowly.

"I bring news, and a question," he said in his deep voice. "I would ask for an audience with your lord as soon as possible."

"And the woman?"

Catheryn smiled at him, although that was the last thing that she wanted to do. "I am the question."

The man looked from Orvin to Catheryn, and back again.

"And your names are?" he asked rudely.

"Orvin, son of Ulfwulf, of the South," Orvin said with a slight bow, "and my lady – "

"Wishes to remain anonymous," Catheryn cut in. "My name is for your lord's hearing, not your own."

The man stared, and then nodded curtly.

"Wait here."

He disappeared inside, and Orvin blew out a breath of tense air.

"Why did you not tell him your name?"

Catheryn shrugged. "It can gain us little for all around to know that I am here. You were right to not tell anyone of my real name, and it is even more important here. If King William is indeed concerned about an uprising in my husband's name, what good do you think we would bring by announcing ourselves to everyone we meet?"

"You are a wise woman," Orvin smiled.

Catheryn laughed. "Well, I do what I can!"

Their laughs halted quickly as the man returned.

"You may enter," he said briefly, "and my lord Richard will see you – "

"Yes, yes, I know the way," Catheryn said impatiently. She quickly dismounted her horse, and strode past the astonished man. Orvin muttered an apology, and quickly followed after her.

But he did not have to walk too far. Catheryn was standing just inside the door, and was staring all around her. The wall hangings that had been her pride and joy – the careful work of generations – were gone. The candle sticks that were dotted about the entrance way she recognised as belonging to their local church. A man stood before her; a Norman style to his hair, and a rich cloak around his shoulders. The brooch that held it together was one of her husband's.

"I am Richard," said the man. He was fat, and the hair that must once been dark was now completely grey. The beard on his face was thinning, and Catheryn did not like the way that his eyes darted over certain parts of her body. "I am the lord here, and all take orders from me. And I do not know you."

Catheryn stepped forward. "And I do not know you, yet you seem to have taken my place here. I am Catheryn, daughter of Theoryn, wife of Selwyn."

Orvin shuffled uncomfortably, unhappy that Catheryn had revealed herself so quickly. Richard's eyebrows rose, but he did not move. "Lady Catheryn, eh? I had wondered whether or not you would return. I came here with Geffrei, and he never did tell me what he got up to with you."

The lecherous meaning of his words was not lost on Catheryn – or Orvin, who drew his sword and stepped forward.

"If you cannot be civil, my lord, then perhaps you should not speak!"

Richard smiled darkly. "Another young man wishing to prove himself against the Normans. Well, be my guest, my body. You would not survive a day after killing me, but you are welcome to try."

"No one is going to kill anyone," Catheryn said hastily, putting a calming hand on Orvin's shoulder. He lowered his sword. Honestly, thought Catheryn. Do men think simply with the sword?

"I have no quarrel with you, my lord Richard," she said quietly, "and as much as I would love to return to my home, I have a feeling you have made it your own. I hardly recognise it."

"Thank you," Richard smiled greedily. "You certainly left enough behind for me to establish my life here very comfortably. But if you do not want to return here, what is it that you came for? My servant tells me that you have a question to ask of me."

"I seek a young woman – " Catheryn began.

"Don't we all?" Richard snickered, and the snicker became a cough. He clasped at his rolling belly as he struggled for breath.

"A woman that was here when you…arrived," Catheryn said over the coughs. Her words almost stuck in her throat, she was so nervous. Was she about to hear the very words that she had been dreading for miles and miles? "A young girl with blonde hair, and a kind face…"

Orvin, realising that Catheryn could no longer continue, spoke up. "We search for her on behalf of her family. Did you come across her?"

Richard stared at them, smiled, and then walked over to a chair by the fire. He said not a word as he moved, and still said nothing as he settled himself down. He looked up at them with a smile, but his gaze was centred directly on Catheryn.

"Of course," he whispered. "It all makes sense now."

"What makes sense?" snapped Catheryn, striding over to him. She stood before him, and it was now that she realised the almost magnetic draw that men had to swords. With a sword, you could force someone to do what you want – and all she wanted now was to find Annis. What did Richard know? "You will tell me, my lord."

"You are lady Catheryn," repeated Richard quietly. "You lived within these walls almost all your life. Your husband was lord Selwyn of the South."

"We know this," Orvin said angrily in his deep voice. "Do you have any information on the girl?"

"There was a girl," Richard said slowly. "Blonde hair. Very beautiful. And she was Anglo-Saxon too, and hated us Normans. She wouldn't even look at most of us. And yet her name was Norman."

All of the hopes that had risen up, unbidden, were suddenly extinguished.

"A Norman name?" Orvin repeated, in amazement.

Richard nodded. "She told us that she was visiting the family here, and that she had been left behind when her father had gone to war. We didn't think anything of it; she was just a woman, and the arguments over who she would wed soon started."

Catheryn physically flinched. "You disgust me," she said quietly.

Shrugging, Richard said, "you may not like it, my lady, but that is the way of the world. You cannot hope to deny it. I, as the most senior, was of course the obvious choice, and yet for three long years, she refused me."

"I cannot think why," Catheryn said bitterly.

"But one night," Richard continued, "I spoke to her about it again, and she became angry. She shouted at me. She said: *you may live in my home, Richard, sleep in my father's bed and give orders to my people, but you do not order me.*"

"Father's bed?" Catheryn said faintly.

"Orders?" Orvin said quickly. "What were you ordering her to do?"

"To wed me, of course," Richard replied, but he was interrupted by Catheryn. She took a step forward.

Catheryn repeated. "Father's bed?"

Richard smiled nastily. "Exactly. Well, from that moment, everything changed. She was clearly the daughter of lord Selwyn, and had not told us her true identity for more than three years. She was a liar, and a thief of my time."

Catheryn smiled, and Orvin could see that she was no longer listening to him. "But then she was alive three years ago! Three years ago my daughter lived!"

But Orvin was not smiling. "You say 'she was a liar', my lord Richard. You speak of her as if…she is no longer a liar."

Catheryn's smile vanished. Richard opened his arms expressively.

"I could not have her here, under my protection, knowing that she had lied to me for so long, that she had tricked me into offering her my hand."

"She was a better match than you deserved!" Catheryn retorted.

"Is she here?" Orvin asked quickly.

Richard shook his head. "She was married to another Norman – Mauger, or Maynard? I forget. It was over a year ago."

Catheryn almost staggered backwards. The shock affected her so much that she just dropped to the floor, sitting there confused and hurt.

"You…you married her off like cattle," she said. "You just *gave* her to another man, and he married her?"

"She was given the choice of him or me," Richard said hastily. "She had every opportunity –"

Catheryn laughed bitterly, tears in her eyes. "Please do not say that she had every opportunity to be happy, because you and I know that is a lie that will stick in your throat. My daughter was – is – a beautiful woman that deserved to have the chance to be happy. And yet you stole that from her, because you saw her as piece of property, something that could be bought and sold and swapped between other men. You disgust me."

Richard stared at her, aghast that there was a weeping woman sitting on the floor in the Entrance Hall.

"My lord Richard," Orvin said quietly. "If you could tell us where this Norman lives – Mauger, or Maynard, or whatever his name is – then we will be on our way."

"Yes," Richard could not take his eyes off Catheryn. She had pulled herself to her feet, and stood resolute, almost regal, and yet still weeping. "North. They went north. He is lord of Ulleskelf. It should not be too difficult to find him."

"And yet what condition will she be in?" Orvin muttered darkly. He took Catheryn by the hand, and began to lead her out.

"Wait!" Richard said, rising in haste, his eyes moving up and down Catheryn's body. "Will you not stay, and rest here overnight? The journey is long, and – "

"I would rather die on the road than spend one more moment here."

Catheryn's voice was dark and full of hatred.
Richard stared with amazement as the lady Catheryn and her companion left. But he smiled as he saw Orvin come back.

"Changed your mind?"

"Never," Orvin said curtly. "I only wished to enquire what name my lady's daughter had taken for herself."

Richard slumped, and gave out a sigh before he answered.

"Avis."

CHAPTER THIRTY EIGHT

"And how many days do you think it will take?"

Catheryn's question unfortunately had no easy answer.

"I think," Orvin said slowly, as they ate their evening meal in another inn, "that if we try to leave before dawn each morning, and continue on into the evening, never stopping to eat or drink but instead going onwards, then we could reach Ulleskelf by this day a sennight."

Catheryn's face fell. "Seven whole days?"

Orvin could not help but chuckle as he finished off the delicious chicken that they had ordered. "When was the last time that you ventured North, my lady?"

Catheryn blushed. "In truth, I have never been much further North than London. I have family there, but they always came to visit us. Is it really that far?"

Orvin shrugged. "During the time of King Edward, it would only have taken you four days; three, if you rode hard. But now there are Norman soldiers manning the roads, demanding to know why you are travelling. You often have to pay to pass certain points, and even then you may not gain safe passage. I think a week is a good time to aim for."

Catheryn sighed in resignation. "I suppose a week will not make much difference to my daughter's life."

Orvin shook his head in wonder. "I thought that you would be happy – that you would be overjoyed! – that you now know your daughter is alive. Annis is alive!"

"You are right." Catheryn's dull expression brightened a little.

"And from what we heard in the inn at Dover, she has certainly been doing good, protecting our people."

Catheryn's smile broadened. "That sounds like my Annis."

"Which proves to me," Orvin continued, "that she is both definitely your daughter, and thriving. Annis has not been destroyed by her circumstances."

Catheryn leaned back in her chair, and sighed. "Annis may not have been defeated by her circumstances, but I think I am. Forced to marry a Norman man? What kind of life is that? It is certainly not what I had wanted for my daughter."

Orvin was silent. Once again, a darkness seemed to overcome him.

Catheryn spoke hesitantly. "Orvin...is there something – "

"We must rest," he cut across her. "Our journey begins tomorrow, and it will be long. You should try to get as much sleep as you can."

As Catheryn and Orvin rode further and further north, the wind became icier, and the temperature dropped. They tried to find safe and warm places to stay each night, but it was difficult; many people seemed to be on the move, although they were all travelling south, in the opposite direction. Many of them looked tired, exhausted, and frightened. Some of them could not control their sobbing.

Catheryn tried not to catch their eyes. The suffering that they had undergone had been largely avoided by her; she had fallen in love with a man very like the ones oppressing her people. She had, in a way, completely betrayed every sensibility and every rule that her people held; and what had it brought her? Nothing but misery.

Orvin had tried to lift her spirits, but with each passing day bringing them closer and closer to a woman bound to a man she was sure to hate, Catheryn could not help but sink further and further into despair.

"What will you do, after you have found your daughter?"

Catheryn shook her head, and looked up at Orvin. It was the sixth day of their journey, and every one of her bones ached.

"I do not know," she said sadly. "If it is true – that she is married – then I cannot see how I will get her away. Her place will belong at his side."

Orvin muttered a dark curse under his breath.

Catheryn hesitated, and then spoke quietly. "What is it, Orvin?"

She received no reply but a look; a look that told her that he did not want to talk to her. But Catheryn persisted.

"I know that something happened," she said quietly, "and I think it involved a woman…a woman that you cared very much about."

Orvin continued to keep his eyes ahead of them, but he did at last relent.

"Her name was Gytha, and she was my sister," he said quietly. "She had hair of flame, and a temper to match. She had never agreed with my father's approach to the Normans, and was not content to simply wait, and watch them take over our lands. But then…"

Orvin's voice trailed off, and Catheryn saw the familiar shadow pass across his face.

"What happened to her?" she whispered.

Orvin swallowed. "A man came to my father. A Norman man. He had seen my sister, and desired her. He told my father that he was willing to pay a price for her, any price, for her to become his wife."

Catheryn's heart sank. She knew the ending to this story.

"I tried to reason with him," Orvin continued bitterly. "I tried to explain to him that accepting King William did not mean obeying every Norman that walked across our path. But he would not heed me, he would not listen to my words. He was so concerned about being an Anglo-Saxon in a Norman world that he sold my sister to a man that he had only known for three days. She looked at me, on that wedding day, and it was as though she had already died. He took her away from us, and within five months, he wrote to my family to say that she had died. Gytha died trying to bear him his child, and by the next Christmas, he was already married again. Another Anglo-Saxon girl, trying to obey her father by taking up a life of servitude."

Orvin finished speaking, and then looked guiltily at Catheryn.

"I am sorry, my lady, you must forgive me; I know that it must be difficult hearing of such a tale, when your own daughter has suffered a similar fate."

Catheryn tried to smile, but she could not summon the strength. She had lived through so much sadness now that she was barely surprised when she encountered more. "Not too similar, I hope."

"We shall find her," Orvin reassured her, "and when we do, we shall kill the man that took your daughter from you, and in the name of the man who took my sister from me, we shall bring Annis home."

Catheryn opened her mouth to reply, but was interrupted by a coarse man, walking in the opposite direction from them.

"Annis, you say?"

Catheryn pulled her horse to a stop.

"Yes," she said fervently. "Do you know her?"

"Know her? Not as such, my lady," said the man. He was of Anglo-Saxon stock, tall, and with blond hair. "But my mother lives in the village that she cares for – she was saved by my lady Annis. Although she called herself Avis then," he hastily corrected himself.

"Where is this place?" Orvin said abruptly.

The man pointed in a direction slightly to the left of the road that they were on.

"'Tis only but a few miles in that direction, my lord," he said deferentially.

Catheryn smiled at him. "Thank you," she said. "I cannot tell you how grateful I am."

The man blushed slightly, and muttered something about it not being a problem – but Catheryn was not there to hear him. She had already turned her horse in the direction that he had pointed, and was forcing her steed forward as fast as it could go.

Within a moment, Orvin had caught up with her.

"Eager?" he said with a smile.

Catheryn finally felt able to smile. "I am ready to see my daughter."

Another rider was moving in the same direction as them, but he had left the road from the opposite direction. His dark hair blew backwards in the wind, and Catheryn could see that he was a young man – but a man of some power. The horse that he rode was fitted with a beautiful saddle, and the cloak around his neck was thick.

Catheryn and Orvin slowed their horses to a walk, as was polite, but Catheryn grew irritated. Should she really be following the rules of decorum when her daughter could be so close? Annis had waited for so long; surely it was only right that she was put out of her misery as soon as possible?

"Well met."

The man's voice was deep, and had a Norman tilt. Catheryn smiled at him, and the smile that he gave in return almost dazzled her. It completely altered his appearance, softening his jaw and bringing a light to his eyes.

"Well met, my lord," Orvin returned. "Where do you ride to?"

"Only on to Ulleskelf," the man returned, "and yourselves?"

"We seek my lady Annis," Catheryn said.

Her words had a strong effect; one that Catheryn could never have imagined. The man immediately drew his horse to a stop, and dismounted. Catheryn and Orvin stopped also, and stared at the man in surprise.

"Why do you seek lady Annis?" said the man darkly, his right hand moving to the long sword that hung by his side. "What business have you with her?"

Orvin dismounted, and carefully rested his own hand on his blade.

"Her safety concerns you?" Catheryn asked. "We also seek her, to ensure that she is safe. She has nothing to fear from us."

The man's eyes darted from Catheryn to Orvin, as if trying to discern whether or not they told the truth – but eventually he merely stared at Catheryn. She grew hot as he looked intently into her eyes, and she was glad that her veil covered the majority of her hair.

Orvin had not moved, but was keeping a careful eye on the man. "Why does my lady Annis come under your protection?"

Melville laughed. "She is my wife."

CHAPTER THIRTY NINE

Before Catheryn could say anything, before Melville could even move, Orvin drew his sword and leaped forward.

"Defend yourself!" he cried.

Melville did not hesitate. Drawing forth his sword, he blocked the initial attack that Orvin brought against him, and immediately began his own. Catheryn could see from her seat on her horse that Orvin was a skilled swordsman, but Melville was older, stronger, and more experienced. Before long, there would be bloodshed.

"Enough!" Catheryn's cry was so loud that both men paused to look at her, and she took advantage of their stillness. Jumping down from her horse, she forced herself between them, one hand on each of their chests. It was clear from the tensed muscles underneath her palms that she was no match for them, but Catheryn knew that they would not dare harm her. Not yet.

"You say that you are Annis' husband?"

Melville was breathing deeply, and took a step backwards, sheathing his sword.

"It is my joy and my honour to tell you that I am," he said in his deep voice. "And I know who you are, though why you would have your man attack me, my lady mother, is currently unknown."

Catheryn blinked. "You...how do you know that Annis is my daughter?"

Melville laughed kindly. "My lady, it is absolutely written all across your face. Not only are your eyes very similar to Annis', but there is no care and concern like a mother's care and concern. She will have many questions for you."

"And we have many for you!" Orvin said with gritted teeth. He had not put down his sword, and he was still balanced on the balls of his feet, ready to advance at any moment. "Why did you force her to marry you? Why is she here – and what do you intend to do with her now that we have arrived?"

Melville stared at him. "I have no idea what you are talking about, my lord."

Catheryn smiled, despite herself. Her eyes had not moved from Melville's since she had forced the two fighting men apart. "Annis; she is well?"

Melville's face broke out into a beaming smile. "She is more than well; she is with child."

Orvin's scream hit Catheryn's ears before his fist forced her to the side. Orvin advanced with a menacing howl at Melville, who quickly stepped aside.

"I have no wish to fight you," Melville said hurriedly, "especially as you are friends with my dear wife."

"Orvin, stop!" Catheryn cried, but her words went unheeded.

"I said that I have no wish to fight you," said Melville, "but it seems you leave me little choice."

With one careful strike, Melville floored Orvin. It was over before Catheryn even realised what Melville had done.

"Now," Melville said, breathing heavily, "let me take you to meet your daughter. It has been too long."

EPILOGUE

The sun was shining, and no cloud blemished the blue sky. As a gentle breeze rustled the trees, the flags rippled from their posts and rope surrounding the village.

Ulleskelf was decorated from the top of each house to the grass beneath the feet of the villagers. Branches of blossom adorned walls, and flowers were intertwined with fresh leaves around each doorway. The smith of the village had wrought small silver bells that jingled merrily in the lilting breeze. All of the villagers were wearing their best clothes, and the children ran round in small groups, tripping up the servants that were trying to set a delectable feast on the trestle tables brought from the house.

Catheryn had found her daughter a year ago, and every single day that she awoke, she could not believe how lucky she was. She had arrived to see her daughter healthy, and loved, and ready to become a mother herself. Annis had seen terrible hardship, but just like her mother, she had not buckled.

Catheryn's new son Melville had declared that a feast was to be held, and the villagers of Ulleskelf had certainly risen to the occasion. She could see from her seat underneath the swaying branches of her favourite tree that some musicians were wandering around, nibbling on sweet pastries and trying not to spill another drop from their tankards of ale.

Melville approached them, and Catheryn tried not to laugh as she saw their attempts to hide their merriment. She could not hear their words, but she could see that Melville put them at ease immediately. It was probably one of the characteristics that she admired most about him: that, and the way that he had completely and utterly charmed his daughter. It was quite obvious, to Catheryn and everyone else, that they were very much in love.

Annis was dancing with some of the girls from the village, and children weaved their way through the crowds, filling their fists with food and laughing. Catheryn rose, and moved towards the group. Annis had just toppled to the ground, and her giggles filled the air, just as they had done in Catheryn's dreams for so long. It was good to hear them again.

Catheryn was just about to reach her when her way was filled by a man on a horse. The livery was that of King William, and the messenger could not dismount before Melville moved to his side.

"Word from the King?" he asked abruptly, before the messenger could even dismount.

"Indeed." The man hauled himself down from his horse, and looked at Melville warily. "You were expecting such news?"

Melville gave a short grunt. Catheryn tried to remain calm. There was no reason, now that Fitz was dead, that King William would know that she had ever left Normandy; no reason to ever care that she had found her daughter again; no reason to interfere. And yet the fear of this man hung over her head like a cloud ready to rain. You had no idea when the sun would disappear and the rain would descend, but you knew that it would.

"I was not anticipating a message from the King until this autumn," Melville spoke quietly to the messenger.

The messenger smiled uneasily. "Then you will be surprised by this letter."

Catheryn watched as he reached into the pack on his horse, pulling out a small piece of parchment that he handed over. Melville took it but made no motion to read it.

The messenger stared at him. "Will you not open it?"

"I thank you," Melville said. "If you would but follow the music, you shall find food and ale awaiting you."

"My lord."

Melville did not open the letter until the messenger was out of sight. Catheryn knew better than to attempt to speak to Melville when he was reading such an important letter, and so she wandered away, finding Orvin standing by a group of children, watching them carefully.

"My lady," he bowed. During their time in the North, Orvin had grown softer, and more forgiving. Meeting Melville, and Robert, and Jean, some of his friends from Normandy – as well as spending time with Tilian and Bronson, Anglo-Saxons like herself that had survived the Harrying of the North – had given her a new understanding of the Norman men that were different from the King. There was even some rumour of Orvin being introduced to Robert's sister, although whenever anyone had muttered it within Orvin's hearing he had strongly denied it, his face always reddening.

Catheryn suspected that another wedding would soon follow that of Jean and Edith's, Melville's friends.

"Orvin, it is good to see you," Catheryn smiled, "although I see that you have been given the task of babysitting."

Orvin smiled. "It does me good to see such youth and hope. The world that we have needs more of such things."

Catheryn nodded. "It certainly does." She smiled as she watched the young ones play, Anglo-Saxon and Norman alike. It would have made Fitz smile also. Her heart did not shatter each time her thoughts dwelled on Fitz, as it had done when the news of his death had first been brought to her, but it was still difficult to accept that he had died for a cause he had not believed in. And yet, that did not mean that she could not live for a cause that she believed in.

Her gaze lifted. There, underneath her favourite tree, sat her daughter, and her husband, and their son. Their family were an example to them all: that hatred and fear could in time give way to love. And love could save this kingdom; as long as hearts ruled.

If you would like to learn more about what happened to Avis and Melville, go back to the very beginning of the series.

Conquests: Hearts Rule Kingdoms
Read it here.

HISTORICAL NOTE

The brutal assault by the Normans on the English in 1066 was seen by many Normans as a right of conquest, and a natural emergence of the brilliance of their people. The colonisation of England became less popular as Norman lords had to divide their time between their families in Normandy and their subjects in England.

Geffrei, Orvin, and Catheryn are all fictional characters. Ursule is also fictional, although based in part on a very good friend of mine. However, unlike the first book in this series, this book contains many historical figures. I have gleaned what I can from the records that have been left for us, and then filled in the gaps myself.

My description of King William is based on historical record, as is my description of his wife. We are lucky enough to have documents concerning the coronation of Queen Matilda; Archbishop Ealdred was the man that performed the ceremony, and he did indeed write a song for the occasion. We know that the objects used in the ceremony certainly existed, and many of the promises that you read spoken by her are historically accurate. Even the banquet is as accurate as it can be: the actions of Marmion were performed by an unknown knight, and the awards that King William gave at the feast in this novel were given at the time. The remainder is my own invention: although I like to think that Queen Edith played some part in the coronation ceremony.

The FitzOsbern family really existed. William FitzOsbern was a cousin of King William the Conqueror; he did have a brother that was an advisor to both King Edward the Confessor and King William the Conqueror; he was married to Adeliza de Tosny; and they did have a son called William and a son called Roger and a daughter called Emma. Some sources mention a second daughter, and some do not, and I saw a chance here to introduce a twin for Emma. I have invented Isabella as a device to get Fitz into the cold, but his son William did have a daughter called Isabella, who was Fitz's granddaughter. Fitz was sick, and so spent much time within Normandy; Adeliza did die of a similar sickness; and Fitz went on to marry Richilde and die fighting for her son's lands. Into this real family I have inserted the fictional character of Catheryn, to demonstrate the tensions and the trials of a Norman family attempting to understand their developing role within the new Norman empire.

The town of Essetesford where Catheryn and Orvin break their journey is now called Ashford, and is a busy town in Kent.

As much as is humanly possible, I have tried to keep to the customs and traditions of both peoples as the story unfolds. A Norman funeral service certainly existed, but we have sporadic records of what they consisted of. I have used my imagination, and my knowledge of Norman Christian rituals to create one.

Any historical inaccuracies are due to my ignorance.

For further reading on this period of history, look for:

Elaine M. Treharne. *Living Through Conquest: the Politics of Early English, 1020-1220.* Oxford: Oxford University Press, 2012.

George Garnett. *The Norman Conquest: a Very Short Introduction.* Oxford: Oxford University Press, 2009.

Hugh M. Thomas. *The Norman Conquest: England After William the Conqueror.* Lanham: Rowman & Littlefield Publishers, 2008.

M. T. Clanchy. *England and its rulers, 1066-1307.* Malden: Blackwell Publishers, 2006.

Donald Matthew. *Britain and the continent, 1000-1300: the impact of the Norman conquest.* London: Hodder Arnold, 2005.

Brian Golding. *Conquest and Colonisation: the Normans in Britain, 1066-1100.* Basingstoke: Palgrave, 2001.

Sarah Foot. *The making of Angelcynn: English identity before the Norman conquest.* Cambridge: Cambridge University Press, 1996.

R. Allen Brown. *The Norman conquest of England: sources and documents.* Woodbridge: Boydell Press, 1995.

David A. E. Pelteret. *Catalogue of English post-conquest vernacular documents.* Woodbridge: Boydell Press, 1990.

William E. Kapelle. *The Norman Conquest of the north: the region and its transformation, 1000-1135.* Chapel Hill: University of North Carolina Press, 1979.

John Le Patourel. *The Norman Conquest of Yorkshire.* Leeds: University of Leeds, 1971.

H. R. Loyn. *Anglo-Saxon England and the Norman Conquest.* London: Longman, 1962.

ABOUT THE AUTHOR

Emily Murdoch is a medieval historian and freelance writer who has worked at the Bodleian Library in Oxford transcribing documents, designed part of an exhibition for the Yorkshire Museum, cared for a historic house with the National Trust, and contributed research for a BBC documentary. She has a degree in History and English, and a Masters in Medieval Studies. Emily is currently working on two new series, one of them set in the past, as well as working as a freelance researcher and copywriter. You can learn more about Emily and her writing at www.emilyekmurdoch.blogspot.co.uk or follow her on Twitter @emilyekmurdoch.

Made in the USA
Coppell, TX
02 January 2022